STONE COLD

Dean Crawford

Copyright © 2015 Fictum Ltd
All rights reserved.

ISBN: 1508823367
ISBN-13: 978-1508823360

The right of Dean Crawford to be identified as author of this Work has been asserted by him in accordance with sections 77 and 78 of the Copyright, Designs and Patents Act 1988.
All rights reserved.

Also by Dean Crawford:

The Ethan Warner Series
Covenant
Immortal
Apocalypse
The Chimera Secret
The Eternity Project
The Nemesis Origin

Atlantia Series
Survivor
Retaliator
Aggressor
Endeavour
Defiance

Independent novels
Eden
Holo Sapiens
Soul Seekers
Stone Cold

Want to receive notification of new releases? Just sign up to Dean Crawford's newsletter via: www.deancrawfordbooks.com

With thanks to Lt. Jack Allen and Capt. John Schaffer of the Great Falls, Montana Police Department, for their assistance during the writing of this novel.

Dean Crawford

I'm like you. And you're like me. Like you, I've made mistakes.

Like you, I just wanted to escape them.

We were both enslaved to our pasts, to the tragedies and histories of other people, not by our own choosing but by events neither of us could do anything about.

I suppose that's what all of us want to do, in our own way, shake off our histories and start afresh. Sometimes it seems to me that people are not really meant to spend their lives together, that enduring life's rigours is easier when there's only yourself to worry about. I didn't always think this way. Maybe it's because I'm an orphan, but I used to dream of the perfect life. Team Family, I used to call it, the perfect little bubble that a fortunate few find themselves cossetted inside, like those charming old couples who have been together since the Dawn of Time and seem effortlessly to sail life's turbulent seas before cruising on into an afterlife of eternal peace. That was all I really wanted.

But in reality it's all a damned sight harder. We all want that perfect life, but none of us really know what a perfect life should look like. We all want do the right thing, and yet we all want to be free. And what is the "right thing" to do anyway? We struggle to adapt to each other, and when a thousand tiny irritations finally blossom into enraged conflict, where no compromise can quench the anger that courses like acid through our veins, so begins what so many of us call "the rest of our lives".

I made a stand. I decided that "good enough" wasn't good enough, that I had one life and I would damned well make sure it became the best I could ever live because life isn't a rehearsal and I'll never get another shot at it. If I failed, I failed.

Don't tell me you've never dreamed of doing it too.

Dean Crawford

1

It was a faint breath of air, the touch of it on the back of her neck that let Sheila McKenzie know that she was not alone in the house. Her skin tingled and she felt the fine hairs on the backs of her arms rise up as she stared at her own reflection in the bedroom mirror, seeing nothing as her mind focused on the sensation.

The air had moved in the house, as it sometimes did when the front door was opened.

Her gaze flicked to the clock on the bedroom wall, outside the walk-in wardrobe where she had been slipping on her shoes. Her husband was not due back until the morning, and the night outside the broad windows was as black as hell and every bit as turbulent, rain squalls hammering the glass as though trying to get inside.

Sheila turned her head, listening for a moment. It was possible that the bad weather had forced her husband to turn around and come back home, but he would normally have called ahead to let her know. He was somewhat fastidious like that, the kind of man who always liked to know where she was and what she was doing. She had used to figure that he was just a little concerned for her whereabouts, that he was a little paranoid and insecure. Now, she wished that he was here.

She turned, her long blonde hair piled delicately up on her head and her pale cream skirt–suit immaculate as she stepped out of the wardrobe and listened intently. The bedroom was large, a King–size double–bed dominating it, and beyond the open door was a broad hall that descended via two opposing spiral staircases to the entrance hall and the front door. No sound came from downstairs that she could hear, further confirmation that her husband had not returned home early. She was about to search the house for any open windows that might have caused the faint breeze when she heard a tiny beep. She recognised the sound the moment she heard it.

The alarm being reset.

Sheila stood in the bedroom doorway and listened. Only she and her husband knew the code for the house alarm, neither of them having any other family members. Her husband would never have given the code away and he would never have crept into the house in this way.

She turned and walked across to her bedside cabinet where her cell phone was charging. She unplugged it and picked it up, dialling 911 as she pressed the cell to her ear. A dull hiss emanated from the phone, a scratching sound. Sheila frowned and looked at the display and realised that the cell was not picking up a signal. Sheila tossed the cell phone onto the bed as she grabbed the land line and picked up the receiver.

Dead.

Sheila set the receiver back into its cradle and stood for a moment beside the bed. She glanced out of the window and saw the trees lining the quiet cul–de–sac gusting in the wind, the street lights across the street glowing as the rain lashed down. She could see the lights of other houses, neighbours, people who could help her if she could just get out of the house.

Sheila slipped off her heels and crept across the bedroom to the doorway. She peered out toward the hall and the nearest staircase. No sounds reached her from downstairs but she knew by instinct now that she was definitely not alone, that somebody had snuck into the house and must surely know that she was inside.

Sheila moved around to her husband's side of the bed and pulled open a drawer. Inside, concealed beneath a pile of handkerchiefs, was a loaded .38, one of two in the house. The other was downstairs in the closet, just off the kitchen. She hefted the pistol out of the drawer, unfamiliar with its weight. Despite her husband's assertions that she should learn to handle the weapon, Sheila had refused: she had always disliked guns and had never really considered the fact that one day, someday, she might have to use one.

For a moment she recalled her husband telling her how to use the pistol, and she clicked open the chamber to see six rounds all ready for use. The chamber clicked shut with a satisfying snicker and she turned again for the bedroom door. Her confidence bolstered by the weapon in her hand, she eased her way out onto the hall and peeked over the bannisters toward the entrance hall below.

The curved staircase meant that she could only see a small portion of the large lobby, but having made certain that the staircase was clear Sheila crept onto the first step and began descending.

Sheila had lived in the house for over five years, and in that time she had become intimately familiar with its sounds and quirks. Although a fairly new property, the staircase still had a few spots where it creaked softly under a person's weight. Sheila detoured around those spots, each foot placed carefully and silently as she descended toward the entrance hall, the .38 held in both hands out in front of her.

The staircase unveiled the broad lobby before her, devoid of any human presence that she could see. She spotted the alarm keypad on the wall opposite, a small red light indicating that it was armed. To her right and below her a corridor turned back on itself toward the kitchen, mirroring an identical corridor on the other staircase, while to her right a door way led into the living room: on the left across the far side of the lobby, another door led into the dining room.

Ahead, a wide oak door led outside.

Sheila stood in silence on the third step of the staircase and leaned over the banister to look back toward the kitchen. The light was off, the entrance to the room enshrouded in darkness. A doorway off that corridor led to a small study and computer room located beneath the staircase itself, also in darkness.

Sheila turned and looked at the front door. Emboldened by the gun in her hand and the silence, she stepped into the lobby and turned away from the front door, crossing instead toward the living room. She had left the light on before heading upstairs and she was able to peek around the doorframe and check the room.

Empty.

She turned and looked across the lobby. The dining room was darkened, but she crept across and with the gun still aimed before her she reached around and fumbled for the light switch. An ornate chandelier glowed into life over a long, polished oak table as Sheila rushed in and swept the room with the pistol.

Empty.

She turned and looked at the lobby. Tiled in a black and white checkerboard design, she realised that anybody entering the house would have left wet footprints wherever they had walked, not to mention at least a minor gusting of rain on the polished tiles. Maybe the weather was cutting off her cell's signal, and the rain and wind outside might well have caused deadfall that could have snapped the telephone wires outside the house or even down the street. Montana got itself some real winds during the winter.

Sheila lowered the .38, but naturally cautious she turned toward the kitchen and kept the gun in her hand as she strode down the nearest corridor.

She reached out for the light switch, one hand creeping around the wall and resting on the switch as she hit it and strode into the kitchen as the light flickered on.

Empty. Sheila sighed and turned to head back for the front door.

The figure lunged for her.

It rushed out of the study and she opened her mouth to suck in air to scream with as she glimpsed a large, bulky figure wrapped in a winter coat, the face hidden behind a black mask, black gloves covering the hands and heavy boots on their feet. Sheila raised the pistol as she staggered backwards but the figure smashed the weapon aside and something hard slammed into the side of Sheila's head with enough force to blur her vision.

The kitchen tilted sideways in front of her as she toppled over and fell without pain onto the floor. The figure filled her vision and a strange, chemical odour tainted her senses as something was shoved over her face.

Moments later, everything went black

***

STONE COLD

Dean Crawford

2

Captain Dale McKenzie was exhausted.

The night shift consisted of several flights, labouring back and forth through turbulent skies between Great Falls International Airport and McCarran International, Las Vegas. Most pilots grabbed sleep between routes, slumbering on sagging couches in tiny staff rooms that smelled of stale coffee and cheap deodorant. There was no glamour left any more for a regional airline pilot, the prestige lost amid the dense air traffic and long, unsociable hours. Rough weather off the mountains, pitch–black zero–visibility flying conditions and increasing fatigue completed the nightmare. Only now was the horizon dimly illuminated by the glow of a new dawn, preceding a day of which he would miss most in the blissful oblivion of sleep. Dale knew of at least four colleagues who had to drive almost a hundred miles to reach home when their shifts ended. He felt lucky that his own home was in the same city.

The twinkling lights of the airport runway shimmered in the darkness as he walked from the terminal toward a private parking lot reserved for staff, the fresh morning air cold upon his skin beneath his shirt as it swept away some of his lethargy. The sound of engines passing overhead made him look up, navigation lights blinking as an aircraft sailed down through the inky blackness and touched onto the runway with a faint squeal of stressed rubber.

Dale pinched the corners of his eyes with finger and thumb as he walked toward a titanium–coloured Mercedes parked in the executive area of the lot. Gusts of faint drizzle dusted the cold air that whipped across the airport, a hint of sleet whipping by on the uncaring wind. Dale opened the car's door and slumped into the driver's seat. There would be little respite. In twenty–four hours he would be expected back here, ready for his next shift.

Dale switched on the engine and primed himself mentally for the drive home. Already the nearby freeways were a river of headlights snaking their way toward the city, straining his eyes as cold rain spilled down from uncaring clouds tumbling through the sky above to smear his windshield. The only consolation was that he was headed in the opposite direction, away from the twinkling galaxy of city lights behind him and out into the darkness, the traffic easing as he left the urban sprawl behind.

The pale dawn revealed sprawling plains and distant mountain ranges wreathed in ribbons of tattered cloud, the road ahead a thin strip of dark asphalt stretching away into infinity and unbroken but for tiny towns scattered like beached ships across endless rolling seas of wheat and rye. Empty and silent. Dale cruised to the edge of the city, a suburban moat around the castle of civilisation separating it from the lonely wilderness beyond. He saw an old water tower and a wind turbine spinning on the cold air, convenience stores and the high school.

The cul–de–sac in which he lived was a leafy paradise tucked down on the city's south side, only a few of the impressive houses showing any activity at this early hour as Dale pulled onto his drive. The double–garage door rose automatically as it detected the car's presence and Dale eased the Mercedes inside, the garage lights blinking on of their own accord. His wife's Laguna was parked inside the garage, shining a pristine electric blue.

Dale climbed out of his Mercedes and walked into the house through the interior garage door, switching off the alarm as he tossed his keys onto a shelf in the hall. The house was dark and silent as he slipped out of his shoes and strode through into the lobby. He wondered if his wife was awake yet.

He stopped when he saw the front door.

A pile of mail sat where it had fallen, probably delivered that morning but not collected. A pulse of alarm shivered through Dale's chest as he picked up the mail and sifted through it. Clearly Sheila had not been home, and yet her car was still in the garage and showing no signs of having been driven in the incessant rain that had been falling for the past couple of days.

Dale picked up the mail as he called out.

'Honey, you home?'

A long, empty silence filled the house. Dale walked back through the house toward the kitchen and hit the lights, and immediately he saw the light speckle of blood staining the floor tiles and a brown envelope left on the dark granite kitchen counter.

Dale opened the envelope and unfolded the piece of paper folded within. A photograph fell out and landed in his palm. His wife, Sheila, walking down a street in the city, all flowing blonde hair and mile–wide smile, talking on a cell phone. As he read the accompanying note his heart stuttered through a couple of beats and cold flushes washed his skin.

We have her already. We require $10 million in untraceable bonds. Await further instructions. If you contact the police, she will suffer. If you fail to deliver, she will die.

Dale stared at the printed words as though he was in some kind of bizarre dream and he could change them by force of will. He dug his fingertips into his eyes, squeezed hard and blinked before reading the note once more.

The words did not change.

The note fell from his hand and drifted gently down onto the deep carpet beneath his feet.

***

Dean Crawford

3

First day at a new job.

Nerves pulled taut, stretching the lines on her face and straining the muscles in her jaw. She must have been grinding her teeth in her sleep again. *Relax*, damn it.

Kathryn Stone hurried about her tiny apartment, checked her hair in a mirror on the way into the bathroom, then checked it again on the way back out. Blouse smart and buttoned up sensibly high, skirt not too short, heels not too high. Hair looks okay. First impressions count. Don't forget purse and car keys.

'Do you think my makeup is too heavy?'

Kathryn heard a faint murmur from the bedroom and hurried through. Her boyfriend, Stephen, had arrived home just as she was getting up. An insurance salesman, he spent hours travelling by car and airplane securing deals and restructuring corporate assurances. The last drive home had been a long one, right through the night he had said. She had to admit that he looked thoroughly exhausted. He glanced at her through one open eye, the other half of his body apparently already asleep. She wondered if he drove like that.

'You look fine, honey,' he mumbled.

'Sure?'

Both eyes were now closed. 'Sure, perfect.'

Kathryn refused to let Stephen's disinterest mar her day. Truth was in his current state she could have taken a blow–torch to her hair and his response would likely have been the same. She had worked damned hard to support their tiny apartment while Stephen travelled to the ends of the Earth for his meagre commission and she had studied equally hard for her diploma. Now, finally, she too would be earning again.

Kathryn walked back into the kitchen as though riding a gentle wave of coffee fumes, bacon and egg. She placed everything that she had cooked on a plate and tray, careful not to splash her crisp white blouse, and carried it through into the bedroom.

Stephen was flat on his back beneath the sheets, eyes still closed beneath neatly trimmed black hair that framed a wide, lightly shadowed jaw. He was annoyingly attractive even when exhausted, or at least he was to Kathryn.

'Breakfast is served, sir,' she said as she rested the tray beside him on the bed.

Stephen grinned dreamily and propped himself up on his elbow to examine the offering. 'What would I do without you?'

'Sleep,' she replied, 'and go hungry. There's more food in the chiller if you need it. Right now, I've got to go to work. Do I look okay?'

Stephen grabbed her arm and pulled her gently to him, kissing her on the lips. 'You look fine, okay? Good luck on your first day.'

'See you tonight.'

Kathryn slipped into her heels and jacket and strode out of the apartment. The air was crisp and cold, the thin lawns outside the block encrusted with ice and the windows of her battered old Lincoln sheened with a light frost. The bitterly cold weather took its toll and it required several grinding, screeching attempts to both get the engine started and keep it running until it was warm enough to risk committing travel. It was like bringing somebody back from the dead.

The drive was not a long one but it required negotiating from the city's east side to the centre, through the usual slog of early–morning traffic. Kathryn drove through town and guided the geriatric car into a parking lot alongside the Great Falls Police Department, rows of patrol cars and a couple of motorcycles parked facing her and the Missouri River flowing cold and dark behind. Kathryn switched off the rattling engine and sat for a moment in contemplative silence. Today was the day. She was on her own. Focus on the future. There is no past. You have a job to do. Check your hair in the mirror.

The car's ancient fold–down mirror distorted her face, making her jowls look larger than they really were and her cheeks poke out as though she were a squirrel feasting on chestnuts. Her long brown hair matched her eyes. Not too much makeup, just a dab here and there. Professional. Smart. The *I–don't–need–to–plaster–my–face–in–gunk* look that she imagined smart guys, like police detectives, might like.

Kathryn reached down to her left hand and removed a silver commitment ring from her finger. It has been given her by Stephen after their first year together, a token of their love. She looked at it fondly for a moment, warmed briefly by the hazy memories of happiness, and then she opened the glove compartment and tossed the ring inside before slamming it shut. It felt as though a breeze block had been lifted from her shoulders.

Now, get out of the car.

Kathryn got out of the car into the cold air, careful not to catch her suit on the greasy door. She slammed the door hard to make sure the catch caught, and then slammed it again when it didn't. Her reflection in the grubby window now looked angular, almost gaunt.

'Miss Stone?'

Kathryn whirled. 'Yes?'

A uniformed officer with short blonde hair peaking from beneath her cap smiled at Kathryn's startled response. 'Easy there, tiger. You're due to meet Detective Griffin?'

'Yes, at ten,' Kathryn replied.

'Don't sweat it,' the officer replied. 'You should have seen me the day of my first arrest: two teenagers lobbing stolen ice-cream into a lido and then at me when I intervened. I looked like a walking vanilla with cherry by the time I'd apprehended them. This way, please.'

Kathryn followed the officer into the station, past the front desk with its armoured glass window and through a security door into the station proper.

A small operations room filled with busy desks constituted the centre of the station's activities, where detectives sat with their heads down talking quietly on phones or searching computer screens with furrowed brows. A municipal law enforcement agency, the overall department was manned by eighty or so sworn men and women supported by some forty civilian staff, along with two canine patrols and the subject of Kathryn's visit: the HRU team.

The HRU or High Risk Unit was considered a *Red Flag* team, qualified and certified for use around the state and region when needed. Routinely activated for calls within the city, it had also occasionally been used outside the city upon request. The unit consisted of four components: entry teams, negotiators, snipers, and medics. Overseen by the TAC Commander, it was comprised of officers throughout the agency doing their day to day duties in patrol, detectives and support services that, upon HRU activation, were alerted and reported for a briefing with their equipment readied before transport to the scene of any crime.

Several weeks before, a pair of riders from the notorious *Bandidos* motorcycle gang had spiked themselves to the eyeballs on peyote buttons after a drinking session in Tuffy's Bar and abducted a nine year-old girl, Amy Wheeler, before holing themselves up in an abandoned farmstead down by the lonely waters of Muddy Creek. Local residents had called the police and the HRU had spent nearly eight hours talking down the bikers, who were armed with sawn–off shotguns and a severe lack of interest in staying alive. A pair of Great Falls detectives had joined the HRU entry team on the request of CCSO.

The HRU team had done a fabulous job. Unfortunately, the bikers had continued to take drugs in favour of using their brains. Drunk on their own biker–gang prowess and the nameless chemicals surging through their bodies, they decided to go down fighting when the HRU team, believing them to be on the verge of a suicide pact, decided to burst in.

In the shoot–out that followed their captive Amy Wheeler was hit by a ricochet and fatally wounded. Both bikers were apprehended, two police officers lightly injured. In the inevitable investigation into the event, although all officers were rightly cleared of any wrong–doing, a forensic examination by the ballistics team had identified the weapon that had caused the shrapnel burst that had killed the little girl.

A shot fired by the sidearm of Detective Scott Griffin, in support of the HRU team.

Kathryn knew the procedures that were performed as a matter of course in the wake of fatal shootings by the police, but she had read the file with particular care in this case. Detective Griffin's gun had been collected as evidence. The Critical Incident Stress Management System had been activated, with a mandatory debriefing of all officers involved taking place within seventy two hours. Detective Scott Griffin had been placed on paid administrative leave for a few days to process what had happened, but had reportedly returned to work a few days later. A GFPD Firearms Use Review followed, along with an internal non–criminal investigation which quickly identified that Griffin's shot was targeting one of the bikers and also identified the unfortunate ricochet which caused Amy Wheeler's death.

The State Department of Criminal Investigation, or DCI, had then conducted a criminal investigation. The following Coroner's Inquest had taken place and had determined that Detective Griffin's actions were entirely justified and that no course of action could have prevented the ricochet.

Throughout the entire process, Detective Griffin's actions and intentions as an officer of the law had been revealed as entirely within procedure and indeed exemplary. If there had been a problem with the officer's actions, then the County Attorney's Office – or, more likely the Montana Attorney General's Officer, if DCI were investigating – would have reviewed the case and perhaps brought criminal charges against the officer. The FBI might also have considered civil rights violations against the officer, and Amy Wheeler's family could have sought damages though a lawsuit against the agency. But none of these things had happened. Detective Griffin had been cleared to return to active duty, his record untarnished by the tragedy.

Two weeks later, Griffin had been found slumped in a bar on the edge of town at two in the morning, incoherent with grief that a shot fired by his own hand had killed a child he was devoted to protecting even at the risk of his own life. Griffin was given a further leave of absence for two weeks, before being reinstated as a detective with the department and offered the support that he needed.

The Great Falls Police Department was on the pioneering forefront of identifying and addressing the issue of Post–Traumatic Stress Disorder, or PTSD. Officers within the department had built a program to alleviate the stigma attached to the condition and educate officers and their families regarding warning signs and how to get help. The Great Falls Police Protective Association, a private association for and funded by the department's officers, had stepped in on Griffin's behalf to arrange for time off, travel expenses and the cost of any treatment. Griffin had refused the more expensive option of a specialized program in Vermont, but had reluctantly agreed to see a local counsellor based in the city.

Kathryn Stone.

Despite the severe nature of the crisis that had brought about the death of Amy Wheeler, the case itself was considered relatively straight-forward, and hence Kathryn had been handed as her first assignment the task of rehabilitating the grieving officer. There was clearly no blame placed upon his shoulders, thus the grief was entirely psychological. Bad things sometimes happen to good people, and Kathryn knew that the search for explanations was fruitless and often damaging. Some turned to God or their families. Others turned away. The weight of a person's guilt and the grief it caused them, over something they could not have possibly controlled, was an oft–underestimated mental health issue. Without boundaries for that grief to be contained it could easily spill into the detective's private life and perhaps consume him entirely if proper perspective were not placed on the event and how he related to it.

Psychology 101: *perspective.*

The officer guided Kathryn to an office adjoining the operations room and knocked on the door, which was adorned with the name Capt. Gregory Olsen.

The captain got up from his desk as they entered. Tall and broad, Olsen shut the door behind Kathryn as the female officer left and extended his hand to Kathryn Stone. Olsen was a long–service officer, his rugged features hewn from granite like mountains and thick white hair like the clouds that topped them, and a magnificent moustache nestled above his upper lip. Kathryn guessed he wasn't far off retirement, and his seemingly eternal presence in the town afforded him as much respect, if not more, than that enjoyed by the mayor.

'Nice to meet you, Ms Stone.'

His voice was so deep it sounded like boulders rolling down a hillside.

'Thank you,' Kathryn said, her hand feeling like a child's being held by a bear's paw.

Olsen gestured to an empty seat beside his cluttered desk as he sat back down. 'Not often we get call for a shrink in this office. Times are changing, I guess.'

'Extraordinary times,' Kathryn replied. 'Big city shoot–outs are not a daily feature of your officers' working lives.'

'No,' Olsen admitted. 'Just as well it was Griffin and Maietta on the scene.'

'Maietta?'

'Jane Maietta,' Olsen explained. 'Griffin's partner. Tough as saddlebags, a street kid out of Illinois made good.'

'And Griffin's a soldier?'

'Former army,' Olsen confirmed. 'Two tours in Iraq so he knows gunfights, probably saw some shit he'd rather not go into. But the shoot–out at the farmhouse was different.'

'How did the ricochet happen?'

'He was shooting at one of the bikers, who'd drawn a bead on an armed officer who had just been hit in the leg and was left exposed. Griffin fired. The bullet hit the wall beside the biker's head, bounced off a metal brace and hit the kid behind him in the left temple.' Olsen pointed to his head, in case Kathryn didn't know what a temple was. 'There was nothing that anybody could do.'

'How did Griffin react, in the immediate aftermath?'

Olsen stared at her for a moment. 'He didn't dance a fucking jig, if that's what you mean?'

'It's important,' Kathryn said. 'The more I know about how Griffin reacted to the event, the better I can understand how he's handling it now.'

'He didn't know he'd killed anybody until he entered the building,' Olsen explained. 'Nobody did until HRU broke through into the building and ended the incident. It wasn't until the kid's autopsy that the bullet was recovered and matched to Griffin's weapon. He was told the day after that.'

'He didn't see the child's body?'

'He did,' Olsen exhaled, his gaze falling from hers. 'He knew the bullet was his, I think, maybe instinct or something. Amy Wheeler died in his arms.'

'Nobody thought to keep it from him?' Kathryn asked.

'Too much red tape,' Olsen explained. 'HRU need to account for literally every round they fire in these kinds of incidents, which meant that we did too. With a dead kid I could plausibly have figured that it made sense to claim that the bikers killed her, but that would have left a round unaccounted for. They went by the book, and rightly so did I.'

'And how is Griffin coping at this time?'

'He's wired up pretty tight,' Olsen replied. 'He's tough enough and smart enough to get through it all, but I don't think he really knows where to begin. Griffin's good, most ex–soldiers are, but likewise he's too proud, thinks he knows best, always wants to work alone and that's what got him into this state in the first place. He doesn't even open up to his partner.'

'And how would you describe his state, exactly?' Kathryn asked.

'Police officers have to be law–keepers, counsellors, fire–arms experts, mediators and often goddamned politicians all at once,' Olsen explained. 'There's no real–life Jack Bauer out there running around playing maverick–cop, no matter what people see on the television. Griffin's suffering from a lack of confidence, no matter how hard he tries to conceal it, so he's built himself a wall to hide behind.' Olsen sighed. 'I guess it's what you folk would call a coping mechanism, right?'

'Something like that,' Kathryn nodded. 'He's projecting his grief outward as anger. Is he working on anything right now?'

'He's been pulled off the front line,' Olsen said, 'and he's not carrying a firearm until he's over this. I've got him looking into our cold–case files. Desk job.'

'How's he liking that?'

'He's not. I'd rather he was in the field, but until the investigation is complete my hands are tied. You think he should be out there?'

'Maybe,' Kathryn said. 'I'll figure that out after I've spoken to him, but generally the more normality that surrounds him the more comfortable he'll feel. Any ideas on his home life?'

'He doesn't talk about it.'

'Fine,' Kathryn said. 'Not talking about it is saying something in itself.'

'That's the kind of talk that'll piss him off,' Olsen pointed out. 'We're straight–talking folk out here, Miss Stone. Griffin doesn't place much stock in all of this fairy–go–lightly psychobabble and nor do I.'

'Noted,' Kathryn replied. 'He won't like me seeing him every day either.'

'You want to stick around that closely?'

'He's a former soldier, a patriot and a police officer,' Kathryn said. 'He's earned the right for me to do a good job for him. What about the parents of Amy Wheeler? Have they been talked to, or met Griffin?'

'No,' Olsen replied. 'They understand what happened was a tragedy and they're good strong folk, enough not to start litigation against the department, but you can figure for yourself that they didn't want a face–to–face with Griffin and he sure as hell doesn't want to see them. As it happens, procedure means that Amy's parents have not been informed of the identity of the officer responsible, and I think it's best to keep things that way.' Olsen watched her for a long beat. 'You think you can set him straight?'

'I don't want to see another veteran's family collapse and let them wander off to a life on the streets, okay? These guys did enough in Iraq and Afghanistan already, let alone fighting crime back home.'

Olsen sucked in a prodigious lungful of air and blasted it out across his desk as he leaned back in his seat.

'I've only got five detectives to play with Miss Stone, and a sixth rotational officer. The sooner Griffin's back on the job, the better. You've got my support if you think this will help him.'

'It'll help him,' she said. 'What's at issue is whether he wants to help himself.'

***

4

'This is the room,' the duty officer gestured Kathryn toward a closed door marked *Interview Room 1*. 'Detective Griffin is waiting for you. Can I get you a coffee ma'am?'

'I'm good, thanks,' Kathryn smiled back.

The officer turned and walked away down the corridor. Kathryn stared at the door in front of her. Get your act together. You're here to help, so *act* like it. She took a deep breath and then pushed down on the handle and strode in.

Bare walls. A brushed aluminium table bolted to a floor of grubby linoleum tiles. A single strip light, harsh and cold, set into the ceiling behind a cracked plastic cover that had been repaired with a strip of gaffer tape. Not the most inviting of rooms and hardly the best place to speak to a grieving man about such delicate matters.

Detective Scott Griffin sat before her, a pair of clear blue eyes flicking up to meet hers. Thick brown hair framed a young face that was lined with world–weariness, the permanent late–night strain of law enforcement. Shoulders set, back straight. Ex–military, she reminded herself. Hands folded in his lap, a little too tightly to be natural. On edge. Uncomfortable.

'Detective Griffin, I'm Kathryn Stone,' she said as she closed the door behind her.

'Pleasure, ma'am.' A soft drawl, but no smile.

'Texas?'

'Odessa,' came the reply, a faint glint of life in the blue orbs now.

'You're a long way from home, soldier.'

'Army got me out and about. Long time ago now.'

'Who are you trying to kid?' she asked with an easy smile as she took a seat opposite Griffin. 'Once a soldier…'

Griffin managed a smile, sort of lop–sided where one side curled up and the other curled down.

'You a local girl?'

'No, I was raised in Nevada.'

'Looks like we're both a long way from home.'

Kathryn retrieved from her bag a small file marked with Griffin's name and opened it up.

'How are you coping with the aftermath of the shooting incident?'

A long silence filled the room before Griffin replied.

'You don't beat about the bush ma'am.'

'I figured that you're probably somebody who probably appreciates straight talking.'

Griffin raised an eyebrow, the crooked smile still touching his features.

'I guess. And in answer to your question, things are fine.'

'Can you define *fine* for me detective?'

'I don't drink any more, if that's what you mean.'

'That's what I mean,' Kathryn agreed. 'You're married.'

'Four years.'

No more details. No elaboration. No mention of the wife's name, although Kathryn already knew it of course. That could also just be straight talking, but she doubted it.

'She coping okay?'

'With what?'

'With you.'

'Should she be having a problem?'

'No,' Kathryn replied. 'Detective, I could take this interview in all kinds of directions, but I prefer to just sound people out at a realistic level. Mind games and inferred psychology seem a waste of time to me. You're a well–trained, upstanding officer and a patriot. If you want the bullshit version I can deal, or we can just cut to the chase and let me figure out how life really is for you and your family right now.'

Griffin stared at her for a long moment, then leaned back as he exhaled noisily. It was like watching noxious fumes spill from a crippled body and then the first inhalation of clean air for months.

'We're working it out,' he said finally. 'One day at a time.'

'Been having problems long?'

Griffin stared at her again, probably wondering whether he could bullshit past her. A soft sigh as he apparently rejected the option, his eyes focused to infinity on the table top.

'You don't just walk away from a war, in any sense.'

'I don't doubt it. Post–Traumatic–Stress–Disorder takes many forms, detective. I won't bother boring you with them as I'm sure you know by now what PTSD is. You've had a hell of a ride over the past few years and sometimes it can take the brain a while to process everything, get it into a context that you can handle. You just need some more time.'

'And my wife?'

'The same,' Kathryn replied. 'We're all people, detective. What affects one person tends to rub off very easily on those close to them, and sometimes that can open wounds which take a long time to heal. Give her space, let her know that you're trying.'

'Like I said, I don't drink now.'

'Getting dry isn't getting better all on its own,' Kathryn pointed out. 'You talk much?'

Griffin shrugged, keeping that steady blue–eyed gaze on her. She felt as though she were being analysed in silence.

'Try harder,' she said, glancing down at the file to break the spell. 'You're young, you've got plenty of time to get past this and move forward.'

'You don't look old,' Griffin observed.

Kathryn almost laughed. 'I'll take that as a compliment.'

Griffin's smile didn't slip as he leaned forward on the table, his eyes fixed upon hers.

'That's what it was meant to be,' he replied. 'You've been through a lot yourself but you're looking okay for it.'

Kathryn's studied calm slipped and she felt saliva pooling in her throat. 'Have we met before?'

Griffin shook his head. 'You sometimes wear a ring,' he said. 'The skin stays smooth after they're removed 'cause the sun doesn't get to it so easy, so I figure you're either recently separated or you took it off before you came in here.'

'I'm happily attached, actually,' Kathryn replied, uncertain. 'Where are you going with this?'

'You're not the only person who can dig into a stranger's past just by looking at them,' Griffin replied. 'Which means your advice is no better than that I could get from friends in a bar.'

'People in bars tend to like talking about themselves more than helping others.'

'You think that I need help?'

'I think that you need time, and space, to process what's happened to you.'

Griffin watched her silently for several long seconds. 'I need to be able to do my job.'

'Which you will, just as soon as I clear you again for full duty.'

'Which will be when?'

'When you're ready,' Kathryn replied.

'Can I ask you something?'

'Anything.'

'You're in an unhappy relationship, no matter what you might say to hide it,' Griffin said. 'So you tell me: if a trained psychologist can't pick themselves the right person to spend their life with, why should I listen to anything they say about me or what I need?'

Kathryn managed to hold the detective's unwavering gaze for long enough to formulate a reply.

'Because I know how to stick with that relationship and make it work,' she said, 'not run away from it and hide behind my anger.'

'That why you take the ring off?'

Kathryn tried to make her jaw work and reply, but before she could do so a sharp knock at the door cut her off as Captain Olsen opened the door and stuck his craggy head inside.

'Sorry, doc'. Griffin, you're up.'

'Can it wait?' Kathryn asked.

The captain shook his head. 'It's pretty urgent,' he said. 'Maietta's caught a time–sensitive case.'

Griffin wasted no time and virtually leaped out of his seat as he flashed Kathryn a relieved smile. 'Nice to meet you, doc'.'

***

5

Griffin strode into the operations room. An Italian looking female detective was walking toward him, long brown hair flowing across her shoulders over a two–piece dark–grey suit. Jane Maietta's lips were a hard, thin line, her eyes dark and her expression uncompromising.

'What's up?' Griffin asked her.

Maietta handed him a case file, brand new and with a name scribbled in black marker across the front. *McKenzie.*

'You just caught a new case, lucky guy,' she said. 'One printed ransom note and a photograph of a missing woman.'

'Seriously?' Griffin asked.

Ransom notes were not everyday events in the precinct, and despite America's infatuation with guns Great Falls had a low crime–rate that had been falling for some years. Griffin read the note and looked at the photograph.

'How did we get this?' he asked. 'The note warns against contacting local PD.'

'The husband sent it,' Maietta replied. 'Shot some images with his cell and e–mailed them to us direct. Neat get–around.'

'Okay, the husband's a smart guy. How long do we got?'

'That's the catch,' Maietta replied. 'The guy's an airline pilot who's been away for at least forty eight hours so the time of abduction is uncertain.'

'Hoax? Wife takes off, tries to disappear, fakes own suicide even?'

'Maybe,' Maietta said. 'Hard to tell until we can figure out a way of talking to the husband, but it's not something we can afford to take a chance on. The woman, Sheila McKenzie, hasn't turned up and I can see the headlines already: *police ignore ransom note, woman dies, police sued.*'

The female detective glanced at Kathryn Stone, who was walking out of the office behind Griffin. 'That the shrink?'

'Jane Maietta, meet Kathryn Stone. I can't wipe my own ass unless she says I'm safe to do it.'

Maietta flicked her eyebrows up at Kathryn in what apparently passed for a greeting in the station. Kathryn managed a tight smile in response.

'Post marked Great Falls,' Griffin murmured as he looked at the envelope. 'The perpetrator either lives here or they're in a settlement close by. That means they're lazy whether they're hoaxing or not. Have we spoken to the husband at all?'

'No, but we checked him out. Dale McKenzie is an upstanding pillar of the community,' Maietta replied. 'No priors or motive so far as we know. He's pinned down in his home and can't come to us without fearing a reprisal by the abductors, so we're talking by e–mail until we can get him in here unobserved or talk to him at his place of residence.'

'Any chance the abductors could be monitoring his e–mails?'

'He's using his cell,' Maietta replied. 'Sure, it could have been cloned, but we don't have the luxury of time to chase that down.'

'Any enemies, disgruntled ex–employees, partners?' Griffin asked.

'I'm running with it now,' she said. 'Dale's a senior officer with Ventura Air out of the local airport. Flies regional.'

'Alibi?'

'Fairly solid. The airline confirms that he was at 35,000ft when the abduction most likely occurred.'

'What about a silent partner?' Griffin suggested.

'I'm pulling what we've got on both the husband and the missing wife,' Captain Olsen said as he joined them, 'but nothing's shouting *solution* at me yet.'

'Which doesn't help us one little bit,' Griffin uttered. 'We need means, motive and opportunity, but we've got no timeline on this because of the disparity between the abduction and the husband's discovery of the note.'

In most abduction cases, there were two well–known rules: that the first forty–eight hours were crucial because after that time frame it was considered unlikely that the victim would be found before death; and that most times the abductor was somebody the abductee knew, often a spouse or family member.

'Nobody has called the husband yet?' Griffin asked.

'Nothing,' Maietta confirmed. 'Either they know we're involved and are in the wind or the deadline's not up yet.'

'Where was Sheila McKenzie abducted from?' Griffin asked.

'Her home,' Olsen replied, 'near as we can figure. The husband said there was evidence that she'd returned home from work, but then been forcibly removed from the house. He said that he found bloodstains on the kitchen floor and some sign of a struggle.'

Griffin read the case notes and frowned. 'McKenzie said that he walked into his home when he got back from work.'

'Yeah,' Maietta replied, 'and he found the ransom note on the kitchen table.'

'And he had to switch off the alarm when he entered the house,' Griffin read from a page of e-mails sent to and from McKenzie.

Maietta nodded. 'The abductor had to know the code and must have re-set it.'

'Maybe,' Griffin said, 'or they coerced Sheila into revealing the code to them, or at least opening the door to them.'

'The security company that fitted the system on the house said that it has two codes,' Maietta replied. 'One is the standard deactivation or arming code, and the other is an SOS code that still operates the alarm but also sends a signal to local police. Sheila could have alerted the police by giving her abductor the alert code.'

Griffin nodded. 'So there's a strong possibility that her abductor did indeed know the correct code and input it directly. That likely puts them inside the house prior to her arrival, which would likely be, what, after work?'

'They also knew enough to isolate the house a little,' Maietta said. 'Phone company confirms that the phone line was cut prior to the abduction.'

'Professional job?' Griffin hazarded.

Maietta shrugged. 'Can't say right now, but they thought about what they were doing. I've got Russell County's HIDTA Drug Task Force in the loop in case this somehow turns out to be a drug or gang related incident, and Cascade County and Teton County are with the jive in case whoever's got Sheila are looking to jump counties. ATF, DEA and Homeland are being filled in on the details via the Bureau as we speak.'

'We've got to assume we've about thirty six hours to work with,' Olsen said as he turned away from Griffin. 'If Sheila McKenzie was abducted after she got home from work, and her husband arrived home to find the letter the following morning, that's forty eight hours minus twelve. See if you can't pin down Sheila McKenzie's last known movements, or who saw her last prior to abduction, and figure out a better time line from that.'

'Find out where Sheila McKenzie works,' Griffin said to Maietta. 'We'll also need to get a support team out to the husband as fast as we can, tap his phones, anything to get ready for a call if it comes in.'

'Perps must have known that the husband would be away for long periods,' Maietta said as she headed for her desk. 'They might have anticipated a delay and be working around it.'

'And find out who fitted the alarm system and who had access to those codes at the company,' Griffin added. 'We need to eliminate any of their staff before we go any further.'

Kathryn watched Griffin for a long moment before speaking. 'Are you sure you want to get involved in a case like this right now?'

'Why wouldn't I? It's my job, and I can't do much damage behind a damned desk.'

'A missing woman,' Kathryn replied. 'Are you looking for redemption?'

'Any reason that I shouldn't be?' Griffin asked as he studied the photograph.

'No,' Kathryn admitted, and then added, 'yes. What if this case turns out to end in a shoot–out, or even failure?'

Griffin did not move but she could see his eyes drift away from the photograph as the detective considered the possibility.

'That's bullshit,' Maietta said as she held a phone pinned to her ear. 'You helping here or hindering?'

'I don't start anything planning to fail,' Griffin replied to Kathryn. 'Do you?'

Kathryn spoke quietly.

'Nobody does, but just like last time it's not your life that might be on the line, Scott. It's somebody else's, and you can't account for everything.'

'You're advocating that I accept failure before I've even started? What kind of support is that?'

'I'm just saying that maybe Olsen should have somebody else should lead this case, one of your colleagues, just for now.'

Maietta chuckled bitterly in the background.

Griffin turned to face Kathryn. 'Sure, that's my line. I hand over responsibility to somebody else so they're carrying the can if it all goes south and I walk away with my hands in my pockets whistling and shrugging my shoulders. Is that what you mean?'

'You know that's not what I mean.'

Kathryn glimpsed Griffin's jaw clench as he struggled to maintain his composure.

'Okay, this is how it's going to go. You're going to leave this building now and come back tomorrow for our little conversations because that's what I have to do in order to stay in my job. And that's all you're going to do. I have an abduction case to concentrate on and you're getting in my way.'

Kathryn was about to reply when a voice called out across the office.

'Griffin,' Olsen rumbled. Griffin looked up as the captain gestured to Kathryn. 'Meet your new shadow.'

Griffin opened his mouth to protest. One of Olsen's thick fingers sliced back and forth through the air in front of his face and cut him off.

'It's non–negotiable,' Olsen said, then looked at Kathryn. 'You want him behind a desk or on the streets, counsellor? It's your call.'

Kathryn looked at Griffin as though sizing him up, when in fact she knew damned well the detective needed to break free of his desk. Keeping him cooped up would do his psyche no good at all.

'He needs to be involved,' Kathryn relented. 'Let him run the case.'

'Fine,' Olsen said, and then looked at Griffin. 'You don't miss a single appointment with Miss Stone. Agreed?'

Griffin shrugged and nodded.

Olsen flashed them both a bright smile. 'I'm glad we're on the same page, detective. You'll make a beautiful couple. Now, get on the case and find the asshole behind this abduction while there's still time.'

'I've got something,' Griffin said as he looked at the photograph.

***

6

'Already?' Maietta asked.

Griffin looked down at the pictures. 'Sheila McKenzie,' he said. 'The picture is grainy and doesn't give us much, but somebody had to take it.'

'It doesn't give us the location,' Maietta said. 'Maybe taken on the east side, which ties in with what you said about the abductors being lazy, but we can't figure out anything else?'

In the picture Sheila McKenzie was walking along fairly non–descript sidewalk. Brick walls, a few parked cars, very little to identify where she was from the images alone.

Griffin gestured to the brick wall behind Sheila McKenzie.

'Look at the wall,' he said. 'There's a patch of faded brickwork. That was graffiti or wall art or some such. I'm pretty sure I used to see it when driving down Division Avenue, before the council scrubbed it down. It's the wall of a massage parlour or some such and there's an intersection nearby, so maybe there will be traffic camera coverage?'

'What will traffic cam' footage achieve?' Olsen asked. 'We know who's been abducted.'

'Yeah,' Griffin agreed, 'and if we can use the footage to identify the person behind the camera, we're one step closer to figuring out who's behind the abduction.'

'He's right,' Maietta confirmed. 'That wall got scrubbed a few weeks ago.'

Griffin looked down at the photograph.

'Good, so we know the shot was taken within the last few weeks and we know where. That means the abduction was premeditated. Can we get traffic camera footage?'

'The chances of catching the photographer are slim,' Maietta pointed out, 'especially if they took the shot from a moving vehicle. We won't know which one to look for.'

'There's a camera,' Olsen called from across the office, one hand cupped over his phone, 'but it's only got forty–eight hours' of footage on permanent record. The disc gets wiped.'

'Run it anyway,' Maietta called back. 'We'll get some donuts in.'

'Great,' Griffin uttered and sat on the edge of his desk. 'That'll lose us another few hours off the deadline. Why not just call the husband and find out when his wife was last walking down that street? If he knows, we can narrow the timeline down.'

'She might walk it every day,' Maietta said. 'Besides, the guy's an airline pilot and probably not aware of all her daily movements.'

'Maybe,' Griffin agreed, 'but right now we need everything we can get and I doubt that she wears the same clothes every day. Maybe we could pin the day the shot was taken down from that?'

'Huh,' Maietta murmured as she reached for a phone, 'I'm on it.'

'And we need a way to sit down in front of the husband and figure out how we're going to help this guy,' Griffin went on. 'If he's not supposed to have contacted us then he needs to continue with his routine as though nothing has happened. Have we got some kind of itinerary for him?'

'He's supplied us with his flight roster for the week,' Olsen confirmed. 'Our best play is to talk to him at the airport, somewhere we can't be observed and any abductors can't get access to. They must have offices, storage depots, things like that.'

'I'll give the airline a call,' Griffin replied, 'see if I can't figure something out. We need a way to get one of our people into his house. Maybe we could get one of our guys to dress up as a fellow pilot or something, come back home with him for a few beers?'

'Sounds good,' Olsen confirmed and then vanished into his office.

'Sheila McKenzie owns an art gallery in a mall downtown,' Maietta said from her desk as she looked at her computer screen. 'You want me to call in and get us an interview?'

'Yeah,' Griffin answered, and then said: 'No. If the perp's an employee it'll rattle them. Find out how many people work for her, then we'll go in without badges as though we're regular punters and see what gives.'

'I'm heading out,' Kathryn reported to Griffin, 'but I'll be back this evening.'

'You mean your bodyguard's leaving you all on your lonesome for the day?' Maietta asked Griffin as she pinned her phone between her ear and her shoulder. 'What ever will you do?'

Kathryn picked up her bag and smiled sweetly at the detective.

'Don't worry, I won't leave him for long,' she said, and then to Griffin: 'Be a good boy.'

*

Kathryn whirled and strode out of the operations room, then released a long sigh of relief as she strode out of the station to her car and checked her watch. She climbed in and drove out of the lot, the sky above now bright and blue and speckled with light clouds.

It should have been a moment to be cherished, a time for reflection on her performance, but Kathryn was far beyond revelling in any kind of success. Too much at stake she guessed, like the rest of her entire life.

She drove into town, parked, and made her way to a coffee shop that she had frequented often while studying for her diploma. Sitting inside the window was a portly woman with a bright smile and a waving hand. Two lattes steamed in front of her as Kathryn walked into the shop.

Ally Robinson was a friend who like Kathryn had studied for a diploma and worked for the same company. English by birth and by nature, she had deliberately sought out small–town America for reasons nobody could really fathom and built a life for herself in Great Falls. She stood and her arms wrapped around Kathryn's shoulders and almost lifted her off the floor as thick tresses of auburn hair wafted across her face.

'Sit down Stone,' Ally commanded as she released her friend.

Kathryn took a seat across from Ally and sipped at her latte. A silence enveloped the table.

'Get on with it then,' Ally insisted, leaning across to peer into Kathryn's eyes. 'What was so important that it couldn't wait?'

Over several days Kathryn had spent countless hours constructing the conversation that she was about to have. The smart, witty opening. The sombre, brooding revelation. The chirpy, *I don't really care much at all* breezing through of the details. Now, in the moment, she found that she could not speak. Instead, she looked down at her left hand.

Ally's gaze flicked down to the same hand and she gasped. 'No!'

Kathryn nodded.

'When?'

Kathryn shrugged.

'Why?'

Kathryn took another sip of her latte.

'How?'

Kathryn finally found her voice again. 'He doesn't know yet. I keep the ring on when we're together.'

Ally's face folded in upon itself as one hand flew to her mouth. '*You're* leaving *him*?'

'You don't have to say it like it's so ridiculous.'

'But, I mean, for Christ's sake Kathryn it's *Stephen*!'

'I know who it is.'

Kathryn's quiet response carried far more weight than she had intended. So much for the carefully imagined responses and elegantly cultivated demeanour she had believed would be required to reveal the greatest catastrophe of her life. In truth, the revelation itself was enough.

Ally's hand reached out and held Kathryn's. 'What happened?'

Kathryn sucked in a breath, felt it quiver slightly as her resolve began to crumble. She swallowed hard and held the grief at bay as she replied.

'Stephen is seeing somebody else,' she said.

'Oh my God,' Ally uttered. Her grip on Kathryn's hand tightened. 'You're sure?'

Kathryn nodded. 'One hundred per cent certain. I wouldn't be sitting here talking to you about it otherwise.'

'Of course you wouldn't,' Ally acknowledged, her brow furrowed as she examined Kathryn's features. 'You want to tell me about it? In your own time, of course. Just tell me what happened, from the beginning.'

Kathryn hid behind her latte for a few moments more and then spoke quietly.

'I found a key in Stephen's belongings, when I was searching for some of my own stuff after we moved into the apartment. Stephen has this little lock–box, and he never really spoke about it to me before but it was always just around in his apartment, before we moved in together. I guess I figured it was personal to him, and maybe he'd talk about what was in it at some point.'

Ally's eyes widened and her lips parted slightly. 'You opened it, didn't you?'

It was strange, how although Kathryn had herself been wronged she still felt somewhat ashamed at having betrayed Stephen's trust. The little mahogany box with its brass lock had always been sitting somewhere in Stephen's apartment, on a mantelpiece or in a cupboard, never hidden and yet its contents never revealed either.

'I knew the key looked about right for the box, so I opened it,' she confirmed.

'What was inside?' Ally asked, leaning forward a little, her drink forgotten.

Kathryn sighed softly, staring at the table as she spoke.

'Jewellery,' she said, 'women's jewellery, and a lock of hair. I know it doesn't sound like much, but none of the jewellery matched so it belonged to different women. I thought maybe that it all belonged to his mother, but Stephen's an orphan so I couldn't be sure and I didn't want to ask. I knew that it could be something innocent, but it got me thinking.'

Ally nodded. 'So you started digging?'

Kathryn nodded. 'Stephen travels a lot and I realised that some of his travel costs don't quite add up.'

'In what way?'

'Gasoline,' Kathryn explained. 'Sometimes he drives long distances to business meetings that last days, but the money he spends on gas doesn't cover the distances so he can't have travelled that far.'

Ally frowned. 'Maybe he gets driven by other people while he's there?'

Kathryn smiled. 'Yeah, that's where I went with it for a couple of months.'

'A couple of months?' Ally exclaimed. 'How long as this been going on, honey?'

'Six months,' she replied. 'I never noticed all this stuff until we moved in together and got the apartment. Stephen travels so much that I offered to do his books for him, seeing as I wasn't working a day job. I had my studies to do but I figured it made sense to help him out, and he seemed really cool about it. Maybe he thought I wouldn't notice.'

'Notice what?' Ally pushed. 'I take it you got further than gas receipts?'

'When I looked further, after I realised it was happening most trips,' Kathryn nodded. 'He'd say he was off to some city, so I'd figure out roughly how much gas he'd need. He always came back with a bill that was for like, half of that much, so I tried to figure out where he was going. Turns out, depending on how much he had in the tank when he left, that he was always going the same distance away.'

Ally's gaze was fixed upon Kathryn's, and she could almost hear her friend thinking hard. Revelation dawned on Ally's face.

'Oh my God you followed him, didn't you?'

'Can you blame me? I had to know.'

'Where was he going?' Ally asked, feigning dispassionate concern but leaning closer to Kathryn with every passing moment.

'The city,' she replied, 'just the other side. I checked the mileage in his car too, and that tallies with the gas used in every trip he's made in the last year.'

'The airport is near the city,' Ally frowned. 'Maybe he flew the rest of the way each time?'

'No parking fees,' Kathryn explained, 'and no tickets. He would have claimed the travel expenses back just like everybody else.'

Ally frowned again, as though uncertain. 'Didn't he used to call you sometimes from other places though?'

Kathryn nodded. 'I get calls from time to time. He was always so sweet, always asking how I was. I guess I was so enamoured that he bothered to stay in touch all the time that it never crossed my mind to wonder about where he was calling from. When it did I traced the number using the Internet. It's surprising, to be honest, how easily you can track such things down these days.'

'Where was he calling from? The city?'

'No, that's the thing, he was often calling from hundreds of miles away.'

Ally's creased features went blank as she stared at Kathryn. 'Okay, honey, you're going to have to run this by me again because I'm not following here.'

Kathryn smiled, and this time she held Ally's hand. 'It's not important right now, okay? And I followed him, remember? He didn't go to the airport.'

'Where did he go?'

Kathryn sighed.

'I'll tell you about it later. Right now I really need you to do something for me.'

Ally appeared not to have heard Kathryn's response. 'You can't tell me all of that and then leave me hanging like this!'

'I'll tell you all I can, as soon as I can, okay?' Kathryn insisted, squeezing her friend's hand a little tighter. 'Right now I'm in the middle of something.'

'Your first day at your new job!' Ally gasped, horrified. 'I'm so sorry, I didn't ask about it and…'

'Don't worry about it,' Kathryn soothed her. 'I didn't exactly give you much of a chance, asking you here on such short notice.'

'Why *did* you ask me here? And what do you want me to do?'

Kathryn felt her jaw tighten as fresh resolve blossomed inside her.

'I'm going to see just what Stephen's been up to,' she replied, 'and I'm going to make sure that he pays for what he's done. I've worked my fingers to the bone since we got together, earning my diploma, looking after the apartment and his damned books, trying to keep everything in order while he's been seeing some other damned woman behind my back!'

Ally's concern melted into delight. 'You naughty bloody cow! What are you going to do to him?'

'One thing at a time,' Kathryn said. 'I might need you to cover for me here and there. I'm going to follow him again and find out what he's really getting up to. All I'll need you to do is cover my back while I'm doing it if he comes calling, and maybe pick up a few things for me.'

Ally quivered, her eyes sparkling with intrigue. 'What's your end game?'

'Later,' Kathryn promised. 'But let's just say the bastard's going to regret everything he's done.'

***

Dean Crawford

7

'You ever been shopping here?'

Jane Maietta stood in front of the gallery, one of a row of boutique shops with broad windows and fashionably minimalist interiors that lined the swankier end of a massive retail park off 13th Avenue South. Bright interior lighting illuminated the works of art mounted on the walls within.

'I can't afford to even look in the damned window,' Griffin said as he surveyed the gallery. 'You think they talk English in this place?'

'Probably not the kind you and I are thinking of,' Maietta replied as she followed Griffin in through the main door, the glass hissing open automatically. 'Sheila's only got one employee, which will make this a little easier.'

The door closed of its own accord behind them and the rush and bustle of passing shoppers was silenced. The interior of the gallery was whisper quiet, like a library that held the world's most expensive books.

Griffin glanced at a large square canvas adorned with what might have been a sunset or something. He couldn't really tell, the canvass adorned with a colourful but shapeless smear.

'What do you make of this?' he asked Maietta, who was peering deeper into the gallery looking for somebody to talk to.

She glanced over her shoulder at the painting. 'Looks like pretentious crap.'

'Yeah,' Griffin agreed. 'I'm just looking for the coffee stains right now.'

A voice spoke in a clear, perfect accent in reply. 'It's a Germaine Verdant original.'

Griffin turned to see a tall woman in a pale white silk shirt and long trousers with heels striding toward them, the heels clicking against the highly polished tiles. Her head was perched on top of a perfect neck, hair pinned up. Fashionable, square–rimmed spectacles balanced on her tiny nose. Griffin figured he was kind of looking at a work of art again, except this one had taken years to perfect.

'Verdant, huh?' he echoed, glancing again at the painting.

'Impressionistic expression,' Saira said. 'The portrayal of the emotion of hope via clean sweeps of vibrant colour amid darkness. It's one of Verdant's finest pieces.'

'Is that so?' Griffin asked, feigning interest. 'And what would one of Verdant's finest pieces set back an ordinary guy who wanted to brighten up his living room?'

Saira managed a small, unconvincing smile. 'Your house, car and the rest of your life's earnings. Both of you. Can I help you? I'm Saira, the sales manager here.'

Griffin didn't bridle at the veiled insult. 'We came into some money, the honey and me.' Griffin nudged Maietta and winked at her. 'Looking to spend some of it here. We were told your boss, Sheila McKenzie, is the woman we need to talk to. She around?'

'Mrs McKenzie didn't come into the gallery this morning.'

'Do you know where she's gone?' Maietta asked.

'Business,' Saira replied with a smile that betrayed no warmth. 'She often slips away for meetings and leaves me in charge.'

'Hell of a gallery,' Griffin said, 'hell of a responsibility for somebody so young.'

Saira could not quite conceal the tiny smile that curled from the corner of her lip at the compliment. 'I'm sure it's just the light, and yes it is a great responsibility, but Mrs McKenzie trusts me implicitly.'

'You got any idea when she'll be back?' Maietta asked.

Saira frowned. 'I don't know.'

'Has she missed any appointments?' Griffin asked.

'Two, both today,' Saira admitted, and then she peered at Griffin and Maietta. 'Why do you ask?'

Maietta flashed her badge. 'Detectives Griffin and Maietta.'

'Oh my God,' Saira mumbled, one delicate hand reaching up to touch her lips. 'Is she all right? I haven't been able to reach her on her cell.'

'You didn't think to report her missing?' Maietta asked.

'She's missing?'

Griffin and Maietta exchanged a glance. 'Presumed abducted,' Griffin explained.

'You didn't even notice she was gone?' Maietta asked.

'Like I said, Mrs McKenzie often goes out of town for several days at a time,' Saira replied. 'She is a very private woman and many of her clients are very private people, so it's not unusual for her to disappear for a couple of days. However, it is unusual for her not to return my calls or to let me know she won't be in. Even stranger that she would miss appointments. Another day or two without hearing from her and I probably would have been in contact with the police.'

'Do you know of anybody who might want to hurt Mrs McKenzie, anybody who might hold a grudge against her, like business rivals?'

Saira's studied demeanour slipped a little and Griffin thought he caught a glimpse of the ordinary high-school girl hidden behind the facade.

'Plenty,' she replied. 'Mrs McKenzie has been in business for over twenty years and has built up this gallery from almost nothing. She started as a runner, you know, working for another dealer who had made his name? Anyway, she fought her way to the top and made a lot of enemies along the way, including her former employer.'

'You got a name?' Maietta asked.

'Alexis Talbot,' Saira said, 'Sheila's main competitor.'

'And how did she upset all of these people?' Griffin asked.

Saira sighed and looked about her, as though worried that there was somebody listening even though the gallery was clearly deserted. Her voice dropped to a near whisper, her tone conspiratorial as she got the rare chance to share some office gossip.

'Mrs McKenzie worked hard to build her gallery,' she said. 'But business has become tough since the economic crisis, and jealous rivals have a habit of playing tough. Her competitors, like Talbot, undercut her to complete sales, approached private collectors and offered them favourable deals in return for…, well, you can guess I'm sure.'

'Sex for sales,' Griffin said. 'This Talbot woman wouldn't be the first person to do that.'

'No,' Saira conceded. 'But Talbot would later spread rumours that Sheila was doing the bed-hopping, trying to drag her name through the mud. She did such things all the time, caused at least two divorces after revealing her activities to scorned wives, hoping to financially cripple business rivals as their galleries were broken up to pay alimony. It caused Sheila terrible heartache. It wasn't that Talbot was outright cruel to people, just that she was absolutely focused on success and that friendships didn't matter in the slightest. *Do or die*, she often used to say as she walked around here, before Sheila took over.'

'When was the last time you saw Mrs McKenzie?' Maietta asked.

'Last night. She locked up here for me as I had to leave early.'

'Can you account for your whereabouts after you left here?' Griffin asked.

'I was at the dentist,' Saira replied, unconcerned. 'Then I went home. I share an apartment with a friend, so she can confirm I was there. It was a horrible night, raining all the time so we didn't go out.'

'Did you and Mrs McKenzie have a good relationship, Saira?' Griffin asked.

Saira sighed, glanced at her shoes before replying. 'She's been good to me. I didn't have much of a life before I got this job, and even though things have been tough financially Sheila hasn't laid me off.'

Griffin nodded. 'What about her husband, Dale McKenzie? You know him?'

Saira's expression brightened a little. 'Oh yes. He's a pilot, flies for a local airline, Ventura I think it is.'

'He come in here often?' Maietta asked.

'Not really. Maybe once a month or so, he's often working unsociable hours so we don't see much of him during the day unless he's on leave.' Saira's expression darkened. 'Is he okay?'

Griffin nodded.

'Mr McKenzie is fine, but he returned home recently to find a ransom note demanding money in return for his wife.'

Saira's hand flew to her lips again and her eyes widened as what was left of her act vanished. 'That's terrible.'

'Yeah, that's what he probably said,' Maietta replied. 'How many people do you think might have wanted to do this to her?'

Saira, her features still pinched with shock, shook her head.

'I don't know. And I don't understand why they would do that anyway, given the way the business is going.'

'Things taking a down turn?' Griffin asked.

'Badly, like I said, the economy and all that,' Saira replied. 'I do the books for Mrs McKenzie, the daily sales. I haven't had anything to record except expenses for over six months. Alexis Talbot's lies have severely affected our trade.'

'How so?' Maietta asked.

'Dealers cutting Sheila out,' Saira said, 'or conspiring together to prevent her from hearing about new auctions because of the lies and the rumours. Alexis Talbot has a lot to answer for, and I'm a big believer in karma. Being a bitch comes back to bite everybody in the ass eventually.'

Griffin fought the urge to smile at Saira's gradual transformation.

'And Sheila still treats you well, Saira?' Maietta asked, 'despite her financial troubles.'

'Well enough for me not to want to kidnap her for ransom, if that's what you mean?' Saira said. 'Besides, knowing her finances like I do, ransom would be the last thing on my mind. It would be pointless.'

'But what about all of these expensive originals, all these Verdants?' Griffin asked. 'There must be capital in the business?'

'Mrs McKenzie has been reduced to the role of a sub–agent,' Saira explained. 'These works are owned by collectors, not the gallery. We sell them in return for a commission. Mrs McKenzie has not purchased an original work for several months.'

Griffin glanced across at Maietta, who folded her notebook and slipped it into her pocket.

'So whoever abducted her for ransom…'

'Isn't going to get very much, at least not from her business,' Saira confirmed. 'And for what it's worth on my part, I actually like my job. The last thing I'd want is for Mrs McKenzie to go out of business. Working here is much better than flipping burgers down the street, if you see what I mean?'

Griffin unfolded a photograph from his pocket and showed it to Saira. 'This is a picture taken of Sheila before she was abducted, and sent to her husband. You got any idea when your boss was wearing this suit?'

Saira glanced at the picture for a moment. 'Three or four days ago as best I recall, late last week.'

Griffin nodded. 'Thanks for your time, we'll be in touch.'

Griffin strode out of the gallery and leaned against the car as Maietta joined him, a leaden sky spitting bitter squalls of sleet around them.

'If she was wearing that suit last week then the footage is no good for an abduction timeline,' Maietta said to him. 'She's in the wind. And from what Saira says, this whole thing doesn't jive.'

'Nope,' Griffin agreed. 'Either her abductors are idiots or they don't know anything about their target, which doesn't make sense if you're grabbing somebody for money.'

'For all they know she could be worth nothing by now,' Maietta said. 'Just like you and me.'

'Thanks sweetheart,' Griffin muttered.

'Hey, c'mon, how much do you think I'd get for ransom?'

'I'd give up all my cash for you, Jane,' Griffin replied.

'I don't know whether to be flattered or insulted.'

'Both,' Griffin said. 'We got nothing here. Saira's got no motive for this unless she's maybe sleeping with the husband.'

'Doubt it if she likes her job and Sheila as much as she says,' Maietta said, 'and anyway if she knocked Mrs McKenzie off and then moved in with Dale it would send alarm bells ringing all over town.'

'We could try Sheila McKenzie's competitors across the country,' Griffin said, 'maybe sound a few of them out? And Alexis Talbot sounds like she might be good for this.'

Maietta chewed on her lip and shook her head. 'This feels like a small–town thing to me. Besides, if Talbot is acting against her she must already know she's put her in a financial hole. She'd be enjoying watching McKenzie go down slowly and painfully, not wrecking the party and implicating herself in an abduction.'

Griffin nodded. 'If Talbot plays out then that leaves us with no suspects right now, except the husband.'

'Dale McKenzie wasn't within five hundred miles of here when his wife disappeared,' Maietta reminded him. 'And there's no motive.'

'Not yet,' Griffin mused. 'Look into Sheila McKenzie's financials, see if she has any interesting life insurances, or maybe owns the gallery premises or something. If our abductors are seeking money then we've got to assume they know something that we don't.'

***

8

Sheila McKenzie sat in silence and wondered how long she had left to live.

The reclining chair in which she was strapped was comfortable enough, one of those heavily padded types that was half–way between a rocking chair and a bed. There was no undue pressure on her body, but nonetheless she was aching all over from a lack of movement, not to mention thirsty, hungry and afraid. Her wrists and ankles were firmly bound and under her jaw was a strap that ran around the back of the recliner to pin her head back.

She could not see. The blindfold obscuring her vision was sufficient to block all light. She could not hear, the bungs placed in her ears blocking all sound. Her sense of smell was unaffected, but the only odours she could detect were those of stale grease and dust. Finally, a gag bound her mouth and prevented her from screaming for her life, which was something she would certainly have done by now because the lunatic who had done this to her had forgotten one other very important sensory input.

Touch.

From time to time Sheila detected tiny vibrations through the metal frame of the chair, as though people were banging things about nearby. The vibrations were incredibly subtle but over time she had sensed regularity to them, the shift between day and night. The horrendously long hours of silence were broken by the clatter of morning, of people at work.

Sleep had come in broken patterns, interspersed by periods during which she experienced horrifically vivid hallucinations as her brain struggled to adapt to the extreme sensory deprivation. Like waking dreams, her fear manifested itself within the tortured confines of her mind until she wept bitter tears against her blindfold.

She had long ago relinquished control of her bladder, unable to bear the pain any longer. Her skin was raw from the prolonged contact with her own bodily fluids and the taint of ammonia stained the air around her.

Sheila spent hours fantasising about rescue, images of police officers bursting into her prison and liberating her. Then, every now and again, she would sense a change in the air pressure around her, just like she had in her home before she had been attacked. It had happened once before, the creeping sensation that there was somebody else in the room with her.

It was happening now. A waft of cold air suddenly drifted across her body and she sensed new, stronger vibrations through the frame of the recliner. Sheila sat absolutely still as she felt the hairs on the back of her neck rise up, a cold tingling sensation rippling across the backs of her arms as though insects were scuttling across her skin. She shivered, her hands gripping the arms of the chair.

The air about her moved almost imperceptibly, a gentle waft on the exposed skin of her legs where her skirt had ridden up. Sheila struggled to contain her mounting fear, but she felt her body trembling and felt rather than heard a whimper escape from her throat and breathe past her dry, cracked lips.

A hand rested on her thigh.

Sheila's tears spilled from her eyes and a muffled shriek of fear leaped from her mouth. This was it, then. Another hand touched her knee. The hands yanked her skirt up to the tops of her thighs, exposing her soiled underwear. Then her panties were dragged down her legs and the bonds around her ankles loosened slightly.

Sheila tried to kick free, but her legs were numb and cold and the hands were too strong. She was about to scream in terror when a soft cloth wiped away the mess from her legs. Sheila froze as her underwear was slid down her legs and removed. The cloth reappeared and cleaned her, and then she felt her ankles being refastened and a warm blanket tucked around her legs.

Moments later, the bungs in her ears were also removed.

Sheila dare not move a muscle. Compared to the silence that she had endured for countless hours, the sudden influx of noise was deafening. The rustle of fabric against skin. The sound of a person breathing, of their shoes against the floor and the distant but unmistakeable sound of machinery.

The voice, when it came, sounded like something out of a horror movie.

'Do not move.'

It was heavily distorted by one of those devices that could be bought in any joke store. It sounded like a cross between Darth Vader and Satan himself, deep and melodious but filled with menace as it went on.

'You will be allowed to eat and drink. If you attempt to call for help, I will leave and you will die of either starvation or thirst, understood?'

Sheila managed a tiny nod against the strap beneath her jaw. Moments later, she felt the gag in her mouth being loosened and lifted away. The touch of a plastic bottle against her parched lips, and suddenly she was gulping down water as though her life depended upon it. It splashed down her blouse, only to be mopped up by her captor.

Sheila gasped for breath as the bottle was taken away. 'Who are you?'

The words tumbled from her lips before she could stop them. Human nature, she guessed. Even though her voice sounded rough and weak, and even though she was quite probably in danger of losing her life, she could not help herself.

'What do you want from me?'

There was no response but for the sound of deep, heavy breathing and what sounded like plastic being crumpled nearby. Sheila waited, and smelled a sudden waft of what might have been chicken and bread.

'Eat.'

The deep voice brooked no argument and Sheila sensed the food hovering near her mouth. She tore off a chunk of sandwich, chewing gratefully despite her predicament. She swallowed the first mouthful and turned her head toward where she guessed her captor must be standing, even though she could not see them.

'I have money, if that's what you want.'

The food was shoved against her lips once more and she took another bite. It crossed her mind that her captor could leave at any moment, abandoning her to the silence and darkness. Sheila slowed her chewing, starting to drag each mouthful out.

'I'll be missed,' she said between chunks of sandwich. 'People will be looking for me.'

The voice, when it replied, was devoid of emotion. *'Nobody is looking for you. You are an orphan.'*

'How do you know that?'

More water sloshed against her lips and she drank, more slowly this time. The sandwich returned, and Sheila managed to drag out eating it for several minutes before the last chunk was placed in her mouth.

She considered lunging forward and biting the hand, but something told her that to do so would be useless. She could smell the leather gloves worn by her captor, which would be tough enough to resist any damage she could reasonably inflict.

The last of the water was drained from the plastic bottle, and for a few moments Sheila feared that her captor would leave. The irony of that fear was not lost to her even in her current state, and she realised not for the first time how much she craved companionship, just as she always had.

'Don't leave.'

The voice did not reply.

Sheila heard the unmistakeable sound of a nearby chair creaking as it was sat upon. Sheila looked blindly about her and then the voice spoke again.

'Your money, where is it?'

Sheila swallowed thickly. Think, woman. Keep them talking. 'It's in the business, and in separate accounts too, shared with my husband.'

A long silence before the voice responded again. *'Does your husband care for you?'*

Sheila's heart froze in her chest. 'What?'

'Answer the question.'

'Yes,' she replied. 'He does.'

'Are you sure?'

Sheila's rage fought its way past her fear and burst from within her. 'What do you want with me?!'

The voice said nothing for a long time, but Sheila could hear the soft hiss of breathing. Her addled mind struggled to focus, to draw some kind of information about her abductor from the meagre clues offered her.

'Your life,' the voice said suddenly, *'depends on your husband following my instructions to the letter. Do you think that he will do that?'*

Sheila writhed in frustration within her bonds, but she could not free herself. 'How the hell should I know? I don't know what you've asked him to do.'

'You're a successful woman,' the voice replied. *'You know what we want of him.'*

'Money,' Sheila spat. 'That's all you people want, isn't it? Cash, but you don't want to work for it. No, you take it from others, like the blood–sucking leeches that you are. Weak, cowardly and lazy!'

Sheila spat in the general direction of where the voice was coming from.

The world beyond the darkness fell silent. Sheila awaited a response, but the longer she waited the more her rage withered and the stronger her fear became. It built up like a poison inside her, cold and clammy until she called out.

Silence reigned, but she could still hear the breathing. When the voice spoke again it was laden with terminal certainty.

'If your husband does not undertake to pay the ransom on your life, I will be forced to execute you.'

Sheila swallowed thickly as her legs began to tremble, but even through her fear some small part of her rational mind recognised the use of I. One person. One abductor. One killer. Maybe working for somebody else? Her business rivals?

'Why?' Sheila uttered. 'I haven't harmed you? I don't know who you are. I can't do anything to expose you so why would you kill me?'

The figure moved, standing again. Sheila flinched but her abductor merely reached up and yanked her bonds tight against her jaw again.

'No,' Sheila gasped. 'Don't leave me here! Please don't leave me to die…'

The gag was pulled tightly into her mouth again, cutting her words off into a stream of strangled cries that degenerated into sobs.

The voice spoke one last time into her ear.

'It's not me who wants you dead.'

Then the plugs were shoved back into place, and Sheila McKenzie was left alone in her lonely universe once again.

***

9

Since she had uncovered his lies, Kathryn had found it extremely trying whenever Stephen had returned home from his business trips. Truth was, she now despised the very moment that he walked back into the apartment, struggling as she had for months now to maintain a facade of delight at his homecoming.

Now, it was even harder to sustain the charade. The desire to burst through the door and beat a confession from him in a screaming frenzy was almost overwhelming, but her new job working for the police precluded any such violent confrontation. Getting arrested for battery wasn't going to do her career any good, despite the no doubt cathartic effect of imprinting Stephen's duplicitous face onto the back of a frying pan.

She took a breath outside the door to their apartment, her door key in her hand hovering before the lock. Just a little while longer, she told herself. You can do this.

Kathryn shoved the key in the lock and walked inside.

'Hi!'

Her greeting was answered from the living room, where she could see the flicker of the television glowing and Stephen's legs resting on the coffee table. The waft of Chinese takeaway filled the apartment, and Kathryn turned into the kitchen and grabbed herself a plate. The food was still hot, so she took her time and dished herself out a helping and grabbed a can of soda before making her way slowly into the lounge.

Stephen was in the recliner chair, his half–eaten lunch resting on a coffee table nearby and a bottle of beer clasped in his hand. She could tell at a glance that he was unhappy. His features were drawn and although he was watching a comedy show his gaze was unfocused.

'Are you okay?' she asked as she perched herself alongside him on the sofa.

Stephen drew a hand down his face and sighed. 'No, not really.'

'What's happened?'

'I got a call from HQ a couple of hours ago. The latest deal went south,' he replied. 'Company could not afford the premiums after all, once their finances were checked out. Damned near in liquidation, so there's no way that they could afford us and no way we'd forward cover to them anyway. Whole thing was a waste of time.'

Kathryn looked down at her plate. 'I'm sorry, I know how hard you worked for that one.'

Stephen nodded slowly, but did not reply.

'What are you going to do next?'

Stephen looked at his beer for a moment as though considering whether to drink it or hurl it across the room.

'I'll head back in the morning. There's an action meeting, if you can call it that, and I want to be there to find out what went wrong. We should never have been involved with a company in such decline. I'm guessing whoever cleared them without running the proper checks first will get a rocket up their ass come tomorrow.'

'Don't you select clients?' Kathryn asked sweetly as she popped a piece of sweet and sour chicken into her mouth.

Stephen shook his head. 'I approach potential clients, but head office audits them before I go back in and negotiate the deals and any contracts are drawn up.'

Stephen looked at her, his face half–lit by the glowing television. She could see he had not shaved and his hair was messy, which was unlike him. That he was under pressure she was in no doubt, and although the knowledge sparked an intense delight somewhere deep inside she still felt as though the emotion was somehow unjustified. He was suffering, and the knowledge made her both powerful and uncomfortable.

'What happens now?' she asked him.

Stephen sighed, his dark eyes reflecting the television. 'I won't make any commission this month again.'

'Even though it's not your fault?'

'Doesn't matter to corporate,' Stephen replied. 'The deal's not done. I got my first–half commission when the company signed up, but the rest is in the wind now.'

Kathryn looked down at her meal.

'So you can't cover the rent again?' she said.

Stephen shook his head slowly. 'I'm sorry honey, I know it's a pain but there's nothing that I can do. I'll cover the other bills and the car with what I've got left, okay?'

Kathryn popped another morsel of chicken that she didn't really want into her mouth. It meant that she could avoid speaking for another few moments. Stephen sighed and took a pull from his beer before he got up and headed without another word to the shower.

Kathryn waited until she heard the water running and then made herself comfortable on the sofa and tucked into her takeaway with relish. Thoughts flashed through her mind as she considered what Stephen had said.

His bosses had called two hours ago, and yet he was unshaven? Stephen had driven home in the very early morning, but it was already one in the afternoon. If he'd slept for a full four or five hours it would only have been ten or eleven in the morning, plenty of time left to have a shower, shave and so on like he normally would do. It was one of the things that had first attracted her to Stephen, the fact that he had always been clean–cut, had always looked after himself. She decided that it was *possible*, given everything that had happened recently, that he had simply let himself slip for an hour or two.

So that left the call itself, from his bosses. The company he worked for was headquartered two hundred miles away. Such was the modern world, where conference calls, cell–phones and the Internet meant that a man on the road rarely had to venture into his boss's office anymore if the work at hand did not require his immediate presence.

Forking noodles into her mouth with one hand, Kathryn foraged with the other across the coffee table until she found Stephen's cell–phone. She picked it up and tapped in his code to unlock the screen. Learning his lock–code had been one of her first acts of subterfuge after discovering his deception, a crime that she defended to herself by citing an *eye for an eye* mentality: Stephen started the lying first, so he had it coming. She had prided herself on not often using her secret knowledge, but now was the perfect moment.

She scrolled down his received calls list and was both elated and somehow saddened when her fears were confirmed. There were no calls logged from the company he worked for. In fact he had not received a single call since late the previous night. On an impulse, she scrolled through Stephen's out–going call list and instantly saw a number that she recognised.

Kathryn returned the cell to its home screen and placed it carefully back on the coffee table, at the same angle and location as she had found it. Quietly, she put her plate down and crept through the hallway toward the front door where the apartment phone hung from its cradle. She could hear the hiss of water from the shower and Stephen splashing about inside the stall as she unhooked the phone and scrolled through its menu.

As she suspected, there were no calls recorded as coming in for the past two days. Nothing had changed since the last time she had checked.

Nobody had called Stephen.

Kathryn crept back to her takeaway and sat watching trash television as she considered the new and important pieces of information. Stephen was lying, which was nothing new, but his demeanour was different. Something was putting him under strain and she figured that whatever it was it concerned weighty matters other than herself.

In the past few months she had come to know Stephen far better than she had before she had unveiled his deception and lies. It seemed strange to her, even now, that the man she was not actually supposed to know was the man she now knew best. Stephen, the man she had met four years ago while working in a small diner in the city, who had asked if *he* could leave *her* his number so that *she* could decide whether to call or text *him*, was in fact a stranger to her. A facade. A figment of her imagination, like a phantom slipping from one dream to the next, hoped for but never actually materialising. The man that she now knew was a manipulator, a cheat, a self–serving bastard who calculated his every move, his every response, for all she knew his every breath in order to maintain a relationship that he probably didn't even want, and all for reasons that she could not fathom.

The only conclusion that she could draw from the whole sorry mess was that the other woman presented a better and brighter future for Stephen than Kathryn herself did, and that he was gradually working his way out of her life. The long absences, the deplorable lack of sexual activity, the disinterest in her life and her achievements.

Simple, really, although tragic none the less.

The man she knew would most likely seek to leave her and hit the road as soon as possible, perhaps on the excuse that if he drove through the night to the other side of the state he would avoid the worst of the rush–hour traffic. It would give him time to think about what had happened, maybe formulate a plan of action when he got there. He'd feel better in the morning, could turn a crisis into an opportunity once again. Except that the crisis never ended, and the only opportunities were those that he presumably took for himself, leaving her to struggle on alone.

'Are you okay?'

Kathryn startled as she looked up to see Stephen staring down at her from the living room door. She realised that she had been stabbing pieces of chicken with unnecessary force, butchering them one after the other.

'Sure,' she replied brightly. 'Was just figuring out how to pay the rent this month.'

Stephen sighed. 'Maybe I'll ask for a raise.'

He walked into the room and picked up his cell phone, slipped it into his pocket. He was dressed for work with his hair neat once again, clean shaven. The bastard looked like he'd just walked out of an aftershave advert.

'You're leaving again?' Kathryn asked.

Stephen nodded as he hunted for his car keys, which were on the window sill, but Kathryn decided not to tell him just yet.

'It's the only thing to do right now,' he replied. 'If I leave now I won't have to worry about traffic in the city later, and it'll give me time to clear my head. I'll stay in a hotel on the company card, get a good night's sleep and probably feel like a new man by tomorrow morning.'

So will I, Kathryn thought but did not say. She stood and reached up to slip her arms around his neck. His cologne smelled expensive and seductive at the same time. It helped Kathryn maintain a smile as she embraced him, instead of tightening her grip and biting his fucking face off.

'You're never here,' she purred. 'Why not stay the night?'

Stephen smiled, his hands resting in the small of her back. 'I'd love to honey, but the sooner this is sorted the sooner we'll be back on track, okay?'

It wasn't a request and she knew better than to argue. Besides, feigning disappointment was enough for her. The sooner he left, the sooner she could get on with more important things.

'Okay,' she sighed miserably and pulled away.

'I'll make it up to you,' he promised as he found his car keys and swiped them up from the window sill.

'I know,' she replied. 'Love you.'

Stephen kissed her on the cheek, whirled and hurried out of the living room. Within moments he was gone, and she heard his car start up moments later and pull away into the cold darkness outside.

Despite everything, her greatest regret was the fact that he had not asked her how her first day at her new job was going.

***

10

Great Falls International Airport was illuminated by a galaxy of lights that flickered against the turbulent grey sky as Detective Griffin drove into the parking lot outside the main terminal.

'McKenzie's on his way,' Maietta said as she dropped her cell phone from her ear and shut it off. 'Ventura's organised us a room out back of the terminal, somewhere we can talk without being observed.'

'Great,' Griffin said as he climbed out of the car and pulled his collar up against the cold air. The sound of an airliner taking off roared through the air around them as they walked toward the terminal, heads down against the gusts of sleet. A bitter grey, icy slush made the asphalt slick beneath their feet as they walked. 'We need his help to try to figure out what the hell's going on with his wife and make some sense of this.'

'Sheila McKenzie's insurance company confirmed that she holds a policy for four million bucks, payable on her death,' Maietta said as she leafed through her notes. 'There's motive there, at least.'

'And she owns that gallery, right?' Griffin asked.

'Has the freehold,' Maietta replied. 'I figure it's a half million or more of prime retail space.'

Griffin frowned. 'Even if the abductors got everything, including the McKenzie's house, they wouldn't get much past five million bucks. It doesn't figure, unless the husband's playing some kind of elaborate game here.'

'Good time to find out,' Maietta said. 'Half the damned state's on alert.'

Because the abduction had occurred within the Great Falls city limits, the case had become a GFPD responsibility, but the FBI had immediately been notified of the incident and investigation. The popular TV drama notion of police departments and Federal agencies being at loggerheads over jurisdictional control of cases was a fallacy: upon notification of the abduction, virtually every agency had leaped at the chance to offer assistance.

BOLOs, *Be On the Look Out* reports, had been sent state–wide and regionally by teletype. Border Patrol and Customs and Border Protection, CBP, for the Canadian Border had also been notified in case the abductors made a run north for Canada, just over a hundred miles away. A Missing and Endangered Persons Alert would be sent out and the

Criminal Justice Information Network, National Crime Information Center and Rocky Mountain Information Network all utilized to disseminate info to law enforcement agencies. To add to that, Homeland Security had been informed and US Marshals Service were being kept apprised of the situation. Cascade County's Sheriff's Office and the Montana Highway Patrol had been issued with images of Sheila McKenzie, and although Great Falls no longer had an FBI Field Office, the Bureau was also discreetly sending out images of the victim across the country.

In short, whoever was holding Sheila McKenzie against her will would find it almost impossible to move her about the country without somebody seeing something.

'Tight as a mosquito's ass,' Griffin agreed with some satisfaction. 'Now we gotta hope they're not smart enough to just stay put with her. What about Talbot, Sheila McKenzie's former boss?'

'She's alibied out,' Maietta replied almost apologetically. 'She's in the damned Bahamas, multiple witnesses, and apparently couldn't care less about McKenzie. I guess she's made her money and is out of the game.'

'So much for Saira's story of her being out for McKenzie's blood,' Griffin muttered. 'We got anybody else?'

'Nobody,' Maietta replied.

They walked into the main terminal and, following directions relayed to Maietta by Ventura Air's staff, found their way past the bustle of the terminal and out to a remote storage facility away from the public buildings. A member of Ventura's staff with a solid alibi for the abduction met them and led them to what Griffin figured was some kind of staff room: Formica table stranded alone in the centre, one shelf with a battered old microwave, a water cooler and stacked mugs grimy with age.

The door closed behind them and a silence enveloped the room as they waited.

'How's Angela?' Maietta asked as she leaned against the wall, her arms folded defensively as though bracing herself for the response.

Griffin shrugged. 'She's fine. Why?'

'You haven't mentioned her much lately, is all.'

'Not much to mention.'

'Are you guys okay?'

'Are you my counsellor now?'

Maietta shrugged and fell silent. Griffin sighed.

'She's a little up–tight, you know?' he said finally.

Maietta raised a dark, delicately curved eyebrow but said nothing. Griffin looked at her. 'What?'

'Nothin'.'

'Crap, I know that look,' Griffin said. 'What, you think I'm to blame?'

'I didn't say that. It's none of my business.'

'Damn right it's not,' Griffin snapped. 'Let's just focus on the case, okay? Let Stone handle my head.'

'How's it going with her?'

'It's not, and that's just the way I like it.'

'She's trying to help.'

'She's interfering and I don't need help. I just need people to stop asking me damned questions about how I am all the time.'

The sound of footsteps outside the door silenced them, and the door opened as Dale McKenzie walked in.

Griffin placed a lot of faith in first appearances. McKenzie was tall, with dark hair and a tan that suggested either mixed parentage or foreign origin. But what interested Griffin more was McKenzie's mannerisms and state of mind: the man was an airline pilot, an occupation of great responsibility, but McKenzie's uniform was somewhat hastily arranged as though he'd rushed to the meeting, and his hair was somewhat in disarray. His gaze was quick but nervous, as though caught off balance. All of this Griffin took in at a glance and put down to the extraordinary circumstances McKenzie had suddenly found himself in.

'Mister McKenzie, thanks for seeing us. This is my partner, Detective Maietta.'

McKenzie nodded at Maietta as the door was closed behind him, his gaze switching between the two detectives.

'Have you found her yet?'

'Nothing yet I'm afraid,' Griffin admitted, noting that McKenzie's first question and concern regarded his wife's welfare. 'But we're already doing everything we can. Please take a seat, sir.'

'What's *everything*?' McKenzie demanded as he sat down.

Griffin sat down opposite McKenzie, Maietta staying where she was, leaning against the wall.

'We've got a team of six officers working the case,' Griffin assured the pilot. 'I'm leading the investigation with my partner Maietta, who is talking to other law enforcement agencies.'

McKenzie seemed satisfied with this, but he was wringing his hands.

'Okay, let's get started Mister McKenzie,' Griffin said.

'Dale.'

'Dale, okay, good. Have you heard anything at all from Sheila's abductors?'

'Nothing,' McKenzie replied. 'I've had my cell with me at all times but there have been no calls at all.'

'Okay, I want you to walk us through everything that happened this morning. Every little detail.'

McKenzie sighed. 'I already went through everything with the sergeant over the phone.'

'Humour us,' Griffin insisted. 'The more sure we are that nothing's been overlooked the quicker we can move forward with the investigation. Anything, even the tiniest detail, can change everything in the first forty–eight hours of an abduction.'

McKenzie nodded and reluctantly began relating the morning's events. Truth was, Griffin had already read the sergeant's report three times and had every single moment of Dale McKenzie's morning mapped out in his mind. Griffin wasn't expecting new details because there wasn't much to go on in the first place, but he did want to see if McKenzie changed anything, altered his story in any way.

McKenzie went through the description of his return flight, journey home, finding the note and calling the police on his cell. There wasn't much to relate, really, and he stuck to his story. No deviation from the details, no tells in his demeanour that suggested to Griffin that he was telling anything other than the absolute truth.

'Would anybody you know of wish to hurt your wife in any way?' Griffin asked when McKenzie had finished. 'Does she have any enemies, any old boyfriends, people like that who might hold a grudge?'

'No,' McKenzie replied without a moment's hesitation. 'She's a hugely successful lady. That's what attracted me to her in the first place.'

'Your wife is the owner of an art gallery in the city, pretty high–class stuff, some international trade.'

'Yes,' McKenzie said, staring into his coffee. 'I appreciate fine arts, but it's Sheila's passion in life. She's been running the gallery for over ten years now and has a strong reputation.'

'And a nice life because of it,' Griffin noted with a friendly smile. 'Your wife's a real wheeler dealer, but she's not in the seven figure range for turnover, right?'

McKenzie shrugged. 'She runs her business, and I fly regional for Ventura Air. I don't have any knowledge of her financial situation.'

'You don't know how much money your wife earns?'

McKenzie offered Griffin a tight smile. 'Our relationship is not about money. Sheila is the big money earner, not me. We are comfortable, financially, which is all that matters to us.'

Griffin noted McKenzie's use of the present tense and the use of *us* when referring to his wife: he believed that she would be found alive and well, and spoke of her naturally as his partner.

Griffin glanced at his notes once more. 'Do you think that you're ten million bucks comfortable?'

McKenzie blurted out a bitter laugh. 'If we were, do you think I'd be working weekends and unsociable hours flying a Dash–8 out of Great Falls?'

'Fair point,' Griffin said, and scribbled a note. 'So why does this abductor believe that you could raise ten million overnight?'

McKenzie shook his head. 'I have no idea, detective. We don't have anything like that kind of money.'

'What about Sheila's life insurance?' Griffin asked.

McKenzie stared at his coffee for a moment and then looked up into Griffin's eyes. 'What the hell is that supposed to mean?'

'Your wife has a life insurance program in place worth four million bucks,' Griffin said. 'Plus what her business premises is worth. That's a lot of money.'

'There's the small matter of her having to die,' McKenzie replied. 'You think that I'd do that to her, for money?'

Griffin said nothing in response, just sat and stared at McKenzie for as long as it took for the pilot to break the silence.

'In case you hadn't noticed, I was at thirty thousand feet and five hundred nautical miles away when my wife disappeared. Who the hell do you think I am, David Blaine?'

'You could be working with somebody else.'

McKenzie slammed a fist down on the table as he glared at Griffin. 'Then why the hell would I go through such a charade? If I was insane enough to pull something like this then I'd just kill her, wouldn't I, and report her missing?'

Griffin nodded. The assumption that he would have to go through the *charade* of an abduction told Griffin, along with everything else, that McKenzie almost certainly had not abducted his wife.

'I apologise, Dale, if my line of questioning seems offensive, but it's just something we have to go through. It's not to accuse you, but to remove you as a suspect as soon as possible.'

McKenzie nodded, but now he refused to make eye contact. The unusual contradiction in McKenzie's behaviour buzzed through Griffin's mind.

'When was the last time you saw your wife?' Maietta asked, speaking for the first time since McKenzie had entered the room.

'Yesterday afternoon,' McKenzie said, 'before I left for work.'

'And she seemed okay, no problems, no apparent concerns?'

'None, she was fine, really fine.'

'Does she have any family beyond yourself?'

McKenzie shook his head. 'No, we're both orphans.' He smiled, a little bitterly, and Griffin thought he detected the faintest hint of grief creasing McKenzie's eyes. 'We've only got each other.'

Griffin felt any last dregs of doubt over the pilot's story flutter away. He glanced down at his notes and added a couple of words. *Both orphans.*

'We spoke to Saira at your wife's gallery,' he said. 'She confided in us that the business was in financial difficulty and that Sheila has made many enemies in the trade over the years. Can you shed any light on that?'

McKenzie seemed non–plussed. 'I wouldn't know about enemies in her trade,' he said, 'although I suppose it's possible to make enemies anywhere in business. As for the financial situation, yes, times have gotten harder for luxury goods since the economic collapse, but we were coping and I was flying extra hours to support us. We're struggling more than we used to, but it isn't a crisis.'

Griffin steeled himself.

'Is it possible, Dale, however remotely, that your wife might seek to stage her own abduction in collaboration with a second party in order to obtain her life insurance policy?'

Dale's jaw almost dropped as he stared at Griffin, and the detective heard Maietta suck in a soft breath of air.

'You seriously think that she would rig something like this?' McKenzie gasped.

'I don't know,' Griffin replied. 'That's why I'm asking you.'

'No, she wouldn't,' McKenzie snapped. 'Absolutely not. Sheila built her business up from nothing, she's no quitter. She'd fight for every last inch of that premises, not risk jail or years' of living in hiding. And besides, who would gain from it? I'm the beneficiary and I sure as hell don't want to see Sheila's business go down the can.' McKenzie scowled as he glanced at his watch and stood. 'I have a flight to catch.'

'Thank you for your time, Dale,' Griffin said as he stood from the table. 'Sorry again for the hard line, it's over now and you're free to go.'

McKenzie turned to leave, his coffee untouched. He shook Griffin's proffered hand, and Griffin recognised all too clearly the shadows of restrained grief in the pilot's eyes.

'Do you think that you can find her?' McKenzie asked, his anger subsiding rapidly. 'Before…'

'They want money,' Griffin cut him off, 'not blood. We'll find her.'

*

'He didn't do it.'

Griffin slapped his notebook down on the Formica table as soon as McKenzie had left.

'I agree,' Maietta said as she pushed off the wall. 'He looked shifty though.'

'He's nervous,' Griffin admitted, 'anxious, afraid maybe, but he sure ain't guilty of this.'

Maietta's eyes narrowed. 'He was hiding something.'

Griffin looked at her. 'Say what?'

'He kept dodging questions.'

'What makes you think that?' Griffin asked. 'He answered everything damned straight, far as I could see.'

'Yeah, but it was the way that he answered,' Maietta insisted. 'It's the dip of their eyes, to the right and down, that betrays the liars, we both know that. They have to think about what they're saying. He wouldn't look you in the eye all the time and kept his head down when things got difficult.'

Griffin shrugged.

'Doesn't look much that way to me. Sure, I thought he seemed a little awkward but he wasn't lying when he said he didn't know where his wife was.'

Maietta did not answer other than to tilt her head in acquiescence.

'What now?' she asked as they left the room and began making their way back toward the airport terminal.

'We get Dale's house wired for sound in case the abductors make a call. We should probably sneak in for a look ourselves, and forensics have got to get in there somehow and dust for fingerprints and such like.'

'That's not going to be easy if the abductors are watching the home. Sure we could get one person in wearing a pilot's uniform, but a forensic team?'

'We'll have to think of something,' Griffin insisted, and rubbed his temples. 'You know, there's a hell of a lot about all of this that doesn't add up. Dale comes home, walks into the house, finds the note, calls us. By then his wife had already been gone for a few hours at least because the bed wasn't slept in and only one day's mail was lying on the doormat. So how come they haven't made contact with Dale yet? Where are the instructions for leaving the money? The abductors can't achieve much if they don't receive their ransom.'

'Maybe these guys are real pros,' Maietta suggested. 'They're letting us sweat on it, waiting until the last minute. Then they'll call in, ask for a reasonable amount of money, something that maybe the McKenzie's *can* afford, and bingo…'

'They walk away with a couple of million,' Griffin finished her sentence as they walked out into the cold air, but he frowned. 'Seems kind of elaborate though, doesn't it? Like all ransoms they're risking identification when the money's brought out.'

'Well,' Maietta said, 'we're pissing into the wind until they make contact. Let's get back and hand over to the night shift, okay?'

Griffin nodded, still thinking about Dale McKenzie and the alarm system in the pilot's house.

***

11

'Ventura four–one–nine–six, downwind for finals to stop, runway two–seven.'

Captain Dale McKenzie held the control column of the Dash–8 tightly in his hands, trying to let the aircraft ride the air currents as the bottom of the cloud layer skimmed past just above him. But he couldn't loosen his grip and the Dash–8 felt twitchy and awkward in his grasp as he squinted into the sunset through ragged bands of turbulent cloud, the past hour of flying consumed by concern for his wife.

On one of the glass screens before him, a digital clock read *16.52*. Twelve hours ago, as near as anybody could figure, Sheila had been abducted. Dale had no knowledge of whether there had been contact from her abductors while he had been airborne, or if her cold corpse had been found dumped in some lonely woods somewhere out on the plains.

The aircraft had just descended out of its cruise, the darkening clouds parting to reveal a gloomy evening below, a stark difference to the brilliant blue sky and burning deserts of Las Vegas from where his flight had just returned. The lights of Great Falls twinkled like a galaxy nearby as Dale watched the runway of the airport passing by off the port wing, following the standard approach pattern into the airport.

'Landing checks,' his first officer said.

Elaine Kingsley was a first–year graduate pilot, fresh out of flight school and eager to impress. She already had the checklist in her lap and was calling out each check for Dale's benefit as she ran through them.

'De–ice on…, flaps retracted…, landing lights on…, fuel as planned plus ten per cent reserve…'

Dale listened to her until she completed the list, then he made his own call.

'Flaps stage one, landing gear down.'

Elaine repeated the calls, the flaps whining into position as the undercarriage dropped out into the airstream. Dale tweaked the trim and throttles to compensate, watching the airspeed decrease steadily.

'Flaps stage two, trim her out in advance.'

Elaine obeyed, trimming the nose down slightly and then deploying the flaps again as Dale held the aircraft steady. Dale felt the Dash settle into its new configuration as Elaine advanced the throttles to arrest the descent, the extra lift generated by the flaps causing the airplane to bob about on the wind more vigorously than before.

'You got anything planned now that the shift's over?' Elaine asked.

Dale shook his head, monitoring the instruments as he replied. 'Nothing special, just relaxing at home.'

'How's the wife?'

Dale opened his mouth to reply, but his brain momentarily froze as he pictured Sheila alone somewhere, maybe in pain or terrible fear, suffering. His grip tightened on the control column as he heard Elaine reply to a call from air traffic control, and he realised that he was breathing more heavily, hot and uncomfortable.

'You okay?'

Elaine was watching him with some concern.

'Yeah, I'm fine,' Dale blinked himself out of his torpor. 'Just feeling a little under the weather.'

'You want me to land?'

'No, I'm good, really.'

Dale checked his instruments one last time as he turned the descending aircraft to the left, the streetlights and rivers of headlights of Great Falls' rush–hour traffic sweeping past below his wingtip as he performed a wide circular flight–path that turned gradually toward the runway to join the final approach.

'Outer marker,' Elaine said. 'On height, on airspeed. You got the traffic?'

'Traffic?'

'ATC called traffic on finals, two o–clock.'

'When?'

'Just now, I called confirmed. They're at…'

Dale McKenzie saw a series of blinking lights flicker just along the bottom edge of Elaine's window, hidden by the Dash–8's steep bank angle.

'Power!'

Elaine lunged for the throttles and Dale hauled back on the control column as a frenzy of voices suddenly blasted through the communications system.

'Ventura–nine–six pull up!'

'Traffic! Pull up!'

'Ventura abort circuit!'

The Dash–8's engines screamed as they went to full power. Dale saw Elaine out of the corner of his eye as she yanked the undercarriage lever to the "up" position to kill drag as the aircraft surged upward.

The sound of another airplane's engines thundered through the cabin and Dale heard a flurry of alarmed cries from the passengers as the Dash clawed for altitude.

To his left and below him Dale saw another aircraft thunder past on finals to land at the airport, barely a hundred feet away, its navigation lights blinking brightly as it sailed on toward the runway.

Elaine's panicked voice sounded over the radio.

'Ventura–nine–six landing aborted, going around to stop, runway two seven.'

Dale pushed the nose of the aircraft down again, his heart thundering in his chest as he blinked sweat from his eyes. Elaine grasped the throttles and hauled them back into their landing settings, the whining turbo–props settling back into a more natural rhythm.

'Captain?'

Elaine's voice echoed through Dale's skull. He turned to her.

'Sir, I have control,' she said.

Dale stared at his first officer for several long seconds, and then he released his control column and nodded. 'You have control.'

Elaine gripped the column and checked all around her for traffic and the airport's proximity before she began to visibly calm down.

'What the hell was that? Didn't you hear the traffic call?'

Dale tried to think straight. 'I.., I must have missed it.'

Elaine peered sideways at him. 'Are you sure you're okay?'

Before Dale could respond the radio came alive with chatter from air–traffic–control.

'Ventura nine–six, please report, confirm status and separation in the pattern.'

'I've got to call that in,' Elaine said.

'No,' Dale snapped, and then forced himself to calm down. 'It was a one–off, I just missed the call.'

'And then missed another aircraft by a few feet!' Elaine shot back. 'Jesus, your head's not in the game, sir.'

Dale felt as though he were gasping for air like a beached fish, unable to think of a suitable explanation or retort.

'It happens,' was all that he could manage to say. 'Let's just let it go, okay?'

Elaine stared at him for a long beat. 'You want me to break aviation law and commit a criminal offence, in my first year with my first airline, because you were staring into space while in the landing pattern?'

Dale stared at his first officer for a long beat, and knew that he had nowhere left to go.

'You do whatever you feel you've got to do,' he muttered.

Dale sank back into his seat and rubbed his eyes as Elaine spoke into her microphone.

'Ventura nine–six, downwind for two–seven, and we would like to report a near–air miss.'

'Roger nine–six, circuit is clear, report to tower after landing.'

***

12

The two case detectives working the night shift had already logged in for duty as Kathryn walked in to the precinct station to see Detective Griffin standing over a stack of papers that littered his desk.

'Anything new?' she asked, by way of conversation.

Griffin looked up at her and shook his head as he gestured to the images.

'Security camera shots pulled down from the street where our abduction image was obtained,' he replied. 'Sheila McKenzie walked up and down here from time to time between business engagements.'

'Shouldn't you have gone home by now?' Kathryn asked as she set her bag down alongside the detective's desk.

'Home's over rated,' he replied, 'and me going home isn't going to help find Sheila McKenzie. Besides, I got a lot of other cases ongoing here okay?'

Kathryn looked down at the black and whites. 'You found a potential suspect yet?'

'Nope,' Griffin said. 'At least nobody that stands out as being out of place, or doing something they shouldn't be, let alone shooting photos of our vic'. Looks like whoever did this shot the image from a moving vehicle and we can't chase up every single person who drove down this through–fare since that wall was scrubbed.'

'Which is probably why they chose it,' Kathryn said. 'They'd know you guys couldn't isolate them.'

Griffin looked up at her. 'You think?'

Maietta, sitting nearby at her desk, looked up at Griffin. 'How could they know she would be there at any given time? They'd have to have been watching, right? Even taking the photograph would have to be planned to some extent.'

'If they already knew Sheila McKenzie was likely to wander up and down that street from time to time, then they're better off timing their shot here than on some dingy side–street or outside her art shop,' Griffin confirmed. 'If it's in the top end of town then there would be other things, like reflections in windows that could be used to identify a driver shooting film if the security camera itself is near the vehicle. Here, where these black and whites were shot, there's just a brick wall. Saira said that Sheila last wore this dress three days ago.'

'Which also confirms,' Maietta said, 'that this abduction was planned over a period of time.'

'There's money then, in the family I mean, the ability to raise cash?' Captain Olsen asked as he strode out of his office.

'Yeah, but that's another thing,' Griffin said. 'These two, Dale and Sheila, bring home about five hundred thousand between them each year, which sets them up real cosy at home but isn't anything like what they'd need to pay off a ransom like this and that's what I don't get. You want ten million bucks out of somebody, you go abduct Paris Hilton on Oprah or something, not an airline pilot's wife.'

'Maybe they're not the real target?' Olsen hazarded. 'Dale McKenzie's a long–service pilot with Ventura, right? Maybe the idea is to get the airline to pay out?'

'That's what we figured,' Maietta said. 'Hit the employee and the employer steps up to the plate. Griffin isn't having any of it, though.'

'Why not?' Olsen asked him.

'Because it's just plain dumb,' Griffin replied. 'Why take the risk that the company might just say no? You're doubling your odds of failure.'

'Or from a psychological point of view, doubling your odds of success,' Kathryn said softly, not wanting to interrupt the conversation but equally unwilling to be ignored on the side–lines. 'If you were to abduct somebody famous, somebody rich and powerful, then that person's family would have sufficient resources to bring the whole world down upon you, maybe even hire hit–men or bounty hunters or whatever. With this guy's wife and a small regional airline, they're pretty much stuck with law enforcement.'

'Thanks,' Griffin smiled without warmth.

'Just sayin'.'

'I don't know, it just doesn't figure,' Griffin said. 'And why so much money? Why not a million bucks instead, something that the airline or even the husband could feasibly dig up?'

'You're projecting,' Kathryn said.

'I'm what?'

'Projecting,' Kathryn repeated, 'putting your mind into the mind of the abductor. It doesn't work. You're assuming they're intelligent when they could just be plain dumb.'

'They were intelligent enough to plan this whole thing. I've got to assume they've approached everything else with the same diligence.'

Kathryn tapped her watch. 'Have you got a moment for me?'

'Didn't we do that already? I'm off duty anyway, time for me to go home.'

'I thought home was over rated?' Kathryn replied. 'Besides, it's two chats per day, remember?'

Griffin glanced at Olsen. The Captain raised an expectant eyebrow, and as though finally accepting the inevitable Griffin nodded toward a nearby vacant office. Kathryn led the way and closed the door behind the detective. He sat down behind the bare desk as Kathryn took the seat opposite.

'So, how are things?'

'Same as this morning. Are we done?'

'We're just beginning. You never told me your wife's name.'

'Angela,' Griffin replied. 'She prefers the full name, not a shortening of it.'

Kathryn made a show of writing the name down in her notebook. 'Good, that's a start.'

'It is?'

'People have different ways of showing things,' Kathryn explained. 'You didn't say your wife's name despite me asking about her several times this morning. Often it's not what people say that defines them, but what they don't say.'

'You think too much,' Griffin said. 'You analyse every tiny detail, every word no matter how insignificant, and draw conclusions when there's nothing to be learned.'

'Does a detective not analyse every aspect of a case because the smallest detail can lead to the biggest results?'

Griffin glanced up at the ceiling. 'It's not the same.'

'It's exactly the same,' Kathryn insisted. 'You're no criminal, but you seek to conceal emotions and worries just as a criminal seeks to conceal a crime.' She smiled. 'You're guilty as hell Scott, and you know it.'

'I'm guilty of trying to do my job,' Griffin replied and tapped his head with a finger. 'I don't think like you do. I don't want to think like you do. I don't want to analyse my dreams or censor every single word I say just because you're here jotting them all down in your little book.'

Kathryn smiled. 'That's why I'm here to do it for you, so you can get on with your job.'

Griffin ran his hands through his hair and shook his head.

'You're a distraction, Kathryn, okay? I can't think straight when you're hovering around me here and second guessing my thoughts.'

'I'm not here to second guess anybody,' Kathryn said. 'I make observations because I want to help.'

'You're not helping.'

'Neither are you. This is something you just have to go through, Scott.'

'It's *detective*.'

'Fine, detective. It's something you just have to accept, that you're not ready to return to full duty and have your firearm returned to you until I deem so. I don't care if I have to sit in this room twice a day with you for the next ten years, I'll do it until I see the real you come back out.'

'What the hell is that supposed to mean? You only met me this morning. How the hell could you know anything about me other than what you've got in those files of yours?'

'What did you talk to Angela about last night?'

'Talk about?'

Kathryn leaned back in her chair and let the silence draw out. Griffin sat with his arms folded and stared back at her.

'We ate dinner, then she went out to a friend's house.'

'Good, and did you speak when she came home?'

'What difference does it make? You know we're not talking much right now.'

'Is that you not talking, or Angela?

Griffin held Kathryn's gaze for a long moment. 'Both.'

'Did she go out just to see a friend do you think, or did she just want to get out of the house for a bit?'

'Away from me, you mean?'

'I didn't say that, but maybe you think so.'

'You're putting words into my mouth.'

'You started it.'

Griffin's features cracked into a faint grin, and he looked briefly down at the table top. 'She goes out a lot of evenings.'

'Want some advice?' Kathryn asked. Griffin looked at her but said nothing. 'Tonight, on your way home, grab some flowers and a bottle of wine, whatever it is that you think you'll both enjoy, and start talking to

Angela. If she sees you're making an effort it might help to break the ice.'

'Angela doesn't do flowers.'

'Angela doesn't? Or you don't?' Griffin said nothing. 'Tell me something, honestly. Does your wife also have some issues you might want to share with me or..?'

'No,' Griffin cut across her. 'She's fine, really.'

Kathryn nodded. 'Then it's you who needs to do something, because it sounds to me like your wife has become either unable or unwilling to, and I'm guessing I don't need to tell you where that will go if things are left unchanged.'

Griffin sighed, his arms still folded.

'Do it,' Kathryn insisted. 'Baby steps, show Angela you're not blind to what's happened to you and that the person she met all those years ago is still in there.'

'Are we done?'

'We're done.'

Griffin stood up and walked toward the office door. Kathryn called after him as he opened it.

'Detective?' Griffin halted, but did not look back at her. 'We're on the same side, remember? I'm not the enemy.'

Griffin looked back at Kathryn.

'I get it,' he said. 'You're trying to help and I'm not receptive to that help. That's because I deal with things in my own way, in my own time, and I'll get there in the end.'

Kathryn nodded.

'I don't doubt that you will, detective. My concern is how much of a life and a family you'll have left by the time you achieve that on your own.'

***

Dean Crawford

13

'It's not that complicated.'

'It's not that bloody easy, either!'

Kathryn sat with her legs curled beneath her on the sofa as Ally sipped a glass of chilled wine and watched her from across the living room.

With Stephen gone on one of his business trips the apartment felt somehow lighter and more airy to Kathryn, even though the blinds were drawn against the cold, dark night outside.

'All I need you to do, Ally, is just say the right things at the right time,' Kathryn soothed. 'I mean, come on, you want to see this happen as much as I do, right?'

Ally smiled over her glass.

'Yes, of course,' she agreed with a giggle. 'Stephen is clearly an individual who needs a damned good seeing too, in every respect.'

Kathryn frowned. 'He's an adulterous shite.'

'He's also your partner, and until this happened he was the best thing that's ever happened to you. You never used to stop singing his praises.'

'Should boyfriends routinely hurry off and sleep with other women?' Kathryn challenged.

'No,' Ally said, 'but as a matter of fact they do it regularly. I think that relationships are not our natural state of being. For the most part men are clearly happier sowing their seed with any trollop that they can find and never seem to grow out of it, so let them. They have used women for their own ends for millennia. I say, screw them: let's use them to make babies and then let them spend the rest of their time fighting over whatever slappers are left.'

'That's a lovely image,' Kathryn uttered. 'You're full of romance, Ally. Maybe you and Stephen should get together?'

'Maybe we should,' Ally shrugged. 'Although there wouldn't be much point I don't think. Fifty per cent of all marriages fail and most of them fail due to unfaithful partners, most of whom turn out to be men. Don't you read the glossies, Kathryn?'

'I prefer real life to magazines.'

'You're the one with the wandering partner.' Kathryn glared at Ally, who giggled and waved her hand airily. 'You know I don't mean it like that. Yes, he's scum, but you're the psychologist ... haven't you asked yourself *why* he's done this?'

Kathryn realised that she was somewhat caught off guard by the question. In the midst of conjuring up her dastardly plot she had forgotten the raw fury she had felt at Stephen's lies, the catalyst for her vengeful crusade.

Kathryn had never had lots of money, had never sought a stellar career in the city or thought that she could be anything more than what she really wanted to be: happy in her life and to share that happiness with a decent, faithful man. What woman ever *needed* anything more than that? Sure, many wanted fame and the adulation of their peers; others sought seclusion through isolation and rarely ventured into the dating game or foraged through the dung mound of men packed inside sweaty, pounding nightclubs. In some respects Ally was a bit like that: she occasionally "got lucky", but generally kept men at arm's length, considering them all to be, as she said, *from the devil*.

In Stephen, though, Kathryn believed that she had finally discovered the gem that so many sought, the Holy Grail of Manhood resplendent before her as though she alone had emerged victorious from a lifelong quest to achieve the peace and happiness denied or eluded by so many others. The term *whirlwind romance* didn't cover it. Stephen was handsome, kind, generous and focused entirely on Kathryn, and she had been swept along in his wake like a joyous dolphin playing behind a cruise liner, and she had made no attempt to conceal or deny it. The rational part of her mind had constantly both sought reassurance and searched for the chinks in her valiant knight's shining armour, and had found none.

Stephen, for all she could ascertain, had been literally perfect.

She had imagined their future marriage. Surrounded by friends, which accounted for their families too as they were both orphans. Photographers and little children dressed in clothes that could not possibly survive the day unstained. The vows. The applause. The alcohol. The first dance. The last dance. The honeymoon.

And then life came along.

Bills. Rent. Jobs. Economic crash. Foreclosures. Jobs lost, once successful businesses floundering. Stephen struggling to earn his commission. Kathryn struggling to get through college a decade after she should have done instead of dropping out and getting the first job that had come along in a cheap Nevada diner. Run down cars and takeaways. And yet through all of it they had each other and Kathryn had drawn such comfort from that, knowing that no matter what happened they would have each other's backs and could probably get through just about anything.

Team Family.

And then had come the revelations, one after the other, that Stephen was not all that he appeared to be. The months of worry, the ache of hope that somehow she was mistaken and that the truth would be a carnival of delight when she learned that Stephen was in fact secretly working double-shifts to earn more money or had another job as a fireman or was in fact a caped, underpants-on-the-outside Superhero saving kittens from burning buildings.

But no. Stephen was a fraud, a liar. A thief. The wolf at the door.

'He's done this because he's not a man,' Kathryn replied finally. 'Not the man I hoped he could be.'

Ally saw the despair crouching in shame behind Kathryn's words and she hurried over to Kathryn's side. She hefted herself next to Kathryn on the sofa and hugged her.

'Kathryn, maybe Stephen's never going to be the person you want him to be no matter what you try. He was good for you, but if it was all a lie then what did you have in the first place?'

Kathryn smiled a bitter little smile that tasted sour on her tongue, but she held her wine glass tight as she replied.

'Would you walk away without trying?'

Ally sighed.

'No, of course not, but maybe you should just confront him with all that you've learned and get it all out in the open. I've seen this before, Kathy. People keep everything inside and it consumes them until they just can't bear each other anymore.'

'I think I'm already past that stage.'

'And that's what worries me,' Ally said. 'What you've got in mind could just as easily blow up in your own face as convince Stephen that he should be here and not wherever the hell else it is he goes.'

Kathryn stared down at the glistening glass of wine in her hand. Truth was, she could not be at all sure that her cunning plan would have any effect on a man who seemed to be a stranger to her. Yet he *knew* her, had known her now for years, and must somewhere in his heart hold a place for her? How the hell could any person achieve the kindness that he had when all the while being a cheat and a thief?

'Some people are lost,' Kathryn said, an image of detective Griffin appearing in her mind's eye.

'Some people are idiots,' Ally shot back. 'For all the good that Stephen was, you deserve better, Kathryn. Maybe I could have a word with him?'

Kathryn smiled, her eyes brimming with tears that seemed reluctant to fall. 'I don't want you to say a word to Stephen.'

'I won't need to speak to him while I'm driving my knee into his family jewels. Come to think of it, he wouldn't have much to say after that anyway.'

Kathryn's smile didn't break but she shook her head. 'I don't think that will help my cause any.'

'Oh I don't know,' Ally grinned. 'Men only tend to start using their brains when their dicks are out of service.'

'And their dicks when their brains are out of service.'

Ally grinned over her wine glass. 'So, what exactly to you need me to do?'

'There's some stuff I need,' Kathryn said, and wiped her eyes on the back of her sleeve. 'Just general shopping really. It's better that I don't buy it myself, as I don't want any chance of Stephen figuring out what I'm up to.'

'Hope you're going to send me the cash,' Ally said. 'I'm up to my neck for eight thousand dollars right now, remember? It's going to take me two years to get that paid off.'

Ally had found herself on the wrong end of a foreclosure on her mortgage when she had been made redundant months before. Like so many, her comfortable life had been shattered in the economic collapse, and now she rented a tiny apartment just as Kathryn did, barely able to make ends meet and in debt to her mortgage provider.

'Of course I will,' Kathryn said. 'I just need you to purchase them on my behalf.'

Kathryn pulled a folded piece of paper from her pocket and handed it to Ally, who unfolded the paper and scanned the list. She frowned almost immediately.

'What on Earth would you want this lot for?' she said, and then her eyes widened as she looked at one of the items. 'Aftershave, for Stephen? Tickets? Where are you going?'

'Just book them using the code I've written down,' Kathryn urged her. 'No questions. I'll send you the money tomorrow.'

'A vacation?' Ally hazarded. 'So, Miss Stone, perhaps you intend this scheme of yours to end happily for *Monsieur* Hollister?'

Kathryn sighed as she stared into her wine glass.

'What we've got is too good to just abandon without trying,' she said. 'I won't just walk away if he comes clean about everything that he's done.'

Ally humphed as she slipped the list into her pocket.

'A man, come clean? Talk about his problems? Admit his love? I look forward to that, just as I look forward to hearing about how Hell has frozen over.'

'Stephen's not like other men,' Kathryn protested. Ally said nothing for a long moment, and Kathryn banged the sofa angrily. 'He *can* be different.'

Kathryn's phone buzzed nearby on the sofa, and she picked it up and read the name on the screen, atop an SMS message.

'It's Stephen,' she said.

'What does he want?'

Kathryn frowned. 'He's coming back home,' she replied.

Ally set her glass down. 'Well, he won't want me here, he's never liked me. You going to start on him when he gets back?'

Kathryn set her phone down and sipped a little more of her wine. 'I've got an idea.'

Ally looked at Kathryn for a long moment. 'You really sure about all of this? Why go through with it at all? Why not just walk away?'

Kathryn sighed. 'I'm an orphan, Ally. I don't have anybody else to fall back on.'

'Humph,' Ally mumbled as she got up and grabbed her coat, 'well, I hope this works out right honey, but in the meantime you make bloody sure you twist his balls up so close to his chin he'll never dare cross you again.'

***

Dean Crawford

14

Griffin hated nothing more than sitting still in his car. Being a beat cop had taught him how much all law enforcement hated sitting watching some criminal's home, or a fearful informer's back, or an even more scared victim's house in case their attacker returned in the night to finish the job.

But now he sat rooted to his seat, unable to move.

The enemy was close at hand.

He looked out through his rain soaked window at his front door, a thin rectangle of light beyond which his wife would be busying herself in the kitchen. Beside Griffin on the passenger seat was a small bunch of flowers he'd picked up on the way home. He didn't know if they were roses, tulips or goddamned Venus fly traps. Foliage wasn't his hot topic. Beside the flowers was a bottle of wine, safer ground. He knew a thing or two about drinking.

Griffin dragged a hand down his face, trying to rub away the fatigue that had plagued him for so many weeks. Sleep didn't come easy. In fact, nothing much came easy right now, and yet he knew what a good thing he had. More than once he'd asked himself just why the hell some days he felt like getting up, packing his gear and taking off. He had a home, a wife, a job, a future. He had what many people strove, fought and begged for. And yet he so often felt trapped. It wasn't like he thought that the grass was greener or any of that shit, he knew too much about real life to spend his time fantasising.

Griffin shrugged. Maybe he really was just a loner, better off on his own and not bothering everybody else with his moods and maudlin thoughts. From somewhere in the back of his mind his military training kicked in, as it always did when he found himself procrastinating. Attack the problem, solve it, and move on.

Get up soldier, and get on with it.

Griffin dragged himself out of his car much as he had often dragged himself out of a warm sleeping bag in the dangerous and bitterly cold wilds of Afghanistan. He walked to the front door as though he were breaching the entrance to Tora Bora caves without the cold comfort of an M–16 cradled in his grasp. Griffin shoved his key into the lock, took a deep breath and pushed the front door open.

Angela was in the kitchen, sitting at the breakfast table reading a magazine and taking delicate bites from a Dorito in one hand. Strawberry blonde hair cut to her shoulders in a fashionable style, an off–the–shoulder cardigan casual and yet somehow perfect. She glanced up at him and smiled.

'Hey.' Her eyes flicked to the flowers and the bottle of wine. One eyebrow arched upward. 'Who died?'

Griffin shut the door behind him to hide the smile that creased his jaw. Angela had always been a smart ass, in every sense of the phrase. He walked up to the breakfast table and set the flowers and wine down before her.

'I figured I haven't been doing a great job of all this,' he said, unable to think of something more profound or moving to say.

Angela seemed suddenly frozen in time, the Dorito still held in her hand. 'Go on.'

Griffin blinked. 'I didn't prepare a speech and the store was plain out of red carpets. I just…'

Griffin's mind was vacuumed of words and his voice trailed off as his lips went numb. Angela stared at him for a moment longer and then she looked down at the flowers. She tossed her Dorito back into a bowl and walked around the breakfast counter to him.

'You're a dickhead,' she said. Griffin opened his mouth to protest, but Angela slipped her arms around his neck, kissed him gently on the lips and beamed up at him. 'Do you remember the last time you bought me flowers?'

Griffin struggled. 'No.'

'That's because you've never bought me flowers, dumbass. What's happened?'

Griffin felt the smile creep back onto his features. Maybe he could do this shit after all?

'I don't know. Nothing. I was just driving home and thinking about the case I'm on is all.'

'Which one?'

'Abduction,' Griffin said. 'Guy went and misplaced his wife this morning and we're having a hard time finding her. I guess it made me wonder how I would feel if that happened to you and me.'

Angela chuckled. 'And there was me thinking you'd lost your romantic streak.'

'I do my best,' Griffin replied.

Angela looked at the flowers and the wine. 'Your best is more than acceptable, kind sir. You open the bottle, I'll finish dinner, 'kay?'

Griffin nodded as Angela moved through the kitchen.

'How's your new friend at the station?' she asked. 'The counsellor?'

Griffin winced. 'A pain in my ass.'

'Was she behind this little gesture?'

Griffin sighed as he rummaged for a bottle opener in a draw. 'No.' Angela hummed her response, and Griffin turned to her. 'What, you think I couldn't have done this on my own?'

'I didn't say that,' Angela replied as she chopped peppers on a board.

'You implied it.'

Angela sighed. 'I guess that this is all a little bit out of the blue, is all, but I don't want to sound like I'm bitching, okay? I'm just..., interested.'

'Interested in my counsellor?' Griffin asked.

'In what she's saying, asking, helping you with,' Angela admitted.

'You're jealous I've been talking to her and not you?'

'Oh crap, you got me,' Angela snapped. 'Of course I'm not jealous. It's about wanting to know what's goin' on up there in that head of yours because I give a damn.'

Griffin winced again. It seemed remarkable to him that he could not, despite years of marriage, fathom how Angela's mind worked. How any woman's mind worked. It was always the same: they sounded like they were accusing him of something, and yet when pressed it turned out they were concerned, or upset or some other shit. Griffin never was able to figure out why they couldn't just talk straight, ask questions, get answers and move goddamned forward.

'Okay, my bad,' he replied. 'Why didn't you just say that bit first, then follow up with everything else?'

Angela waved the knife in the air. 'Because women like to build up to these things.'

'And men like to get to the point.'

'Do they, Scott?'

Irritation lanced Griffin like a blade. He couldn't help himself. 'What's that supposed to mean?'

'That you can't just waltz in here with a bunch of flowers and a bottle of wine and figure that weeks of misery will just evaporate from my mind like a hangover.'

Griffin stared at his wife for a long moment. *'Misery?'*

Angela sighed, struggled for the right words. 'It wasn't all misery, I didn't mean it like that. Things were…'

'But there was plenty of misery in there, right?' Griffin challenged her. 'I don't know how you cope, life with me being so damned harsh and all.'

The knife blade buried itself in the chopping board as Angela jabbed a finger at him.

'There you go again! Everybody's got it worse than you, Scott, isn't that right? You served in war zones and got caught up in a shoot–out and suddenly the rest of the world is just a bunch of complaining losers compared to The Almighty Griffin.'

'That's bullshit,' Griffin winced. 'And what the hell do you mean "got caught up in a shoot–out"? A little girl died because of me!'

'You didn't shoot her Scott!' Angela screamed. 'You didn't fucking shoot her, just like you didn't start a fucking war in Afghanistan! You joined the military and then you joined the goddamned police force, because you can't stop telling me that it's what you love to do! So stop complaining when the dangerous jobs that you love to do start having dangerous things happen in them!'

Angela burst out of the kitchen and barged past him. She grabbed her coat from a rail near the front door and swung it over her shoulders.

'Where are you going now?' Griffin snapped. 'Running away from this won't do any good!'

'I'm not running away from this conversation,' Angela shot back as she grabbed her keys and handbag. 'I'm running away from you, Scott. You're so damned big on how people should get their story straight all the time, but one moment you're bringing me flowers and the next you're telling me that I don't know what I've got here. Well I'll tell you what I've got here: every which way to misery, just like I said!'

Angela yanked the front door of their house open and vanished down the front path as Griffin hurried after her and stood in the doorway.

'You go to that damned sister of yours again and you can damned well stay there!'

Angela did not reply as she stormed across the front lawn. Her car's lights flashed as she deactivated the alarm and opened the driver's door.

'This is it Angela!' Griffin shouted. 'You go now, you don't come back!'

'Fine,' Angela shouted in reply. 'I'll do what you ask, and be decisive!'

Angela slammed her car door shut, and moments later her car pulled away and vanished into the night.

***

Dean Crawford

15

'It's a surprise, okay?'

Kathryn got into the driver's seat of her tired old Lincoln and started the engine as Stephen climbed in. The interior of the car was cold enough for their breath to condense on the air. Kathryn turned on the blowers, sending shafts of even colder air blasting past their ears.

'Thanks, that's working wonders,' Stephen uttered.

'I'm doing my best,' Kathryn shot back, willing the engine to warm up a little more.

'Why don't we just grab a take–away?' Stephen complained. 'It's a freezing night and I'm starving.'

'Because we don't ever do anything like this anymore,' Kathryn replied. 'Come on, how often do we get out of the house and enjoy ourselves a little?'

'Hardly ever,' Stephen admitted, 'because we're broke.'

'Not for long,' Kathryn smiled cheerily as she drove out of the apartment lot and onto the main road. 'I've got my job now, so things will be better.'

Stephen closed his eyes and dragged a hand down his face. 'I'm sorry, I've been so wrapped up in things that I forgot all about it. How's your job been going?'

'Glad you asked,' Kathryn replied, willing to give him a break seeing as he was clearly exhausted. 'It's been going well. I'm assigned to a detective who's suffering from Post–Traumatic Stress Syndrome.'

'I know how he feels.'

'The hell you do. He's a former soldier, served tours in Iraq and Afghanistan with the army.'

'Sounds like a barrel of laughs.'

'Don't you ever let up?'

Stephen sighed. 'It's hard to forget about work, you know? Things aren't going so well, case you hadn't noticed. I'm sure this detective is a stand–up guy, but it's hard to think about his problems when we've got so many of our own.'

'We have problems?'

'Me,' Stephen corrected himself. 'I have problems, at work. Keeps me awake at night.'

'So talk to me about them. We've got all night.'

'I need to be up early in the morning.'

'If you're not sleeping, you will be anyway.'

'Very funny.'

'We've got time right now, is all I'm saying,' Kathryn said as she focused on the route ahead. 'Tell me about it.'

Stephen rubbed his forehead with one hand. 'It's not interesting, just stuff going missing.'

'Missing? You lost something?'

'No, paperwork on deals, figures, files, crap like that. We need them to seal deals and nobody can find them. Where are we going?'

'It's a surprise.'

'It'll be a surprise if your car gets us there.'

'It's worth the risk,' Kathryn replied. 'Like I said, it'll do us good to get out of the apartment. We can pretend we're different people for the evening, enjoy ourselves for a change instead of worrying about everything.'

'Jesus,' Stephen uttered. 'I'll be worrying about starvation by then. Have you seen the traffic at this time of night?'

'You'll enjoy it all the more when we get there then,' Kathryn said.

Stephen remained silent and still for several moments. The car was warming up nicely as Kathryn drove, and on an impulse she switched the radio on. A gentle lullaby of country music swelled from the dusty speakers set into the doors.

'Why don't you have a nap while I'm driving?' she suggested. 'You won't be so tired when we get to the restaurant.'

Stephen did not reply, but she saw him lean back in his seat and close his eyes.

Kathryn drove through the galaxies of blazing streetlights, of queuing traffic and busy shop fronts. The blinking navigation lights of aircraft arriving and departing from the airport filled the sky ahead as she drove.

From time to time Kathryn glanced across at Stephen. Although his eyes were closed, she could tell by the depth of his breathing and the intermittent flickering of his eyeballs beneath the lids that he was not even remotely asleep. The fact that he could pretend to be so for such a long time without becoming bored surprised her immensely, and she wondered what thoughts were drifting through the vaults of his mind. Did he suspect already that she had uncovered his deception and lies?

Kathryn consoled herself with the thought that it didn't matter much either way. Stephen was not here to enjoy himself. He was here to suffer.

Kathryn drove through the city centre, past the diners and the bars that were packed with teenagers, all with their lives stretching ahead of them. The bright lights and festival air hinted at the possibilities of the future, and of those that Kathryn had abandoned long ago. She gripped the steering wheel tighter as she drove on, and saw the signs for the restaurant she sought just up ahead. The place was called *Isaac's*, and boasted a vast range of international cuisine, the kind of place where wealthy people went just to say they'd eaten squid, or octopus, or whatever the hell was fashionable to eat at the time. Stephen had eaten at *Isaac's* twice with the other woman in the time that Kathryn had followed them here.

'Which one are we going to?' Stephen asked from beside her.

He was feigning coming awake from a doze, squinting his eyes and stretching his legs into the foot wells.

'Just up here,' Kathryn said. Stephen was already staring at the restaurant as though it were a North Korean labour camp.

Kathryn affected a disappointed tone. 'Have you been here before?'

Stephen hesitated a moment before replying. 'I think so, maybe once, with work.'

Kathryn pulled into the lot and parked, switching off the engine and getting out. The wind was bitterly cold as they walked to the restaurant entrance.

'Do you have any idea how expensive this place is?' Stephen asked.

'Relax,' Kathryn said. 'I'm enjoying myself. Let's not let money spoil the evening, okay?'

Stephen said no more, hurrying ahead to open the door for her. Kathryn smiled dutifully as she walked in and spoke to the girl at the desk regarding her reservation. Within moments they were led to a secluded table for two half way down the restaurant, which was dominated on one side by a wall of water flowing down a glass screen through vibrant and shimmering beams of light like rainbows.

'Wow,' Kathryn said and glanced at Stephen. 'How could you forget being in here?'

Stephen glanced at the spectacular display. 'Maybe it wasn't here before. They've probably just sprung a leak.'

The waiter showed them to their seats, and as they sat down he looked at Stephen. 'Nice to see you again, sir.'

Stephen looked up at the waiter. 'And you.'

As the waiter turned away, Kathryn looked at Stephen. 'I thought you said you hadn't been here recently?'

'I said it was a long time ago, with work I expect. They seem very professional, maybe they're trained to remember people?'

'Maybe,' Kathryn said as though it didn't matter. She surveyed the wine list, rueing her decision to drive.

They selected drinks and their courses, and as the waiter departed Kathryn looked at Stephen over the glowing candles and sparkling wine. For a moment, just the briefest instant, she could see them both as they had once been. New lovers, charged with excitement and the joy of each other's company, each the centre of the other's world.

'So, what shall we talk about?'

Stephen shrugged. 'I don't know.'

'How about us?'

'Us?'

'Us.'

'What about us?'

'Where are we going, Stephen?'

'Ah,' Stephen said, and took a sip of his wine. 'So that's what this is all about.'

'Shouldn't it be?' Kathryn replied. 'We've been together for three years. I've got a job now, you're employed at the very least. My studies are over. Maybe it's time we started thinking about the future?'

Stephen eyed her from behind the candle flames. 'In what way?'

Kathryn shrugged, enjoying herself. 'Where do we want to be in another three years' time? Where do you see our relationship going?'

Stephen swallowed. She could see it from the way the candlelight hit his throat. She couldn't be sure if it was fear of being recognised by somebody or a genuine fear of the magnitude of her question. His discomfort entertained her immensely.

'I'm not sure,' Stephen replied. 'I haven't had much chance to think about it lately.'

'Oh come on,' Kathryn chided with a gentle smile. 'All that driving, all those business trips? You must have had enough time to figure out the origin of the universe by now. Surely you must think about *us* sometimes?'

'Well of course, but...'

'And then there's where we're going to live,' Kathryn interrupted smoothly. 'I mean, I don't suppose we'll be living in that teeny little apartment for much longer now that we're both earning.'

'No, I don't suppose we will, but...'

'I was thinking of moving here.' Kathryn gestured to the city outside the restaurant windows with an airy wave of her hand. She saw the tiniest flare of panic in Stephen's eyes. 'So much more lively, don't you think?'

'So much more expensive,' Stephen replied, 'and then there's the commuting and...'

'Children.'

Stephen's eyes flew wide with alarm as though somebody had fired a live current between his buttocks. He stifled a cough. 'Children?'

'They're like us,' Kathryn said, 'but smaller.'

A waiter carrying their starters appeared and bought Stephen some time. Kathryn leaned back in her seat as her *hors d'oeuvre* was placed before her. She didn't really know what the term meant and didn't care.

'I hadn't thought about that,' Stephen managed to utter as the waiter left.

'Is it too soon?' Kathryn asked, affecting a concerned expression. 'I mean, we've been together three years Stephen, it's certainly crossed my mind that at some point we may like to start a family together.'

'Well, of course, but...'

'Which would mean we'd need a larger house,' Kathryn went on, 'depending on how many children we're going to have. Some people say that two is perfect, you know, one of each, but I say throw caution to the wind and try for three. Which would mean we'd need at least four rooms, a decent back yard and...'

Stephen sat back and held up a hand. 'Okay, slow down there just a minute.'

'What?'

'You'll be discussing our retirement plans next. We've only been in the restaurant for ten minutes and you're already planning an empire. Where's all this coming from? And where's the *money* for all this coming from, while we're on the subject? You know that a child costs about a hundred thousand bucks to raise to the age of eighteen, right? So you're already committing us to three hundred thousand, plus the new house. I'm guessing that's a house in this city, right?'

'Of course,' Kathryn replied with a bright smile. 'We need the best for our kids.'

Stephen chuckled and shook his head, glancing at the spectacular water display nearby. 'So we're in for eight hundred thousand before we've even finished the starter. Has it escaped your notice that we can't even afford to replace your car?'

'That's *now*,' Kathryn said as she popped a morsel of something that tasted a bit like pork into her mouth. 'I'm talking about *later*, when we're married.'

'Oh,' Stephen said, 'forgive me. I'd forgotten about our white wedding and honeymoon in the Bahamas.'

'You're taking me to *the Bahamas*?!' Kathryn almost leaped out of her chair and her voice carried right across the entire restaurant as she radiated delight. 'Oh my god that would be fantastic! You see? You *have* been thinking about us!'

Stephen glanced left and right as panic fluttered across his features. The smiling faces of perhaps thirty or so other diners glowed back at him.

'Well, I hadn't actually…'

'The Bahamas,' Kathryn whispered, her eyes sparkling as she stared at Stephen and retook her seat, her smile as broad as the day was long. 'And this white wedding you mentioned, how would you feel about it being in the Bahamas too and with a…?'

'Look, Kathryn,' Stephen said, forestalling her question with a raised hand. 'I don't know if we can afford to do anything like that right now, okay? I was just being sarc...'

'Being *what*?'

Kathryn dropped the smile as though it was poisonous and glared at Stephen, daring him to speak another word. She let her eyes dance across the plates in front of them as though picking a suitable missile.

'Romantic,' Stephen replied. 'I was being romantic, dreaming of what could be if we just had the money to do it.'

Kathryn kept her gaze on Stephen, revelling only in the warm buzz of excitement swirling in her belly. Her disappointment at Stephen's retraction was not entirely faked. Truth be told, the idea of a lengthy vacation in the Bahamas was entirely agreeable with her. Minus the wedding. And minus Stephen.

'And the *will*,' she suggested tartly as she stabbed another piece of meat with her knife.

She could feel Stephen watching her across the table. She could tell that he was uncertain. Off balance. She realised, quite suddenly, that she had never really seen Stephen lose his nerve before. Nor had she felt so in control of her life.

He took another long sip of his wine before he replied. 'You're asking me if I intend to marry you?'

Kathryn smiled at him with her lips only. 'You don't get a big house and kids without marriage, darling.'

'You don't get any of them without money.'

'Money isn't everything.'

'No, but it's a fair proportion and we don't have any.' He seemed to sadden slightly. 'I couldn't even afford a ring right now, to be honest.'

Kathryn raised an eyebrow in response but said nothing as she pecked at the last of her starter. She noticed that Stephen had barely touched his despite having claimed to be starving when they had left. His wine glass, on the other hand, was almost empty.

'It's not like I don't want to get married,' Stephen added.

'Could've fooled me.'

'What's that supposed to mean?'

'We never see each other,' Kathryn said as she set her fork down on her empty plate. 'You live out of hotel rooms and I virtually live alone. What I'm saying to you, Stephen Hollister, is that if we're going to stay in a relationship then we need to start building a proper life together.'

Stephen blinked, thrown off balance once again.

'Jesus, now you're threatening to leave me? You only just asked me about marriage!'

'It's called an ultimatum,' she replied with another smile.

The waiter appeared as Stephen stared at her as though she had just revealed that she was in fact a man. The fact that she could not photograph his expression in that one moment was one she guessed she would probably regret for her entire life. The waiter cleared their plates and vanished, probably sensing the aura enveloping the table. Kathryn sat quietly, waiting to see what Stephen might dredge up to escape his predicament.

His jaw gaped a few times before any cohesive noises broke free from his lips.

'You're telling me to propose, or leave?'

Kathryn shrugged but said nothing, sipping her glass of sparkling water instead. Stephen gulped down the rest of his wine and exhaled the fumes, then looked at her as though seeing her for the very first time.

'That job has changed you,' he said finally.

'Yes it has,' she agreed. 'It is my future. It is what I want my life to be. You're either a part of it or you're history, Stephen. Decide.'

Stephen gaped at her in astonishment. Kathryn remained motionless, but inside her guts were swirling like warm chocolate and she was bursting with the need to laugh herself into a cardiac arrest.

'I'll give you 'til the main course arrives,' she finally blurted. Then she stood up, grabbed her handbag and strode confidently away from the table.

On an impulse she swayed her hips a little more than she usually would as she strode between the tables to the rest–room and was both surprised and delighted to catch the eyes of several male diners.

She barely made it into the rest–room before she threw a hand over her mouth to catch her own delighted giggles. She hurled her handbag onto the counter in front of the mirrors and rested one hand beside it as she bent over and laughed.

'Somebody's having a good night.'

Kathryn looked up to see a young girl emerge from one of the stalls, her pupils dilated and a dreamy look on her face. Expensive clothes, designer label handbag, expertly dyed hair. She had "rich–kid" written all over her and cocaine smeared across her left cheek, but her smile was genuine and filled with playful curiosity.

Kathryn spilled the beans before she could even think about it. 'I just gave my boyfriend five minutes to either propose or leave.'

The girl's eyes widened and she chuckled. 'Ain't you the woman, honey!?'

Kathryn managed to gain control of her mirth, and then she looked at the girl. 'You look like you enjoy a laugh. Would you mind doing me a favour?'

'You got it, girl.'

***

16

Kathryn strode out of the rest-room as though she was being announced at the Oscars and a big band was playing. More heads turned as she swayed her way between the tables, focused only on Stephen and his furtive features as she closed in on him like a falcon hunting a hare.

Stephen shifted in his seat, his second glass of wine already drained. An awkward smile slapped itself across his face as Kathryn set her handbag back down on the table and slid silkily into her chair.

'Well, Mister Hollister?' she asked. 'What will it be?'

Stephen, one hand pinching the stem of his wine glass, swallowed thickly before replying.

'I think that...'

'You have to *think* about it?'

Her voice was just loud enough to raise attention to them again. Stephen's eyes swivelled left and right and he raised his spare hand to placate her, still unwilling to release his pride anchor.

'Would you rather I rushed in and made a fool of myself?'

'You mean you're not making a fool of yourself now?'

'I...,'.

'Save it,' Kathryn cut him off before he could say anything more. 'I suspected that you would be like this, so I've saved you the trouble.'

'Wait,' Stephen said as Kathryn shot to her feet. 'Don't leave, I want to...'

Kathryn raised her hand to silence him.

The girl from the rest-room appeared right on cue, a microphone in her hand. She passed it to Kathryn, who spoke without hesitation into the microphone as the tinkling of the background music in the restaurant suddenly faded out.

'Ladies and gentlemen.'

The sound of her own voice amplified across the restaurant startled Kathryn, and she hesitated before she gained control again, asserting her confidence over Stephen, who was sitting in terror on his chair and holding onto the table edge as though for his very life.

A hundred people were now all watching her attentively as she spoke. Cocaine Girl giggled as she hurried out of the way.

'I hope that you don't mind me interrupting your meals,' Kathryn said, her heart fluttering in her chest as she tried to keep her voice calm. 'I wanted you all to know that my partner Stephen, who's sitting here, and I have been together for three years and that we're at such an important point in our lives. I've just started a new job that I really love, and Stephen's working as hard as he can to help support us. So, I want this to be a very special night.'

Kathryn turned to Stephen, looked down at him and dropped her voice an octave as she spoke.

'Stephen, you said that my new job has changed me. You're right. I've decided to take control of my life and do the things that I want to do. I guess we don't really know who people are until they're forced to reveal themselves, and I don't want to hide any more. I want this to be the very first night of my new life. I'm not much for tradition, so...'

Kathryn reached down to her handbag and retrieved from within a small, elaborate box. A ripple of whispers fluttered through the assembled diners as Kathryn popped the box open and revealed a sparkling silver ring with a small, cleanly–cut diamond.

Stephen's eyes widened and she saw the colour drain from his face as she moved around the table and offered the box out to him.

'Stephen,' she said softly into the microphone, 'make this the first day of our new life.'

Stephen stared at the ring as though it were a thermo–nuclear device. One hand reached up furtively from the table and plucked the ring from the box as Stephen almost fell from his chair onto one knee. Kathryn saw conflicting emotions race across his features like raging seas as he mastered whatever he was really feeling and forced a smile onto his face.

His words, when he spoke, were thin and reedy compared to Kathryn's mighty microphone–amplified oratory and barely audible even in the silence that surrounded them.

'Kathryn Stone,' he gasped, 'will you marry me?'

Kathryn looked around her at the rapt diners watching them, and then gave a small shrug as she glanced at Stephen. 'Maybe.' A ripple of laughter tinkled through the restaurant as Kathryn smiled brightly and thrust her outstretched hand straight into Stephen's face. 'Of course I will!'

A blast of thunderous applause flooded the restaurant as Stephen slid the ring onto her finger and got unsteadily to his feet to put his arms around her.

'Can we just eat dinner now?' she heard him say in her ear above the tumultuous applause surrounding them.

Kathryn stood back from him, her face flushed with excitement. 'Just one last thing,' she said, and nodded over his shoulder.

Stephen turned, and Kathryn hugged him tightly to her as Cocaine Girl's camera flashed brightly. Kathryn felt Stephen's entire body stiffen as the photograph was taken.

'They're going to put it up in the restaurant bar for *everyone* to see,' Kathryn smiled as she held Stephen tightly beside her. 'Right up until we get married. Isn't that great?'

Kathryn could not hear Stephen's response above the clapping.

***

17

'Wow,' Maietta said as she climbed from the vehicle.

'Yeah,' Griffin replied. 'That about covers it.'

They stood in front of the broad Colonial–style house, fronted by perfectly–manicured lawns that glistened with frost in the pale glow of the sunrise. The threatening rain clouds of the previous day had vanished, the sky a pearlescent dome as cold as ice above them.

The pool car they were driving was marked with Ventura Air's logo on the doors and Griffin looked resplendent in his pilot's uniform, the darkness and the cap's low peak helping to disguise his identity.

'We're in the wrong job,' Maietta said as she adjusted her cap, apparently uncomfortable in the uniform.

'What do you think?' Griffin asked. 'Me captain, you my co–pilot?'

'Bullshit,' Maietta snapped. 'I'll take the left hand seat.'

Griffin smiled, but he pinched the corners of his eyes as he shut the car door and rubbed his face with his hands.

'You okay?'

'Long night.'

Another night had passed painfully slowly in the wake of Angela's departure. Jesus, at the one point in his life when he had believed that things just *couldn't* get any worse… He dragged a hand down his face, felt his stubble thick on his chin. He needed to get himself sorted out, he knew. It wasn't like he couldn't see what was happening to him or was oblivious to his decline, and yet somehow whenever he decided it was time to do something about it all then something else more important got in the way.

'Want to talk about it?' Maietta asked.

Griffin saw in the windows of some of the other houses the occasional movement, people watching from within. Easy way to change the subject.

'Pity we can't question the natives.'

Maietta nodded as she glimpsed a woman watching from a window in a house on the opposite side of the street move out of sight again. 'They might have seen something.'

'Maybe,' Griffin replied. 'But we can't take the chance right now that one of them isn't involved somehow.'

'Well, the security company confirmed that nobody on its staff had any access to the alarm codes,' Maietta said. 'The occupants are always required to enter new, personal codes once the system has been fitted in order to activate the system. All of their fitters and maintenance staff have cast–iron alibis.'

'That rules out a presence, not assistance in the crime,' Griffin pointed out.

'Not much we can do about that,' Maietta replied, 'until we have a suspect.'

They walked up the garden path and climbed the steps to the front door. The door opened for them and they walked inside, the man who had let them in careful to remain out of sight.

A broad foyer greeted them, a grand staircase facing them that split half way up and climbed to opposite landings above the foyer. Two doorways to the left and right in the foyer led to the living room and dining room, and two corridors either side of the staircase led to the rear of the house and presumably the kitchen.

'Kinda pokey,' Maietta quipped.

A sergeant dressed in casual attire appeared and gestured with a jab of his thumb toward the living room to their left.

'Owner of the house is in there.'

'Forensics cleaned up?' Griffin asked. 'Find anything?'

A small forensics and technical team had been sent into the house under cover of darkness, while Dale McKenzie was out, to both check the house for evidence and install a phone–monitoring system.

'Just the spilled blood. It's being analysed as we speak, but chances are it's Sheila McKenzie's.'

Griffin nodded as he followed Maietta into the living room. Sumptuous carpets inches deep, couches yards long, an immense fireplace large enough to sit in and a plasma screen mounted on one wall that would have shamed a small–town cinema. Dale McKenzie sat on the enormous couch, his hands clasped in his lap.

On the coffee table, a phone was wired to a laptop computer being monitored by a technical officer. If the abductors called about the ransom, it would give law enforcement a chance to pin down their location.

'Detectives,' McKenzie said, standing and glancing at their uniforms. 'Anything yet?'

'Nothing,' Griffin said, 'but we're investigating every possible avenue.'

Dale McKenzie was wearing casual clothes after his day on duty, but Griffin could tell that he was hiding considerable emotional strain.

'Of course,' he replied quietly.

Griffin had to maintain the essence of a man isolated on his own, to keep McKenzie as far from any suspicion of police activity as possible. The men in the house with him would be gone soon and would monitor his phone line remotely.

'This won't take long,' Griffin assured the captain. 'You have a flight to take?'

'Daily schedule to Las Vegas,' McKenzie replied, 'due out in about an hour.'

'Just stick with your normal routine,' Griffin said. 'Anything changes, the abductors are going to suspect you've come to us and that could become a real problem. You just keep holdin' it together, okay?'

McKenzie nodded. 'It helps not to be sitting about here,' he said. 'I feel better if I've got something to do.'

'Okay, I'll make this quick,' Griffin said, checking his notes. 'You were away from home for just over forty–eight hours during the period in which your wife was presumably abducted.'

'Presumably?' McKenzie echoed. 'I showed you the ransom note, remember?'

'Yes sir I do, but a ransom note does not necessarily mean that there is a ransom *demand*.'

McKenzie's eyes narrowed as he looked at Griffin. 'You still think that Sheila is somehow behind all of this?'

'I didn't say that,' Griffin pointed out. 'We have to explore any possible motive or outcome. It's what I imagine you'd want us to do?'

'I want you to find my wife!' McKenzie snapped. 'How the hell could I have anything to do with this?'

'Sometimes there's a partner involved,' Maietta said. 'Somebody who can do the dirty work while providing a convenient alibi for the brains behind the crime.'

McKenzie stared at her for a long moment.

'And supposing I was the brains behind some kind of bizarre abduction scheme, and a benefactor paid on my behalf for my wife's liberation? What then? I couldn't launder the money, because I wouldn't know where to start. I couldn't spend it, because to do so would expose me as the guilty party. I would be utterly unable to touch a single dime.'

'Patience,' Griffin said, 'is a virtue.'

'And mine is running out,' McKenzie snarled as he stood and jabbed a finger hard into Griffin's chest. 'My wife is missing and yet again you're standing here questioning a victim!'

'Don't do that,' Griffin said as he batted McKenzie's hand aside. 'You don't want to end up in a cell yourself, right?'

McKenzie backed off, apparently surprised by the threat. Maietta moved in, taking her cue naturally from Griffin. Good cop, bad cop.

'Mister McKenzie we're not here to accuse you, we're here to find answers and if we miss something, your wife might not return. Do you understand?'

'I'm not an idiot,' McKenzie snapped, clearly trying to restrain his anger and keep his voice down. 'I know what you have to do, but these theories make no sense at all and you're wasting what time we have. Forty eight hours, isn't it? Before the chances of an abductee surviving their ordeal are drastically reduced? It's been more than twenty four already, we've had no contact from the abductors and you're no closer to finding my wife than when I first called!'

Griffin slipped his notebook into his pocket and looked the pilot in the eye.

'Is it possible, captain, however unlikely, that your wife might somehow have leaked the security codes from your alarm system to somebody else?'

'I doubt it,' McKenzie replied. 'Sheila is very paranoid about security, especially at home.'

'Any reason for that?' Maietta asked.

'Like I said, she grew up an orphan,' McKenzie replied. 'She's used to having nobody to fall back upon but herself. I imagine her childhood was quite lonely, intimidating even. People like that grow up security conscious.'

'Like you?' Griffin asked. 'You're an orphan too, you said?'

'I am,' McKenzie replied, 'but we men are not quite the target that attractive, successful women can be.'

'Sheila's abductor was either allowed into this house or knew the code well enough to enter the property and then re–set the alarm before they left. Somebody, somewhere, knew the code.'

'I don't know how that could be,' McKenzie insisted. 'I'm the only other person who knows it.'

'I think that you may know something, even if you're not sure yourself,' Griffin pressured him. 'Could Sheila have been unhappy in her life, decided that she would skip town maybe, and then decided that she would arrange an abduction situation to extort you for money?'

McKenzie shook his head.

'No, it doesn't make sense, she wasn't unhappy. We were due to celebrate our fifth wedding anniversary, she was making plans. Everything was fine.'

'Can you define *fine* for me, Mr McKenzie?' Griffin asked.

'Scott,' Maietta said, 'that's enough.'

'Jesus, you really want to pin this on me don't you?' the pilot asked in horror. 'Is that why you're here?'

'I'm here,' Griffin said, ignoring his partner, 'because I cannot fathom why anybody who was planning an abduction or extortion would have targeted you or your family. If I were an abductor I'd target somebody wealthy, famous and ideally stupid and neither you nor your wife fit that category.'

At once both insulted and complimented, McKenzie wasn't sure how to react. He settled for glancing at his watch.

'I have to go,' he uttered.

Griffin watched the pilot walk away as Maietta turned to him. 'What the hell was that?'

'That was my job,' Griffin replied with a shrug.

'You were interrogating our victim,' Maietta snapped. 'Not exactly the caring and sharing policy Olsen likes us to project onto the community, Scott.'

'I don't care about the damned policies,' Griffin shot back. 'I care about finding that man's wife as soon as possible, and right now I don't have a damned clue how to go about it.'

Maietta watched Griffin for a long moment before she replied. 'What's eating at you?'

'Nothing,' Griffin snapped in reply.

'Well, take a hint,' Maietta replied, 'poking Dale McKenzie in the eyes isn't the way. You're on thin ice right now, Scott.'

Griffin offered his partner a tight smile as he checked his watch. 'It'll be a lot damned thinner if we don't find Sheila.'

***

18

Kathryn awoke earlier than usual.

Maybe it was the buzz in her heart, the first flush of true excitement over her new and bold undertaking that aroused her from a deep and dreamless sleep. Stephen had spent the night facing away from her, his legs curled up in a foetal position that she had once found rather endearing. Now, she wondered if the experiences of their previous night's escapades had shrivelled his masculinity and left him huddled protectively around what was left of it. Whatever.

Stephen had awoken early and left before dawn, leaving her to enjoy the luxury of their bed on her own. Sunlight streamed into the room between the blinds. Christ, for once it wasn't *bloody* raining, as Ally would say, her British obsession with the weather remaining fully intact. There were, it seemed, suddenly no end to the wonders blessing Kathryn with every passing day.

Kathryn got out of bed and walked to the bathroom. She turned on the shower until steam puffed around her in clouds and stepped in, luxuriating in the heat. It was bizarre, ridiculous and certainly not real, not in a *real* sense, but she had not felt so alive in what felt like years. Decades, perhaps, even. Her skin tingled with delight and she lathered herself from head to foot, humming tunes to herself.

When they had returned home from the restaurant the previous night, Kathryn glowing with delight and looking constantly at the ring she had bought for herself the day before, Stephen subdued and troubled, she had taken it upon herself to soothe his suffering. Magnanimous in victory and revelling in her new found power over him, she had decided that he should endure no longer. Or not exactly *suffer*, anyway. Even lying, cheating bastards needed a break sometimes, and her grand design required a certain degree of finesse to play out the way she wanted.

Despite his protestations, she had pinned him against the wall of their bedroom and unzipped him before sinking to her knees and giving him precisely the kind of attention no man would be able to ignore for long. She had undressed herself at the same time, tossing her lingerie to one side as she yanked his pants off and then stood up and shoved Stephen toward their bed. And then she had ridden him as though he were the last man alive on Earth, bouncing up and down as though she were a teenager until he climaxed inside her.

Exhausted and quite probably stunned into a disbelieving silence, Stephen had promptly fallen asleep, which suited Kathryn fine. The quieter he was, the better she felt about things.

Kathryn stepped out of the shower and towelled herself down. She was halfway back to the bedroom to fetch her clothes when she heard the front door of the apartment open and close and Stephen walked into the bedroom.

'You're back?' she asked, surprised.

'Sorry,' he replied as he lifted a bag filled with food. 'Thought you might want some breakfast?'

Kathryn blinked in surprise once more, and smiled as she took the bag from him. 'Sounds good to me.'

She turned and made her way into the kitchen and prepared breakfast. Bacon and eggs, sausages, mushrooms, coffee and orange juice â€" the whole nine yards.

The aroma of food had the desired effect, and she heard Stephen plod his way into the shower and the hiss of the water as he splashed himself out of his torpor. As much a man as he ever was, he appeared in the kitchen just minutes later as though carried aloft by the scent of food.

Kathryn breezed by him and reached up on tip–toe to kiss him on the cheek. 'Did you sleep well?'

'Like the dead.'

Don't tempt me. Kathryn gestured at him with the flickering blade of a bread knife. 'Sit.'

Stephen plonked obediently down into a chair and stared at the splendid array of food before him. 'I feel like I'm living in a dream.'

'Glad you approve,' Kathryn said as she sat down opposite him and nibbled a piece of toast. She reached out for a brochure and began flipping the pages.

Stephen tucked into his breakfast and coffee, but it took him only moments to notice the brochure.

'What's that?'

Kathryn leafed casually through the pages without looking at him as she replied. 'Baby clothes. I picked it up the other day in town.'

'Baby clothes?'

'They do wear clothes you know,' she replied. 'Little ones.'

'Yeah, I know, but we don't have one.'

'Not yet we don't,' she winked and smiled in reply. 'If I were you though, I'd brace myself.'

Stephen stared at her, a dribble of egg yolk heading south for his chin. 'We only...'

'Last night?' she cut across him, and then leafed through another page of the magazine. 'I know, first time in about a month wasn't it. The thing is, we were having sex so rarely that I came off the pill a while back.'

Stephen coughed. One hand flew to his mouth to keep his food inside it as he swallowed. His eyes glistened with tears from the strain. 'You're not taking any contraception?' he wheezed.

'No,' she said, still munching happily on her toast. 'Were you?'

Stephen appeared stunned once again. 'Were you planning on telling me this sooner?'

Kathryn searched the air above her head for a moment as though looking for an answer. 'No, not really.' She grinned mischievously. 'Last night changed everything.'

Stephen looked as though he didn't know whether to laugh or cry.

'Kathryn, we only just got engaged.'

'*Engaged*,' she echoed in a delighted whisper. 'Don't you just *love* how that sounds?'

'It sounds expensive,' Stephen muttered as he cut into a sausage.

'Oh you're so romantic sometimes,' she chided. 'Look, we've only got one life and I'm damned if I'm going to sit around waiting for the things that I want to happen to just fall into my lap. I want to get married, Stephen. I want us to have children. Hell, I might even buy a little dog.'

'The hell you will.'

'It's my money, remember?' Kathryn said. 'I earn my own salary now and I can spend it on what I want.'

'And me?' Stephen asked around a mouthful of sausage and egg. 'What about my money? Apparently you've spent about half a million for us already, what with your new house, children, dog and what not. You going to cover all of that?'

Kathryn flashed him a devil's smile. 'That's why it's called marriage, darling. Husband *and* wife.' She held the smile for a moment, the bread knife still close by. 'Til *death* do us part.'

'Now who's being romantic?'

'It's not just children we need to think about,' Kathryn said as she switched to another brochure. 'Life's not been easy for us this past year, and when the children arrive it'll be tough for us to get away. I thought that we should book a vacation while we still can. I thought that maybe we could combine our wedding with your idea of the Bahamas and get married out there.'

'Get married,' Stephen replied, 'in the Bahamas, before we have children and get a giant new house in the city. Is this before or after we buy Montana?'

Kathryn chuckled and then pulled an excited face. 'Oooh, that reminds me, there's a travel company doing big discounts at the moment. I'm not sure which one it was, hang on a moment…'

Kathryn turned to her handbag and yanked out a thick wedge of brochures. She flipped through several of them before finding the right one.

'Ah, here it is. Great Escapes. Have you heard of them?'

Stephen shook his head, one hand holding his fork close to his mouth, the other gripping his knife.

'Maybe we could head over there this afternoon and chat to their staff, they're headquartered on the other side of the city.'

Stephen, his mouth full of food, shook his head vigorously.

'What?' Kathryn asked. 'It could be a real bonus if we could get a deal on travel and accommodation through them. It can't be every day that customers walk through their doors and besides, after our triumphs of last night, maybe we'll get even luckier?'

Stephen shook his head again and swallowed his food with some effort.

'Don't you think you're trying to do everything just a little too quickly?'

'Look, right now we're at least free of any other obligations, right?' Kathryn said. 'In future years, we'll have a mortgage, kids and everything that goes with having a family. My thinking is that right now is the time to have a little fun before it's too late for both of us.'

'I think that we should take our time a little, think about all of this.'

Kathryn shrugged and closed the airline brochure. Then she waved airline tickets in the air with one hand. 'So what do you want me to do with these then?'

Stephen looked at the tickets and his eyes flew wide. 'Jesus, you haven't?!'

Kathryn grinned. 'I have.'

Stephen's shoulders slumped. 'Kathryn, we can't just take off on holiday!'

'Why not?' she asked. 'Why not just say "to hell with it all"?'

'Because then my boss will say "to hell with him" and we'll be even more broke than we are now!' Stephen sighed. 'Look, I know you're trying to do the right thing for us, but that's too much Kathryn, really.'

Kathryn dropped the tickets back into the brochure and set it aside. 'Okay, okay, I'll get a refund.' She switched back to the images of babies for a moment. 'Would you prefer a boy or a girl?'

'Kathryn, I don't know that….'

'Twins!' Kathryn gushed. 'Imagine that, if we had one of each right off the bat!'

Stephen sighed. 'I'd prefer some time to think about it.'

'You didn't need much time to think about having sex last night.'

'That's because you were…!' Kathryn raised an eyebrow. '… encouraging me. Anyway, it takes two to tango.'

'Just as I was saying,' Kathryn agreed cheerfully. 'Make sure you get plenty of that breakfast down you. I've got to get to work.'

Stephen frowned as he munched on his bacon. 'Why so early?'

Kathryn drained the last of her orange juice and stood up. Her gown dropped away from her shoulders to reveal the slenderest of thongs and a matching bra that she had slipped on after her shower. She turned away from the table and sauntered back toward the bedroom.

'My client needs me,' she said, and then looked over her shoulder at him. 'What about you, darling?'

***

19

Sheila squirmed on her seat, lost in a desperate delirium of blackness and solitude.

Her wrists were sore, as were her ankles, rubbed raw by the tight fabric pinning them in place. Her eyes itched beneath her blindfold and a dull headache throbbed behind them, a mixture of dehydration and tension fuelled by the grinding terror of not knowing her fate at the hands of a murderous stranger.

The faint sounds beyond her prison had alerted her to the fact that it was probably morning again, but beyond that she had lost all track of time. Visits by her captor were unpredictable, something that she dimly recalled reading was often a deliberate tactic used by military troops against prisoners of war: a captive's resistance was dramatically reduced when denied knowledge of the passing of time. All that she had were the senses that no captor could supress. In her world of absolute darkness and silence, endured for so many long hours, Sheila McKenzie's sense of touch and smell had become almost supercharged.

With nothing else to occupy a mind starved of stimuli, and afraid of the bizarre and vivid visions that flashed into existence like living dreams in her mind's eye, Sheila had focused on the vibrations from whatever was going on outside her tiny prison.

That her captor, or captors, had chosen to conceal her within probably sight of working people was a dash of brazen confidence that unnerved Sheila. A basement, a cellar or some remote farm would have surely been a wiser choice, but instead she was hidden almost in plain sight, the last place anybody would think to look for her.

She had learned to sense when vehicles were driving past, to differentiate them from each other. Some were, she believed, fork–lift trucks, others ordinary cars. That the vibrations from their passing seemed to reverberate not just through her chair but also through the air suggested to her that she was in a confined space. The fact that she had on occasion detected the whiff of diesel fumes when the fork lift passed by hinted that she was on some kind of storage sight.

Anonymous. One of dozens in the city or in any town.

If it was one of the cheaper ones there probably would be limited surveillance, easily disabled or perhaps even avoided. Sheila was used to moving in higher places than the world of storage units, but she knew enough – she had not been born wealthy, instead working her way up the ladder in the art world from an employee of a gallery to a trader to a dealer to a gallery–owner herself. Despite her wealth, Sheila McKenzie had never forgotten her roots.

The silence of her world was shattered by a much stronger vibration that sent zig–zags of electrical signals dancing across the blackness behind her eyes. Shutter doors, she recognised, a rattling motion and a deep thump. Something about the motion was too steady to be human: electrical motors. The motion was reversed, the doors shutting again, and Sheila once more felt the presence of another human being in the unit with her.

The gag between her lips was loosened and the plugs in her ears removed once more. The gag tore at the soft skin on her lips, dried saliva as stiff as glue pulling on them. She winced, and then felt the tip of a bottle pressed to them as water splashed down her neck. Sheila drank gratefully, swallowing deeply and letting the chilled water flow across her tongue like the finest wine she had ever tasted.

'*Be quiet,*' the throaty, digitised voice commanded as she drank, '*or I will leave immediately.*'

Sheila emptied the bottle, gasped for air as it was removed and another took its place. She drank more slowly this time and smelled the aroma of food nearby, but she dared not speak without being commanded. To her disbelief, she wanted the bastard who had done this to her in the room with her, rather than be alone for countless darkened hours.

Sheila drained the second bottle, and then was fed as her captor cleaned her once more and removed a sheet that had lain across the seat beneath her legs. Like a child who still wet the bed in the night, Sheila was relieved to be clean again and yet humiliated beyond compare.

On impulse, she spoke as her captor finished.

'Thank you.'

'*Shut up,*' came the reply. '*You won't thank me if you're dead.*'

Sheila obeyed, falling silent despite the thousands of voices crying out to be heard in her head. Who are you? Why are you doing this to me? What do you want? She held her tongue, and was awash with relief when she heard the sound of the chair being dragged across to her.

Her unseen captor sat down. For a moment, Sheila could hear their breathing, rough and heavy through the digitiser.

'*You are a very successful woman,*' the voice said.

Sheila tried not to let her fear and grief overwhelm her, but as she thought of the long years of labour she had endured to build up her business, of the sacrifices and the things that she had had to do to ensure her success, she felt tears flood her eyes and her lips quivered as she replied.

'I've worked hard.'

'Haven't we all,' the voice replied. *'You're not special.'*

'I've never claimed to be.'

'How much money do you have?'

'How much do you want?'

'Answer the question!'

'I have my house,' Sheila blurted. 'The business is failing and doesn't hold any capital. You've abducted the wrong person because I don't have much money!'

'How much?'

Sheila sobbed as she tried to calculate how much she could raise. 'Maybe three quarters of a million, no more.'

'And your husband?'

'What about him?'

'How much does he have?'

'Nothing, he's an airline pilot but he doesn't have much capital either.'

'How much would he stand to gain if you were to die?'

Sheila felt as though her heart had stopped beating. Her breath came in short, sharp gasps as she thought of her life insurance policy.

'Four million,' she whispered. 'Is that what this is about?'

'Shut up and answer my questions,' the voice snapped. *'How would the money be paid to him? A monthly allowance or a lump sum?'*

'Both,' Sheila replied, struggling to gain control of her wildly flying emotions and start thinking straight, 'a lump sum of one million and then an annual payment for the life of the policy.'

A long silence followed, only the sound of her captor's heavy breathing filling the darkness. Sheila bit her lip and asked the question that had bothered her ever since the last visit.

'Who wants me dead?'

The heavy breathing continued for a moment, and then she heard her captor stand and push the chair back into what she assumed was the corner of the room. Sheila felt the gag against her lips and she opened her mouth to scream.

'No, please, let me…!'

The gag was fastened into place and her cry choked off. Sheila, tears drenching her blindfold, heard her captor squat down alongside her, heard the heavy breathing close to her ear, and she smelled a waft of something from their skin that she recognised.

Just before her captor spoke, Sheila heard something that she also recognised: above the sound of diesel–powered vehicles outside, she heard the unmistakeable sound of a jet aircraft taking off, loudly enough for her prison to be fairly close to the airport on Great Fall's south side.

'Don't worry, Sheila,' the voice rasped. *'This will all be over for you very soon.'*

Before Sheila could consider the unthinkable, the ear plugs were shoved back into place and she was abandoned again, alone with the sounds of her own miserable sobs.

***

20

Down to the last twelve hours.

Griffin sat at his desk with his head cradled in his hands as other detectives bustled around him or talked on phones. His eyes ached and itched from a lack of sleep and his brain felt fuzzy and lacking in focus. Think, dammit!

There had been no contact from Sheila McKenzie's abductors. The detectives monitoring the phone line had confirmed that there had in fact been only three phone calls to the McKenzie's landline since the tracking equipment had been installed, all of them for Sheila McKenzie from clients interested in works of art for sale and leaving messages asking for her to contact them.

A family targeted for a ransom that they could not hope to pay. No contact from the abductors. No body. Something was missing from the whole equation and for the life of him Griffin could not see it.

He rubbed his eyes and looked down again at a series of old files he had pulled that morning after returning from Dale McKenzie's home. He was studying them when the aroma of fresh coffee infiltrated his thoughts and he looked up to see Maietta standing in the office doorway, two mugs of steaming coffee in her hands.

'Figured you could use the boost,' she said.

Griffin took a proffered cup from her with a brief smile. Maietta returned it as she walked by him to her desk and dumped her handbag and keys there and began shuffling through mounds of paperwork. Griffin watched her. A street-wise kid from the wrong side of the block, Maietta had fought her way through life from her first diaper. Tough, resourceful and proactive, she had joined the force right out of school, determined not to follow so many of her friends into lives of crime, drugs, prostitution and who-knew what else.

It wasn't often that Griffin found her to act shy of him.

'You okay?' he asked.

Maietta glanced up at him. 'Sure.'

'You seem a little, y'know.'

'Y'know, *what*?'

'Quiet.'

'Figured you'd like the change.'

'Nice to get a word in now and again.'

'Shut your face.' Maietta smiled as she sipped from her coffee and gestured to his monitor. 'What you working on?'

Griffin shrugged.

'Cold cases,' he replied. 'One of them kind of reminded me of Sheila McKenzie's disappearance.'

'Care to share?'

'Sure,' Griffin said. 'Remember a suspicious drowning from about ten years ago? Young woman found in her bathtub downtown?'

'Just about,' Maietta said. 'I was a patrol officer back then. Coroner said she'd died naturally, probably fell asleep in the bath, right?'

'That's the one,' Griffin confirmed. 'Detectives working the case found a glass of wine by the side of the tub, no sign of struggle, no history suggesting enemies or vendettas against her. The suspicious side of things was that her bank accounts had been wiped clean that same night, every penny she possessed completely withdrawn.'

Maietta perched on the edge of her desk, still some distance from Griffin. Something had changed, that was for sure. Like any curious cop she'd normally have wandered over to take a look at the screen, refresh her memory. Now she kept her distance from him.

'Yeah,' Maietta replied. 'I remember now. The money was shifted into another account, then that account was emptied for cash. Nobody was able to trace it and the person who did it was in the wind.'

'Took the money as cash and hid it well,' Griffin nodded. 'Uniforms spent weeks canvassing for information on who might have had a motive to kill the victim and steal her money, but no evidence of foul play was found. It says in the case file here that there was a boyfriend, apparently, that nobody was able to trace. Got a few vague descriptions but it looks like he took off before the body was found. The victim's friends all said that they had heard of this boyfriend but that he kept himself to himself and hardly any of her friends had met him.'

'Suspect number one,' Maietta said. 'What's your angle on this and McKenzie?'

'I decided to look a little further into it, see if I couldn't find any similar cases, maybe an MO that fit other unsolved homicides. I got lucky.'

'Yeah?' Maietta asked, raising an interested eyebrow, but she did not move.

Griffin, finally convinced that Maietta wasn't going to stand up and join him, grabbed a sheet of paper from his desk and handed it across to her.

'Three near–identical homicides that occurred in Nevada, one a year for three years,' he said. 'Two more girls drowned in the bathtub, the third in a swimming pool in her backyard. No sign of struggle or forced entry in any of the cases, and no evidence on the bodies of strangulation or forced asphyxiation of any kind. They all just died in the water. In each case, their bank accounts were cleaned out around the time of their deaths.'

'No arrests,' Maietta said. 'Not even any suspects.'

'Except the one guy, a mysterious boyfriend in all of the cases who appears in the victim's life, hangs around for a while and then vanishes right about when they die.'

'No names,' Maietta said, 'looks like Mr Mysterious hid himself pretty well, avoided being identified and took each of the girls for around thirty thousand.'

'Hits four women, one after the other about a year apart, and then disappears,' Griffin related the rest of the case report. 'How the hell does that make sense? Serial–killers generally escalate their attacks or become increasingly sloppy. Murders for money are generally equally opportunistic and often carried out by spouses and family members eager for a slice of somebody else's financial pie.'

Maietta looked up at him over the sheet of paper. 'How does this fit with McKenzie?'

'I'm starting to like him for the abduction,' Griffin replied. 'There hasn't been any contact from his wife's abductors and they're leaving it too long now for this to be a test of wills. These cold cases kind of reminded me of Dale McKenzie because the victims were all orphans and so is Sheila McKenzie.'

'That's thin, and besides the MO is different,' Maietta said. 'Our case is an abduction, not a homicide, at least we're fairly sure it still is. If McKenzie was a serial–killer he would hardly have married his damned target. There's no link here Scott, it's a totally different case.'

'But what if maybe McKenzie had found his perfect partner? Maybe he would stop slaying and settle down? Sheila's wealthy and successful, maybe he figured this time he'd go for the big bucks, y'know? Stop messing around with ten thousand here and there and go for six or seven figures?'

'I don't know,' Maietta said, shaking her head. 'There's nothing linking McKenzie to these murders, nothing that suggests he's even remotely psychotic himself. He's an airline pilot for Christ's sake, they take tests for things like that don't they? Make sure they're not going to nosedive an airliner full of people into a mountain just because they're having a bad day.'

'Maybe McKenzie's smart enough to pass tests like that? We should put a tail on him, see what it gives us?'

'Using what manpower?' Maietta asked. 'Olsen's already got every spare hand working cases, including ours, and how the hell do we tail McKenzie if he's doing five hundred knots at thirty thousand feet? I don't suppose Nevada's PD are going to send officers to watch McKenzie's back based on something as thin as this.' Maietta set her coffee down and handed the sheet of paper back to Griffin. 'McKenzie's not our guy. He's got a cast–iron alibi and we've already checked his financials going back five years or more. He's clean, Scott. Sure, he's up–tight and he's under pressure but that's hardly surprising.'

'It was you who said he was hiding something,' Griffin pointed out.

'Doesn't mean he's hiding a murder or four,' Maietta replied.

Griffin sighed, and rubbed his forehead with one hand. 'I figure it's worth a look.'

'Everything's worth a look,' Maietta agreed. 'You just gotta know when to let it go and put your time and effort into something else.'

Griffin did not reply, still staring down at the documents on his desk.

Maietta glanced across the office as Kathryn Stone strolled in. 'Time for your treatment, right?'

Griffin looked over his shoulder at Stone, then scowled as he turned back. 'Great.'

***

21

'You seem tense.'

Kathryn had drawn the blinds over Captain Olsen's office in an attempt to provide some level of privacy for herself and Griffin, and the surroundings were far more appropriate to a counselling session than the cold walls of the interview room.

'I've had a few bad nights,' Griffin replied without looking at her.

He was slumped in his chair, his hands clasped together out of sight in his lap, although Kathryn could tell he was tensing them because of the set of his shoulders. His neck bulged against the collar of his shirt and his jaw was shaded from the previous day. The dark rings beneath his eyes stood out all the more for his piercing blue eyes.

'Couldn't sleep?' she hazarded.

'Didn't much try.'

Kathryn noted the lack of eye contact and the short, disinterested responses. She figured that Griffin and his wife had probably had some kind of row.

'You want to tell me what happened?'

'You want to fuck off?'

Kathryn flinched internally but she kept her expression neutral. Griffin still hadn't looked her in the eye and she realised that he was holding her responsible for whatever had happened.

Sometimes guys, especially proud guys like Griffin, found it easier to weave an imagined avenue of blame back to somebody or something else, anything else, than admit that they'd screwed up. It didn't matter whether it was putting up a lop–sided picture or forgetting their wife's birthday – when it came to trivia it was always somebody else's fault.

But present them with a major issue, a truly traumatic event for which they remained blameless, and *wow* did the chip hit the shoulder. Suddenly, all the burdens of the world were weighing down upon them and nothing short of a miracle could liberate them from their sorrows.

'You tried something, didn't you,' Kathryn said.

Griffin looked out of the window, anywhere but at her, and said nothing.

'I'm right here detective.'

'I know where you are,' Griffin uttered.

'You don't want to be in this room with me, do you?'

'No.'

'Good,' Kathryn said, 'because it's right where you're staying.'

'You're an asshole,' Griffin shot back. 'I think that people like you do this job because you enjoy seeing other people suffer.'

'I do this job because I enjoy seeing people overcome their suffering,' Kathryn countered. 'You going to tell me what happened?'

Griffin bit his lip and looked away again.

'Look, detective, what happened isn't just going to vanish,' Kathryn said. 'I'm not going to vanish. You can't just pretend we're not sitting here. You have to go through this process to be able to get back to work properly. I know it, Captain Olsen knows it and I think you know it too.'

'How very perceptive.'

'Is that all you've got?' Kathryn asked. 'A few snippy lines, all lip and no balls?'

'Just because I have to be here doesn't mean I have to be here talking to you,' Griffin snapped. 'I could request a different counsellor.'

'Go ahead,' Kathryn said. 'You'll just be sat here having the same conversation with somebody else. It doesn't matter who you're talking to, just that you talk. You get somebody else, all it means is they'll have to start over with you, prolonging the suffering. You want this to be done with, right?'

Griffin seethed and stared out of the shutter blinds as he spat out his response. 'Of course I do.'

'Then talk. Tell me what happened.'

'I did what you said. I went home, picked up some flowers and a bottle of wine on the way for my wife.'

Kathryn nodded slowly. 'So far, so good. Then what?'

'Then what?' Griffin echoed. 'I took them to her, I apologised, and before I knew it she blew up in my face and stormed out of the house, that's what fucking happened! So much for you and your goddamned master plan!'

Kathryn took a breath. *Always think before replying*, her course principal had often said. *Never say an unconsidered word*.

'I didn't offer you a master plan, detective,' she soothed. 'I suggested going home and talking to your wife. Did you talk to her?'

'Yes, I talked to her.'

'So what happened between you apologising and her walking out?'

Griffin kept his gaze off her as he replied.

'It was going fine, but then she started picking holes, mentioned how miserable things had been, shit like that. Before I knew it we were shouting at each other.'

Kathryn glanced down at her notes before she spoke.

'Scott, you were doing the right things but a bottle of wine and a bouquet do not a life–changing event make. Angela probably was hoping that you would sit down with that bottle of wine and talk all night about what's been happening.'

'Yeah,' Griffin blurted, 'I don't doubt it.'

'She wants reassurance,' Kathryn went on, 'she wants to know that you still care about her, that she's not going through life on her own. She wants *you*, Scott. She wants the man that she married, the man that she fell in love with, and she hasn't seen that man in a very long time.' A silence descended upon the office as Kathryn became aware that she could just as easily have been describing herself. She shook herself free of the realisation. 'Neither have you.'

Griffin bit his lip again and Kathryn saw the first fractures cracking the detective's armour, the first hint at untold oceans of grief seething behind an icy exterior.

'That man is gone.'

'No,' Kathryn cut across. 'That man is you. You've just forgotten how to show it. You're holding inside all of the things that you need to let go of, and if you don't do it before long you'll wake up and realise that everybody you care about has given up on you and vanished. That's how these things happen, Scott.'

Griffin shook his head, his cold blue eyes glistening. He ducked his head, shook it again.

'No, I've got this.'

'You've got nothing,' Kathryn said. 'You're losing your wife and you're losing yourself.'

'I tried!' Griffin snarled. 'There's only so much that I can do!'

'For whom?' Kathryn asked. 'Scott, you fired a shot that killed a nine–year old girl.'

'I know what I did…'

Griffin's voice cracked, wrenched with grief as his features creased and then crumbled. The harsh sunlight beaming through the blinds cast his misery in deep shadows that he fought to conceal from her.

'But *you* didn't kill her,' Kathryn said. 'You, Detective Scott Griffin, did not kill that girl. She died because of where her abductors placed her. Had they not done so, you would not have been there and she would not have died. Had they surrendered, she would not have died. Had they been decent, upstanding and honourable men like you, she would not have died.'

Griffin dragged an angry forearm across his eyes.

'That shit's easy to say from behind a desk,' he growled back. 'Try it when you're holding that nine year old kid in your arms and trying to stop her head from falling apart.'

Kathryn felt her guts surge in sympathy both for Griffin and the poor child whose life had been cut so brutally and horrifyingly short. She sucked in a breath.

'I don't know that I could, Scott,' she replied. 'If it happened to me, I'd need help too.'

Griffin's grief surged over again and he shielded his face with a hand, his elbow thumping down onto the desk as he leaned on it.

'This isn't an interrogation,' Kathryn said softly. 'There's no wrong answer here.'

'There's no right answer either.'

'But either way, you can't keep hiding from this. You know how to spot a liar detective and so do I. You've just got to let it out.'

'I don't want to let it out!' Griffin shouted out loud and shot to his feet. He hit the desk hard, spittle flying from his lips as he bellowed into her face. 'I don't want to ever let it out! You understand me?! Ever!'

The door to the office flew open as Maietta and Olsen burst in.

Kathryn, still sat in her chair, kept her eyes fixed on Griffin's as they blazed rage before her.

'Everything okay?' Olsen asked.

Kathryn swallowed once. 'Everything's fine,' she replied, barely managing to keep the fear from her voice. 'Detective Griffin was just leaving.'

Griffin glared at her, every muscle in his body drawn like a tensed bow. In a flash he whirled and stormed out of the office as Olsen and Maietta twisted out of his way.

'That's enough Griffin,' Olsen called after him. 'You're suspended until you get your shit under control, is that understood?'

Griffin didn't reply as he stormed away.

'Hey,' Maietta protested to the captain. 'There's no need for that. He'll be fine.'

'He's off,' Olsen insisted. 'I'm not having him threatening staff. You got a problem with that?'

Kathryn let out a blast of air and her shoulders sagged as she slumped back in her chair. Maietta shot her a dirty look.

'How's that gentle touch workin' out for you there, Stone?'

Maietta whirled and hurried away after her partner.

Kathryn sighed as Olsen looked across at her. 'You okay with this? I can get somebody else in to…'

'No,' Kathryn said. 'I'll be fine. I just didn't know that…'

'He could be violent?' Olsen finished the sentence for her. 'He's a former soldier. What did you expect? The tearful type?'

***

22

Griffin burst out of the precinct doors and scattered two uniformed officers who had been making their way inside. They took one look at his face and slipped quietly past him and into the station.

Griffin stormed down the steps and hauled in a lung full of air, blew it out as though trying to void himself of the dizzying rage seething through his veins.

The sky was a bright blue, the air cold and crisp enough to crack with his knuckles. A thin sheet of frost glistened like diamond chips on the trees and on the roofs of cars parked in the lot. The cold air and blue sky reminded him briefly of Afghanistan, but something else seeped in there too - memories of his childhood, growing up in the woods and hills of Texas. Frosty mornings out hunting with his pa', closing in on Christmas. The excitement of that time of year, the warmth of his family around him, the fresh air and the wilderness.

Griffin felt his thumping heart ease inside his chest, felt some of the pain lanced from his festering soul.

'You okay?'

Maietta's voice came from behind him, a little ways away. He guessed she figured he might turn around and throttle her to death if she came too close.

'I'm fine,' he replied, 'just needed some air.'

Maietta sauntered up to stand beside him, her hands shoved into her pockets. She surveyed the cold morning before them, watched a few cars drift by.

'She got you pretty riled up there, soldier.'

Griffin did not reply. He plucked a cigarette from his pocket and lit it, blowing a cloud of fumes out into the perfect blue sky.

'Didn't know you smoked again,' she observed.

Griffin nodded. He had been partnered with Maietta for three years and had never smoked a cigarette in that time. In fact, he hadn't smoked one since joining the force. Becoming a police officer was meant to have been a new start, a new life. He'd stopped smoking and barely drank at all. Life had been better, back then.

'Guess I dropped off that wagon too,' he said finally.

Maietta looked across at him. 'You're not quitting, are you?'

'I only just started again.'

'Not the smoking.'

Griffin exhaled noisily, blue smoke drifting on the cold air. 'No.'

'Good,' Maietta replied. 'Because right now I get the feeling that you're at the threshold of something and if you can just hang on a little longer you'll pull through just fine.'

'What, you the damned shrink now?'

'I'm your partner,' she shot back. 'I've worked with you every day for the past three years. You think that what happens to you doesn't affect me too? I was there with you Scott. I saw that kid die. You think I don't wake up some nights and wish I could go back in time and do something different?'

Griffin shook his head. 'You didn't fire the shot.'

'I didn't fire *that* shot!' Maietta snapped. 'I'm watching you go down the can Scott, a little bit further every day, and I don't like it.'

'Well what would you like?'

'For you to stop blaming yourself and everybody else around you for something that nobody can change.'

Griffin shook his head, Maietta's words falling away like storm waves battering immoveable cliffs. His partner stepped in front of him, grabbed the collar of his jacket and yanked his face toward hers. A pair of sun–flecked green eyes glared into his.

'You *didn't* kill her, Scott,' Maietta growled at him. 'She was dragged into a dangerous situation by two coked–up bikers who are both now serving twenty–five to life. *They* killed her, Scott. They did. Get *that* into your thick head and stop fucking your life up over it.'

Maietta pushed him away with an angry shove and turned for the precinct door. Griffin turned and watched her go for a moment before he spoke.

'I can't.'

Maietta slowed and stood on the precinct steps. She looked over her shoulder at him, her long brown hair shielding her face as though it was something to hide behind.

'Why not?'

'I don't know.'

Maietta turned back and walked to Griffin's side. 'You've got to get over this and start moving forward. That shrink in there, Stone. She's there to help you do that.'

'You're doing a better job,' Griffin said with a shrug.

'But it's not my job,' Maietta pointed out. 'It's Stone's. You need to figure out whether what she's telling you is getting you riled up because it's true and you just don't want to hear it.'

Griffin's jaw tightened and he shook his head.

'She's just another shrink who thinks that she can lecture families when she doesn't even have one.'

Jane raised an eyebrow. 'Well you do have one Griffin and right now you're losing it, so whatever you've been doing up until now hasn't worked.'

'Angela walked out on me.'

Griffin's abrupt and unexpected statement caught Maietta unawares. She took a moment to digest what he had said.

'I'm sorry,' was all that she could manage in response.

'Yeah, me too.'

'She comin' back?' Griffin shrugged, and Maietta shook her head.

'You wanna talk about it?'

'Not so much. I don't even know how it happened.'

'I guess we don't really know people until they're forced to reveal how they really feel.'

Griffin looked at her. 'Are you talking about me or Angela?'

'Maybe both. It's what Stone's trying to get through to you. You don't tell people stuff, how the hell can they help you?'

'Who says I want any help?'

'You think that Angela did?'

Griffin flicked his cigarette away and exhaled noisily. 'The hell with it all.'

Griffin stormed away toward his car.

'Where are you going?'

'Anywhere but here. I'm suspended, right? I can do what I like.'

Griffin got into his car, fired up the engine and pulled out of the lot and away down the street.

The precinct seemed quiet as Maietta walked back inside in the aftermath of Griffin's temper. He had a reputation for it. Maietta sat down at her desk and stared out of a window, wondering whether or not she was about to do the right thing.

Trust was everything in law–enforcement. For cops, detectives, attorneys, judges: those for whom upholding the law was a job were themselves required to be the pillars and the foundations of that law. A betrayal of that trust, of any kind, was the rot that could bring the whole house tumbling down.

The world ain't built for you to like, honey, her dad used to tell her back in the day. Immigrants always had it tougher, even when sheltered in their own communities. Hard knocks and tough breaks were a way of life for Maietta, but this wasn't the usual run–of–the–mill disappointment, like a missed grade at college or a dumb–ass mistake on the job. No, this was something that she had to do and the aftermath might be with her for the rest of her career.

She turned the problem over in her mind for a few more moments and then stood up and strode to Captain Olsen's office door. Maietta hesitated, wondering if this really was something she shouldn't just drop for now.

'What is it, Jane?' Captain Olsen asked. 'Or do you just want to stand there and fantasise about me?'

Maietta cursed herself and opened the captain's office door, striding in and closing it behind her.

'Sorry to bother you,' she said.

'What the hell's that?' Olsen asked her, raising his eyebrows. 'Last I heard, Jane Maietta hasn't apologised to anybody since 1986. What gives?'

'Got something on my mind.'

'No shit.' Olsen gestured to a chair. 'Park your ass and unload.'

Maietta slumped into the chair and stared at Olsen. 'It's a difficult one.'

'You going to propose to me, Maietta?'

Maietta let out a long sigh. 'I think Griffin might be looking to skip town.'

Olsen's studied humour slipped and his enormous moustache twitched. 'You might want to elaborate on that, detective.'

Maietta nodded. Having said one thing, she may as well say it all. 'His wife walked out on him.'

'Hardly a chapter of Revelations, detective. Get to the point.'

'He's depressed, angry and confused. Last I spoke to him just now he sounded like he didn't really want to be on the job anymore.'

Olsen raised an eyebrow. 'You gonna keep tugging my fly or are you going to get those lips working? Spit it out.'

'I think he's off the wagon again.'

'And?'

'He needs help,' Maietta said. 'I can't be with him when he's suspended, and I don't know what he'll go and do without the job to keep him occupied.'

'I'm not following.'

'Only because you don't want to,' Maietta said.

Olsen's icy eyes fixed like lasers onto Maietta's. 'Are you suggesting what I think you're suggesting?'

'I want a tail on Griffin,' Maietta said finally. 'Even if it's me. He's not himself and I don't know how far he'll take this.'

'I don't know,' Olsen said. 'You really think Griffin's likely to take his own life and...?'

'You any idea how many vets have offed themselves after returning home from war zones?' Maietta cut across Olsen.

Olsen rubbed his temples. 'It's a long shot Maietta and frankly it makes no sense at all. Griffin's been through hell lately but he's straight as an arrow.'

'Everybody has their limit, sir,' Maietta said. 'Maybe Scott's reached his, and now he's been trying too damned hard to pin the abduction case on Dale McKenzie. He even pulled out some cold cases and tried to put McKenzie in the frame for 'em.'

Olsen's moustache twitched from side to side.

'I can't do anything about this, Jane,' he said finally. 'It's circumstantial. The only way you'll get anything on him is if you...'

'Follow him myself,' Maietta agreed. 'That was what I was going to do, but you saw how he went for Stone earlier. He's on the edge, captain, and if he sniffs me out while I'm tailing him into God–knows–where and he was in a bad enough mood...'

Maietta let the suggestion hang in the office between them for several long and silent moments.

'You've been his partner for three years,' Olsen said to her. 'Surely you've figured out by now whether he would do something like that?'

Maietta shook her head.

'If there's one thing that this job has taught me, sir, it's that no matter how well you think you know somebody, you don't know 'em at all. I read about some psychologist once, who said that all patients lie because there is one thing people fear above all others, one thing that will drive them to unbelievable acts.'

'What's that?'

'The fear of other people learning what they're *really* like,' Maietta said. 'Of seeing their innermost thoughts, their most deprived fantasies or most bizarre fetishes.'

'Christ, Maietta,' Olsen muttered. 'You're giving me wood here.'

'It's your corner,' Maietta said as she stood.

'You still going to follow him?'

'If I have to, yes. You good to sign off on it, officially?'

Olsen nodded. 'I'll make sure he doesn't get to carry again on duty even if Stone clears him, but there's nothing that I can do about it outside of the department, Maietta, you understand? He's an ex–soldier. He's bound to have a piece in a drawer somewhere at home.'

'That's what worries me,' Maietta said.

She made for the office door when the captain called after her.

'You know this could all be a scam, right? Maybe Sheila McKenzie's pulling the wool over all our eyes?'

Maietta opened the door. 'Yeah,' she agreed. 'Somebody's definitely screwing with us, and when I find out who I'll knuckle them myself.'

***

23

'You did *what* in the middle of a restaurant?!'

Ally's voice broke out loudly enough for several people in the cafe to look up.

'Quietly,' Kathryn hissed. 'It's not like I want this to be on live television.'

'Noooo,' Abby chided. 'Of course not. You just want it to be in front of the entire city.'

The cafÃ© was only half full, businessmen and women on their lunch breaks at scattered tables, gossiping about colleagues and texting on their cell phones as they did so. Kathryn had never much liked that sort of office feel about lunchtimes in town, as though working for some crummy business that nobody cared about was the central feature of people's lives. The office affair, whispers over the fax machine or the water–cooler, people being nice to their colleagues with strained smiles and soft voices even though they hated each other with a passion.

Kind of like living with Stephen, she realised.

'So, come on then, spill it all,' Ally insisted with a beckoning wave of her hand. 'Leave no details unspoken.'

Kathryn related the rest of the previous evening with Stephen at the restaurant, and of how on a final and deeply vicious impulse she had a young girl photograph her together with Stephen. She had then asked the staff at the restaurant to frame the picture for them and place it on the wall until Stephen made good on his proposal.

Ally listened in stunned silence, not something that Kathryn witnessed very often, before she finally replied.

'I feel certain that I speak for all womankind when I say that you should be knighted, handed an Oscar and awarded the Nobel Prize for Outstanding Bitch.'

Kathryn nearly choked on a slice of cucumber. 'He started it, remember?'

'Sure he did,' Ally agreed, 'and it's coming back to bite him in the ass, but I don't see where you can go from here. There's not much you can do to top your last performance.'

Kathryn peered at Ally over a sandwich as she smiled. 'You sure about that?'

'Oh do tell right this instant or I swear I'll call the police.'

'That's blackmail.'

'And last night's set–up of Stephen wasn't?' Ally grinned as she sipped a sparkling drink. 'I never knew you had it in you, Kathy.'

'Nor did I.'

'You have unleashed the wrath of your inner bitch my friend, and lo has it struck the mighty Stephen down.' Ally bit into her sandwich. 'So, what's next? A public flogging?'

'I'm going to check out the other woman's house.'

Ally's mouthful of sandwich nearly blasted across the restaurant as she fought to control herself. She managed to swallow her food, tears swimming in her eyes. 'Oh sweet Jesus, I think I might have peed myself. They have a house together? And *how* are you going to get into their house?'

Kathryn giggled. 'Stephen keeps a key in the apartment. He's such a douchebag, probably thought that I wouldn't notice it with all the others on his key ring. I had a copy made and will make my way up there when he's away with work.'

'What about the other woman?' Ally asked seriously. 'What if you get seen?'

'I'll pick my moment,' Kathryn said, picking at her food with a fork. 'There's no real rush.'

'No real rush?' Ally echoed. 'Where is all this coming from? One moment you're the shy and retiring college student, now you're a psychological terminator with no soul.'

'I'm not *that* bad.'

'Miss Stone,' Ally announced, 'in the history of bad–ass women you are among the *baddest* and *assy–ist* I've ever encountered. You're making Boadicea look like Mother Theresa.'

'Boadicea fought for a cause she believed in.'

'So did Mother Theresa,' Ally agreed. 'But she didn't cut men down by the hundred with a giant sword and then put their villages to flame.' She thought for a moment. 'Are you sure this admittedly wonderful plan of yours is going to actually work?'

'It is working,' Kathryn replied. 'He asked me to marry him.'

'Under duress,' Ally reminded her. 'It's the man you want, right? Not a piece of paper and a shared husband. What good is it if he's with the both of you?'

Kathryn thought for a moment. 'Maybe you're right. Maybe I need to get him away from all of this for a bit. The tickets I already bought didn't go down well.'

'What, a dirty weekend instead?' Ally smirked. 'How naughty.'

'Maybe. If I can time it to be as inconvenient as possible for Stephen it'll put him under more pressure and keep him away from *her*.'

'And what will you do on this dirty weekend?' Ally hazarded. 'Force him to confess? Oooh, you could tie him up and *then* force him to confess!'

'Ally,' Kathryn chided. 'I'm being serious.'

'So am I! You'd be amazed what a man will agree to do when you're rubbing a cheese grater up and down his…'

'Will you cut it out?!' Kathryn snapped, and then peered at Ally. 'Really? A cheese grater?'

Ally nodded as though it was nothing, but then she leaned in conspiratorially. 'The big deal was that he actually asked me to do it.'

'The big deal is that you obeyed,' Kathryn murmured in reply. 'Although the idea of slicing Stephen's most valuable asset does have some appeal.'

Ally smiled, her joviality fading. 'This isn't about hurting him, only punishing him and ultimately winning him back, right? You want something left to play with afterward.'

'I suppose.'

'So, when are you going to quit this charade and spill the beans? You run it too long he'll figure it out. He's not an idiot.'

'I'll come clean in the end,' Kathryn promised. 'The question is whether he will first.'

'He could have been with this other woman for a while, I figure, but I doubt they're married. People don't generally get hitched overnight.'

'You married a guy in Vegas once,' Kathryn reminded her friend.

'We were drunk,' Ally replied, 'and we were drunk for the next six years too. We only got divorced when we sobered up.'

The thought of drinking and divorces made Kathryn suddenly think of Griffin. His life was spiralling out of control.

'What?' Ally was looking at her with a concerned expression.

'Just reminded me of something at work,' Kathryn said. 'A client of mine.'

'Do tell,' Ally said.

'It's *work*, client confidentiality and all that.'

'So, you can hint and you can allude, can you not?'

Oh, I can *allude*, can I?' Kathryn mimicked her. 'You're so *bloody* posh, you know.'

'Shpill it Shtone,' Ally threatened in what sounded like a mock–Chicago accent, 'or I'll shing like a canary.'

Kathryn shrugged. 'Let's just say he's a decorated veteran going through a particularly hard time.'

'Police officer,' Ally said clairvoyantly.

'How the hell did you know that?'

'I didn't,' Ally beamed in delight. 'But there are no army bases around here, only Air National Guard so I figure he must be retired, you're a trauma specialist so he's either suffering from PTSD from his war experiences or he's had a big trauma while serving on the police force, because that's where a lot of ex–military end up.' Ally took a sip of her drink. 'Close?'

'What, you're Sherlock now?'

'To your Watson,' Ally agreed. 'Go on.'

'There's nothing to say,' Kathryn said. 'He's suffering, his marriage is breaking down, he's being watched by his superiors because they're concerned about his ability to do his job. I'm there to help him.'

'And are you helping him?'

'Not so much,' Kathryn sighed. 'Not yet, anyway.'

'That's the problem with people like you and your policeman friend,' Ally shrugged.

'What's that supposed to mean?'

'You're do–gooders,' Ally said without a hint of malice. 'You know, police, soldiers, psychologists or whatever. You're all brilliant at helping everybody else and useless at sorting yourselves out. Look at you. You're going through a major crisis of your own and yet you're sitting here worrying about some cop.'

'I can't help who I am,' Kathryn said in defence. 'Nor can Scott.'

'Scott, is it?' Ally asked as Kathryn cursed. 'On first name terms already, are we? Handsome, is he?'

'Cut it out,' Kathryn said. 'He's married.'

'Unhappily, apparently,' Ally added. 'And you didn't answer my question.'

'Yes, he's handsome. But so is Stephen and look where that's ended up.'

Ally briefly inclined her head and then drained her glass.

'You think this Scott will get over whatever it is he needs to get over?' Ally asked. 'You think that you will too?'

Kathryn sighed and stared at her plate. 'I honestly don't know. Griffin's a soldier, somebody used to dealing with stressful situations. I don't know that I can.'

Ally looked at Kathryn for a moment longer and then reached out and squeezed her arm.

'Sometimes, you've just got to know when to quit,' she said. 'We all do. There's a whole world out there waiting for us, if we've got the guts to get out there and find it. Stephen's already a lost cause, Kathy.'

'I won't give up until I'm sure,' Kathryn said.

Ally released her arm and glanced up out of the restaurant windows. Kathryn turned and saw an airliner climbing out from the airport on the other side of the city, its lights flashing until it was consumed by scattered clouds rolling in from the west on chinook winds.

'You see that?' Ally asked. 'It's like a highway, heading off into the unknown. That airplane is too. Somewhere else. Anywhere else. You've got to be willing to take your chances and try again, while you're still young enough to do it.'

'Like you did?' Kathryn asked.

Ally smiled. 'Exactly like I did. I left an unhappy life in England to come here and start over. I've never looked back. Almost everybody dreams of starting over at some point in their lives, with a clean slate, somewhere completely new. But few people have the strength to go and actually do it.'

Kathryn sighed.

'I know,' she said. 'But I want *this* life to work.'

'Fine,' Ally replied. 'There's a place called Hunter's Lodge, out west of the city on the plains toward Freezeout Lake. It's a tourist retreat, horse riding, hiking, all that crap. It's close by, cheap and easy and tickets are easy to come by, especially at this time of year. But make it work fast between the two of you or get out, because this can't go on much longer, you understand? Make a decision soon about just how much you want Stephen before he figures out what you're up to.'

Kathryn sighed and made her decision.

'I'll check out their house and their life, and what I see will determine what I do next.'

***

24

It took Kathryn half an hour to drive through the city, most of it spent trying to control the writhing sense of naughtiness squirming in her belly.

Kathryn was by any woman's standards appallingly sane. As far as she could remember she had never broken a law, never struck another person and had hardly ever had the need to tell anything more than the whitest of lies. She recognised that this was something that made her interminably boring to many. Most of her friends had lost their virginity before their sixteenth birthday and paraded the fact with some pride, regardless of their supposed religions or their parents' insistence otherwise. Most were drinkers, many were smokers and quite a few had been familiar faces in the local precinct until they settled down with husbands and families.

Most shockingly of all, about a third had indulged or were positively up to their necks in extra–marital affairs, at least one of them with another woman. Kathryn had long puzzled over this, as so many of the women she knew seemed otherwise remarkably sane, rational and family–loving individuals whom she might have considered far above such indiscretions. More to the point, some of their husbands were genuinely lovely men whom Kathryn would have been proud to marry. Of course, many others were also slovenly, chauvinistic bastards who spent more time in their local bars than they did raising families, but still…

Kathryn figured that sometimes people were just not meant to be together, despite being in possession of all the ingredients that supposedly made up the perfect couple. Convention, tradition, family pressure and faith often took precedence over personal happiness, and the entirely human fear of embarrassment and social rejection sustained the suffering over months, years and even decades. Few were strong enough or brave enough to break out and start over, even when their supposed beloved husbands frequently enjoyed battering them after a night on the booze.

Ally's advice to give Stephen a wide berth echoed through her mind as she negotiated the dense city traffic, and once again she saw the airliners lifting off and vanishing into the distant darkness. Somewhere else. Anywhere else. Better places, filled with happier people doing happier things with happier spouses and beautiful children in lovely homes with bright, shiny futures. Kathryn knew that the imagery she was creating was in truth filled with the same daily worries about money, jobs, bills and the kid's futures as any other, but what was the future but a fantasy? What was aspiration without a dream to follow? Life *could* be that good, surely? It just boiled down to how badly somebody wanted it and what they were willing to do to achieve it.

Kathryn gripped the steering wheel a little tighter as she drove toward the suburban district on the opposite side of the city to the airport. The streets and homes became cleaner and quieter than the bustling metropolis, leafy cul–de–sacs and gated mansions with glowing lanterns outside.

She had prepared herself to find something a little more luxurious than the cramped, damp apartment she shared with Stephen, but as she drove she found herself gaping at the sheer opulence before her. Some of the homes probably had bathrooms bigger than her entire apartment, gardens the size of football pitches, with pools and games rooms and televisions the size of tennis courts sunk into gargantuan walls.

The GPS beeped and a digital voice told her she had arrived. She drove past the house and turned into a side road, then pulled the Lincoln into the sidewalk and switched off the lights and clattering engine. Kathryn got out of her car and locked it, not for the first time wondering why she bothered locking a car that was barely functional, before strolling back along the road until she reached the house.

The house was not gated like some of the others, but perfectly manicured lawns stretched up to a broad, grand Colonial style home. Two giant trees flanked the house like ancient guardians. Stone lions sat either side of an ornate flight of steps that led up to a broad, dark oak front door. The place looked like something out of Beverly Hills.

Kathryn walked up the garden path. She scanned the windows of the house but everything was dark inside. She reached into her handbag and retrieved the key she had copied from Stephen's collection, and then with her heart beating hard and fast in her chest she pushed the key into the lock and turned it. The lock clicked and the door swung smoothly open to reveal a vast and dark interior of unknowns.

A dim flashing light blinked on and off as she stepped onto the expensively tiled foyer, and she turned to see a touchpad set into the wall. The alarm system. Kathryn stepped across to it and touched a series of keys, memorised from a file in Stephen's laptop that she had surreptitiously accessed some nights before as he showered. The alarm beeped softly once and the flashing light vanished. She smiled to herself, turned and gently pushed the front door closed again.

A wide, sweeping staircase ascended opposite the front door to the upper rooms, while to her left and right were doorways to adjoining rooms. Either side of the staircase were passages leading toward the rear of the house. The foyer itself was larger than her and Stephen's apartment and much higher. An ornate chandelier style light, with faux candles, dominated the ceiling above her. Kathryn reached out for a bank of switches on the wall near the alarm system, and the chandelier glowed into life and illuminated the grandly decorated foyer.

Dark wood panels, tastefully subtle magnolia painted walls, modern art canvasses adorning the corridors. A bouquet of flowers on a glass table, a couple of expensive looking *American Contemporary Art* magazines tossed casually alongside the vase in the way that nobody ever does unless they actually want people to see them.

Kathryn followed the left hand passage, her sneakers making no sound on the polished tiles as she moved past the staircase. To her left, an open door led into a spacious office where a widescreen monitor stood on a mahogany desk with a wireless keyboard. No wires or cables. A roller–ball mouse was set into the surface of the desk alongside a glossy black phone. Everything polished and perfectly aligned, more like a show home than a working office.

On the wall, a picture of Stephen and his wife on a paradise beach somewhere, him in shorts and shirt, her in a long, flowing dress that looked as though it were some kind of native attire, like a sarong, all flowing waterfall shades of blue and green that matched her eyes. Kathryn studied the image of the woman for some time before moving on.

Kathryn moved into the kitchen at the rear. Granite worktops, black–tiled floors and ice–white cabinets and dÃ©cor. Everything was flawlessly polished, dusted and tidied away. Kathryn figured the place was disinfected every day and probably fumigated by the Centre for Disease Control once a week. Even the chiller was bigger than Kathryn's shower.

She crossed the kitchen and followed the other corridor back toward the foyer, passing on her left a doorway that led into a beautiful games room. A billiard table in the centre near an ornate chess–board with carved ivory figurines of goblins, kings, dragons and princesses.

Kathryn walked back into the foyer, an unsettling nausea poisoning her innards as she turned left and walked into a grand dining room. A long, immaculately polished table with ten seats: four down each side and two at each end. Lovely soft carpets, indirect lighting casting soft patches of light across the walls, a mirror–polished serving set arrayed in the centre of the table.

Kathryn stared at the table for a moment and then moved back across the foyer and into the room on the opposite side of the house.

In Kathryn's apartment, Stephen had once used a cushion to demonstrate how it was possible, just, to swing a cat without touching the walls. In Stephen's other house, she would have been able to demonstrate how it was possible, just, to throw a cat the length of the room.

A giant, cream leather sofa and two matching armchairs were still dwarfed by the wide open lounge that led onto broad French windows at the far end of the room. A faux mantelpiece contained a fireplace into which was set a glossy–black screen that she guessed was probably some kind of electrical fireplace.

Above it, set into the wall, was what looked like a three–thousand inch plasma screen. Miles more soft carpet, a smoked–glass coffee table large enough to lay down on, scattered with more sickeningly modern art catalogues and magazines and a telephone wired to what looked like a modem or similar. A canvass was mounted on one wall that looked like thirty deranged chimpanzees had hurled coloured paints at it for half an hour, yet was probably worth more than Kathryn earned in a year.

Kathryn felt a pinch of grief sting the corners of her eyes as she turned away and walked back to the staircase. She switched off the lights, just in case somebody showed up, and stared up at the staircase for several long minutes before she finally walked up the steps one at a time and turned onto the landing.

She could see in the half–light that there were several bedrooms, most with the doors shut, but two large doors opened out onto what could only be the main bedroom. She walked across to it and stood in the doorway.

Like everything else in the damned place it was overbearingly large. The bed was big enough for Venus Williams to practice serving on. An on–suite that Kathryn could not be bothered to look at was visible through an open doorway and looked to be larger than her bathroom anyway. Walk–in wardrobes featured on both sides of the bed.

Kathryn walked across to one of them, the side that she knew belonged to Stephen's wife by the romance novel and small box of tissues on her bedside table. Kathryn slid the doors open and like the Tardis it opened out and a light came on automatically to illuminate its cavernous interior.

Clothes, clothes and more clothes above endless orderly ranks of shoes. Enough fabric to dress the population of Spain, enough footwear to make a queen blush. Kathryn edged into the wardrobe, ran one hand along the impossible soft and clean dresses and business suits hanging in their hundreds. As she surveyed them, a flash of blue caught her eye. She moved toward it and parted the dresses to reveal waterfall colours flowing down a dress.

The dress that she had seen in the photograph, in the office downstairs.

Kathryn ran her hands down the fabric a few times, and then with a flourish she grabbed it off the hangar and rolled it up under her arm.

The temptation to take fire and sword to the entire house was overwhelming, to burn it to the ground as she danced in the garden before the raging inferno of Stephen's secret life while singing happy songs and laughing manically as the police arrived. Maybe there was an expensive car in the double garage she had noticed on the way in, something that she could douse in paint or drag her keys down. Or perhaps she could take a chainsaw to Stephen's no-doubt equally expensive clothing collection.

On an impulse she hurried across the room to the other wardrobe and yanked it open.

Smaller than the first, a light came on to reveal a few rows of suits, most of them dark in colour. A half-dozen pairs of polished shoes along with countless sneakers. Some jeans and shirts, nothing out of the ordinary.

Only one thing caught her eye.

One of the suits had two thick, gold bars high up on the shoulder. She stepped toward it and pushed the suit aside to see a pair of gold wings pinned to the breast. Above the suit, on a shelf, was a smart looking cap with identical wings embroidered onto the front.

Kathryn blinked. For all the world, the suits looked like the kind that an airline pilot would wear. For a few moments she wondered just how much money Stephen must be making in his other life, and the means by which he was able to call her from cities many hundreds of miles away and yet burn no fuel getting there was finally explained.

Finally, Kathryn understood. Stephen was not seeing another woman: it was *Kathryn* who was the *other* woman. Kathryn was the affair.

Kathryn turned and walked out of the wardrobe, and then moved across to Stephen's wife's bedside table. She opened it, and inside lay what was unmistakeably a woman's diary. Excitement pulsed through

Kathryn's stomach as she lifted the diary out, and she made herself comfortable on the edge of the bed and opened the first page.

It was perhaps a mark of the woman that there were no doodles of flowers, or clouds, or any sort of absent–minded sketches that usually adorned a woman's diary, including Kathryn's. No. This diary was more like an itinerary, a series of formal lists detailing events as though they were being spilled out in binary code.

Sold two canvasses, both below auction price.

Lunch at Travelli's. Melinda worried about her kids, poor souls, both poorly with flu.

Dinner out, alone again. DH on late duty, probably. Did not enjoy being leered at by men in the bar so left early.

Kathryn spent almost an hour leafing through the pages of the diary, delighting in its revelations. She reached the end and closed it just in time to hear the distant sound of a car pulling up outside the house as a flare of headlights swept through the bedroom.

***

25

Kathryn's heart leaped up into her throat.

She rushed out of the bedroom, only just remembering to shut the wardrobes behind her as she ran for the staircase. She was half way down when she realised that there was no chance that she would be able to slip out of the house before whoever it was outside got to the front door.

Half way down the staircase and with panic running like poison through her veins she heard the slamming of a car door that sounded as though it came from right outside the front of the house.

Kathryn whirled and dashed back up the staircase and then ran out of sight as she heard the sudden crunch of keys in the front door and it swung open behind her. She crouched down on the landing and tried not to breathe as she heard footsteps on the tiles of the foyer downstairs.

She heard the front door slam loudly and a set of keys crash down onto the glass table in the foyer. The soft beeping of the alarm system was silenced by what sounded like angry jabbing at the keys and a muffled *shut the fuck up*.

Stephen.

Kathryn, her heart still pounding in her chest, huddled over the stolen dress she still gripped in her hands as she heard the figure below her step away from the alarm. Moments later the foyer and landing were flooded with light as the chandelier and what seemed like every other light in the house blossomed brightly into life.

Kathryn remained still, forcing herself not to move and perhaps betray her presence. She had to make a decision.

The first, and most honourable choice, was to stand at the top of the stairs with her hands on her hips and demand to know what the hell was going on. Play the stricken fiancÃ©e, the enraged and wronged girlfriend, the downtrodden, insulted woman of wrath. Who was also the illegal trespasser and near–lunatic.

She scratched that option off of her list. There was no telling what Stephen would do. In fact, she realised with some alarm, she knew virtually nothing about Stephen. He had been living two lives for years and she had never known a thing until now.

Kathryn's train of thought led her to option three: get the fuck out of the house as fast as she could and never, ever come back again.

The sound of heavy, angry footfalls coming up the staircase galvanised her into action. Kathryn withdrew silently along the landing and realised that she had nowhere left to go but back into the master bedroom.

She bit her lip in frustration as she hurried back into the darkened room and looked desperately about for somewhere to hide. The underside of the immense bed looking wonderfully inviting, as did the walk–in wardrobe of Stephen's wife. Indecision swamped her mind as panic constricted her throat and clenched her stomach in a painful spasm. Kathryn shuffled around the bed and away from the door.

To her horror, in the darkness, she realised that she had not shut the wife's walk–in wardrobe door properly and that a sliver of light was visible beneath it. Kathryn gasped, but there was no time now to reach the door and hide inside, or even shut the door properly. Stephen was walking along the landing, breathing heavily as though irate. Kathryn dropped onto the thickly carpeted floor and rolled beneath the bed, holding her breath as Stephen's feet appeared in the bedroom doorway.

There was a brief hesitation and then she heard his voice ring out like a claxon.

'You stupid bitch!'

Kathryn clenched her eyes shut tightly as she realised that Stephen must have seen her. The light in the bedroom burst into life and she flinched as Stephen's feet stormed toward the bed.

Kathryn opened her mouth to speak.

'How many times did I tell you?' Stephen growled.

Kathryn's mouth hung open in silence as Stephen stormed past the bed and slammed the wardrobe door shut. 'Close the fucking wardrobe doors!'

Kathryn held onto the breath she had taken as Stephen's feet turned and walked back to the bed. She saw him stand there for a moment, heard what sounded like a tie being ripped off and tossed onto the bed. Then a shirt.

Stephen's pants dropped to his ankles and he lifted his feet one by one and removed them. Then his socks were torn off and finally his shorts were flung across the room.

'Useless bastards,' she heard him utter. 'Useless fucking bastards, the lot of them.'

Stephen turned and padded away toward the en-suite, his bare feet slapping the tiles as he walked in. Kathryn let the breath she had been holding slip from her lips as she heard the sound of the shower being turned on. Slowly, carefully, she began to edge toward the far side of the bed, determined to remain concealed as much as possible until she could make her dash for the bedroom door and out of the house.

She heard a clatter of bathroom implements being scattered angrily about as she crawled from beneath the bed and hunkered down alongside it. She peeked over the top and saw clouds of steam billowing from the en-suite, Stephen's clothes scattered across the bed along with an open briefcase filled with cell phone, spare clothes, notebooks and what looked like some kind of pills.

Kathryn edged toward the briefcase and reached out for the pills.

The cell phone suddenly trilled and vibrated on the bed as though screaming for Stephen. Kathryn almost yelped with fright and shoved her hand over her mouth as she heard Stephen shout from the en-suite.

'For Christ's sake!'

She heard Stephen's feet slap against the tiles and she ducked down flat behind the far side of the bed again as she heard him burst back into the bedroom. Stephen stormed across to the bed and she heard him rifling through the briefcase for his cell phone. His heavy breathing and irritation vanished as she heard him take a single, deep breath.

'Hello?'

Calm. Controlled. Accessible. It was as though he had transformed into a different man in the blink of an eye. Kathryn, laying now as flat as she could behind the bed, was surprised to hear the warbling voice of the caller loud and clear through the bedroom – Stephen must have switched his phone to speaker.

'I received the report about yesterday's flight, captain, and I'm afraid we're extremely concerned about what happened. There's talk of the incident being investigated.'

She listened as Stephen replied.

'I'm very sorry for what happened, but I got turned away from work today because of it. Surely that's an overreaction?'

'Not these days it isn't. Health and safety officials from the Federal Aviation Administration are already crawling all over the ATC tapes. They're advising us to suspend you from flying duties until their investigation is complete.'

'I'm sure that won't be necessary, it was a procedural omission, nothing more.'

'That's not how it looks here, captain,' the voice countered. *'You had twenty six passengers aboard when you ignored both an ATC command and your co–pilot's warning and turned into the path of incoming traffic.'*

'I can appreciate that sir, but…'

'We can't afford these kinds of lapses in concentration, not from somebody with your levels of experience. It puts the airline in a bad light.'

'It's the first time it's happened in my career, sir,' Stephen protested.

'Yes it is, you have an unblemished flight history and we want it to stay that way.'

'It will, sir.'

'Good, I'm glad you agree. We believe that it's best for now if you're temporarily suspended from flying duties until this is all over.'

Kathryn heard Stephen snatch the cell phone from the bed and answer it directly.

'That's the last thing that I want, sir.'

More warbling down the line. Stephen sighing heavily.

'I'd rather not be sitting here all day, sir. No, I agree, the sooner this is all over the better things will be but…' More warbling and then a resigned sigh. 'Yes sir, of course.'

More warbling, decisive this time, abrupt and firm.

'Yes sir, I understand. Just a few days. Yes, I'll take it easy, thanks for your concern.'

Stephen shut the phone off and tossed it onto the bed. 'Asshole!'

Kathryn, her head turned to look beneath the bed, saw Stephen turn and storm away toward the en–suite. Moments later the door slammed shut.

Kathryn levered herself up onto her hands and knees and edged her way around the bed until she was within six feet of the bedroom door. She listened to the noises coming from the en–suite and heard the splash and slap of water on skin as she reached the end of the bed.

Her eyes caught on the briefcase and she saw the pills she had glimpsed earlier.

Kathryn had never known Stephen to take pills before and certainly not to carry any around with him. She leaned over the bed and peered at the bottle, and realised that it was not a bottle of pills at all but a medicine of some kind, a fluid inside. The label was printed with a name she did not recognise: *Pancuronium bromide*.

Alongside the bottle, she saw a pair of syringes still in their sealed plastic surgical bags. She peered at them curiously, wondering what on Earth Stephen might be using them for, when she caught sight of a tablet computer lying inside the briefcase.

Kathryn reached for it and quickly tapped the power button. To her relief it was still switched on, the screen coming to life as she opened the Internet and tapped in a website address. As quickly as she could, she accessed the page and logged in. Immediately, she then logged out and closed the window. She closed the lid and slid the tablet back into place in the briefcase.

The splatter of water from the en–suite was abruptly silenced.

Go, *now*!

Kathryn lurched to her feet and hurried out of the bedroom and along the landing. She turned and descended the staircase toward the foyer, saw the front door ahead of her. The alarm system was off, deactivated when Stephen had returned home. She rushed for the door and yanked it open, felt a rush of fresh cool air wash over her as she staggered out of the house, closing the door quietly behind her before running down the garden path and out into the night.

***

26

Maietta drove slowly, her headlights off as she let her eyes adjust to the faint morning light that glowed across the eastern horizon.

She had waited a long time through the darkest hours of the night, and her back and legs ached from not moving for such a prolonged period, but now she would get her answers.

She had followed Griffin the previous evening, tracking him from a bar on Great Fall's west side where he drank alone for a couple of hours. With no sidearm, Griffin had no fear of being hauled before a committee for being intoxicated in possession of his weapon, but to her surprise Maietta had seen him consume little alcohol and only a couple of cigarettes.

Griffin had gotten into his car late in the evening, and for a moment Maietta had allowed the hope to blossom that he would simply drive home and get his head down. That hope had evaporated when Griffin had driven out of town, heading through Sun Prairie and out onto the lonely plains.

Maietta, haunted by the notion that Griffin might take his own life, had followed. Griffin had pulled off the main road and down an old track toward Muddy Creek, and Maietta had parked up in the cover of ancient trees bent over by the annual chinook winds, and waited through the long hours of the night.

Despite an overwhelming desire to follow Griffin down the track she had resisted, and experienced an intense relief when hours later he had driven back out and turned toward Great Falls, his tail lights vanishing into the gloomy dawn.

Maietta started her car's engine, and pulled into the track.

The trees were black against the sky, the track narrow and winding as it descended toward the river. Broken scrub sprouted from the gravel and grit beneath her car's wheels, signs of how long ago this lonely spot had been abandoned. Few cars came out here, and often in the winter the deep snows effectively not only shielded the track from view but actually prevented any kind of access for months at a time.

Maietta eased the car down the winding track, her foot off the throttle to silence her approach, the other holding the car back on the brakes. The light was just enough to make out the woods thinning ahead, opening out onto a small beach where once, back in the day, cotton boats had unloaded onto wharfs and smaller vessels with shallower hulls to take the goods into the city for sale in the markets.

Maietta's car rolled softly out of the woods as she pulled up and killed the engine.

It was utterly silent out here. The city was but a glow against low, torn clouds that hurried across the cold dawn sky as though fleeing the sunrise. Maietta climbed out of the car, pulled the collar of her jacket up close about her neck as she quietly shut the door. The light was brighter now. She could see the old mill further down the river, the rickety and collapsing wharfs and jetties, and the old farmhouse entombed in shadows before her.

Maietta walked across the gravelly surface of the embankment toward the farmhouse, her eyes seeking movement. She saw nothing and heard nothing, save for the lonely rumble of the wind as it gusted across the river and whipped the surface into tiny ripples.

She stopped near the farmhouse, and squatted down as something in the dust at her feet caught her eye.

The dust was rippled with geometric patterns, the tell–tale mark of where a vehicle had pulled in. Maietta glanced up at the sky. It had been raining on and off for several days, the weather blustery, changeable. The tracks must have been made recently, at most in the last twenty four hours.

Maietta's practiced eye followed the tracks. Griffin's vehicle had pulled into the farmstead and swung around, pulled up near the edge of the treeline to face out, back toward the track from which it had come. Maietta glanced at her own car, facing her with its trunk to the track.

She looked alongside the tracks, and saw where a shallow depression had been formed as dust and gravel had been piled up. The same vehicle, making the same manoeuvre over and over again. Many visits, over some period of time, had left a depression that the rain could not quite conceal.

Maietta moved across to where the vehicle had often pulled up, and squatted down again. There, ground into the dust at her feet, were several cigarette butts.

Maietta got up, drew her service pistol, and held it before her as she eased her way toward the farmstead. The entrance was wide open, a black maw beckoning her inside to discover whatever horrors lay in wait.

She eased her way inside, the cold gripping her as though in an embrace, the farmstead a crucible to loss and pain. The floorboards beneath her feet creaked, their timbers creased and turned up at the edges. The wind from outside whispered through empty rooms as she made her way through to what had once been a kitchen, stripped bare now but for aged cabinets and the rusting hulk of an old gas stove.

Maietta lowered her pistol as she saw strips of old police tape fluttering in the wind, and on a doorframe that led into what had once been a living room was a bright blue ring of paint circling a chunk of wood now missing from the frame where hinges had once been screwed in place.

The metal off of which Detective Scott Griffin's bullet had ricocheted.

Below the cabinets on the opposite side of the kitchen were more blue rings, this time signifying the spilt blood of Amy Wheeler that still stained the aged tiles

*

Kathryn awoke early in the morning, the incessant beeping of her alarm clock violating her slumber as her eyes opened to see the pale dawn breaching the bedroom curtains. But she did not groan, or mumble or curse. She shook herself awake and hurled off the duvet.

There would be little time for her to do what she now knew she must.

Visions of the previous night's revelations flashed repeatedly through her mind, the dawning knowledge that Stephen was not just seeing another woman but was in fact married to her, and that he was far from who she had believed him to be. Kathryn knew, somehow, instinctively, that she needed to get as far away from Stephen as she could, and the memory of the strange fluid she had found in his briefcase bothered her immensely.

Kathryn drove to the precinct station and searched for Detective Griffin. She had been tempted to call in when she had got home the previous night and get Griffin's number from the night staff, but had resisted the temptation. They might not understand and probably would not give out a personal cell number to a caller anyway. Besides, she and Griffin were not on the best of terms and the chances of him returning any of her calls outside of work hours seemed remote at best.

'Have you seen detective Griffin?' she asked the desk sergeant as she walked in.

'Not in yet,' he replied gruffly.

Kathryn was about to concoct a reply when the operations room door opened and Maietta strode through and beckoned for Kathryn to follow her.

'Where's Griffin?' Kathryn asked as she followed Maietta into the operations room.

'Called in sick.'

'But he's up to his neck in the McKenzie case, he needs to be here, as much for himself as anybody else. I need to talk to him.'

'Yeah, because that went well for you both last time.'

Kathryn frowned. 'What's that supposed to mean?'

Maietta whirled to face Kathryn, who flinched in anticipation of a flying fist. The detective glared at her for a moment and then pointed at Olsen's office door.

'A word,' she said.

Kathryn obeyed in silence and walked into Olsen's office. Maietta strode in behind her and kicked the door shut.

'What do you want?' Kathryn asked.

'You're a psychologist,' Maietta said, 'you can figure out what drives people, right?'

'It's what I'm paid for.'

Kathryn's face was tinged with a hint of anxiety that she could feel burning on her skin. She was reminded of her school days, when she would see the same look as Maietta's in the eyes of other pupils just before she was punched by them.

'Griffin keeps doing a vanishing act,' Maietta said.

Kathryn's anxiety shifted to her guts as she realised both that she was not under threat and that Maietta was sharing an important piece of information.

'How long has this been going on?'

'I don't know,' Maietta said, 'I'm not his mother. Only noticed it in the last couple of days.'

'Have you followed him?'

Maietta nodded, not making eye contact with Kathryn.

'And?' Kathryn pressed.

Maietta sighed, swatted some of her long hair out of her face with one hand. 'Heading out of town to an old farmstead down by the river.'

Kathryn felt herself stiffen, not really wanting to hear the answer to her next question. 'What's there?'

'What do you think? You read his file.'

'It's the site of the shoot–out, isn't it?'

Maietta's shoulders slumped as though a weight had been removed from them. 'He's even got a sleeping bag down there. Shit, he's gone crackers and I don't know what to do about it. I followed him, waited him out for a few hours until he left early this morning. I guess he goes home to eat, change or whatever.'

'You want me to go down there and talk to him?' Kathryn asked.

'Hell, no! He'd spot you a mile away and probably shoot you on sight if he's armed. Jesus, I want you to figure out why he's doing what he's doing. You're so damned smart? Put me one step ahead of him.'

Kathryn stared at Maietta for a few moments, then chose her words with care. 'He's not crackers, he's trying to be close to Amy Wheeler. It's a coping mechanism, okay? He's just trying to find a way through all of this.'

Maietta shook her head. 'I reported to Olsen that I was afraid Griffin would attempt to take his own life.'

'And now you think if you fill Olsen in on the rest, you'll be the reporting officer and Griffin will find out about everything.'

'Shit,' Maietta shook her head and pinched the bridge of her nose between finger and thumb. 'I shoulda known better.'

'It's not your fault,' Kathryn said. 'You're only looking out for him, just like he would for you.'

'Thing is, what the hell do I do about it now? I can't tell anybody about it, but he's gotta stop or sooner or later it'll all get out. Without his badge and his job he'll be in freefall. He's already drinking and smoking again.'

Kathryn looked at her watch as though pressed for time.

'You got somewhere you'd rather be?' Maietta challenged.

Kathryn reached into her handbag and pulled out a notebook and pen.

'I need an address from you,' she said. 'You know how often he goes down there?'

'Anytime he's not working I guess. You going to help me with this or not?'

'I don't think I can help,' Kathryn said, 'and neither can you.'

'What the hell's that supposed to mean? He needs help, that's your job and I want to know what you're going to do about it?' Maietta demanded.

'What should have been done a long time ago,' Kathryn replied. 'I'm done with procedure. I'll head out now, and meet up with you later at the site, okay?'

***

27

Sheila McKenzie lay in silence, her body tense and exhausted as she watched a kaleidoscope of bizarre colours and images twist in nauseous whorls before her closed eyes, her brain playing tricks on her as she awaited the unknowable.

To her dismay her addled brain had begun blocking out the distant sounds of activity outside her prison, the faint and irregular movements too vague to maintain focus on, and the vibrations through the reclining chair were also becoming harder to detect.

Sheila wriggled her head wearily from side to side, as she had done for many hours, in the hope of somehow loosening the blindfold, but it was useless. The tightness of her bonds was excruciating after so many long and lonely hours, and her head throbbed. She knew, somehow, deep inside that she could not take much more of the isolation, the silence, the loneliness and the pain, and feared the sleep would be the end of her.

Even as the thought crossed her mind to just let herself go, the lights before her eyes flared with vivid colour and she heard the sound of the doors being raised. A waft of cool clean air from outside, scented with fresh rain and snow, drifted across her as sweet as anything that she could ever recall smelling. A dull thud, and the blissful odour vanished.

Sheila stiffened, sensed movement around her, and once again the ritual began. Her captor cleaned Sheila, the violation of her body now a simple matter of fact requirement of her captivity. Sheila closed her mind to the activity, but after a few moments she realised that she was missing an opportunity to learn something.

She inhaled deeply.

Too late. Her captor moved behind her as one hand tugged the gag free from her Sheila's mouth and then removed the plugs from her ears.

'*Sit still*,' the deep–throat voice growled, '*say nothing.*'

Water spilled against Sheila's lips and she ate and drank again, missing not a morsel of the precious food. Her captor mopped the last dribbles of water from Sheila's chin and blouse, and then stepped away. Sheila said nothing, but secretly she was hoping that her captor would once again stay a while, talk for a bit and provide Sheila with the meagre crumbs of human contact and communication she so desperately craved. *Stockholm Syndrome*, she realised, the development of an emotional bond of sympathy for the abductor by their victim, but it was too strong to fight off.

To her relief, she heard the chair nearby being dragged into position, heard weight being shifted onto it and the rustle of fabric on skin. Sheila waited as the silence drew out, and eventually she had to break it.

'My arms and legs,' she whispered. 'I can't feel them.' Her abductor did not move. The silence drew out longer. 'Please, could you let me move them, even just a little bit? If I stay here much longer without moving I could end up with deep–vein thrombosis. I won't be much use to you if I'm dead of a cardiac arrest.'

Her abductor shifted position and moments later Sheila felt the bonds on her legs loosened slightly. She gasped in relief as she was able to move her legs, bending them and stretching them. Her wrists remained fixed in place.

'My arms now, please,' Sheila asked.

Her captor refastened Sheila's ankles in place before loosening the arm restraints. Sheila stretched her arms above her head, heard tendons pop and click as her muscles were tested properly for the first time in days.

A strong hand grabbed one of Sheila's wrists and yanked it back into place. Moments later the other was likewise rebound and her abductor moved back to the nearby seat.

'Have you come here to kill me?' Sheila asked.

'I wouldn't have fed you if I were here to kill you,' the deep–throat voice replied.

'Maybe it was my last meal?'

'Maybe it was.'

Sheila shivered. 'You take the time to clean me and feed me,' she said. 'I don't think you intend to kill me.'

'What I intend to do to you is my business and it will happen whether you want it to or not.'

A cold sweat tingled across Sheila's forehead. 'I can't stay here forever. People will know that I am missing. My staff at the gallery, my friends. They will report me missing.'

'It is too late for that.'

'What does that mean?'

'Your husband has betrayed you.'

Sheila froze in her seat and she momentarily stopped breathing as an image of Dale flashed into the field of her awareness once more.

'What do you mean?'

'We told him that you would die if he went to the police,' the voice growled. *'He is working with the police now.'*

Bastard. Sheila knew enough to be sure that Dale was, to all intents and purposes, one of the most selfish, self–serving, chauvinistic men she had ever met. If it wasn't about Dale then it wasn't important at all. Of course, he had only revealed this less palatable side to his personality *after* they had married. Prior to that fateful day he had been the man she had long dreamed of: professional career man, devoted fiancé, attentive lover.

Within a year of their marriage she had developed the first suspicions that he had been cheating on her. The absences, the feminine scents wafting from him in their house that did not match any perfume she wore. Of course, Dale was a handsome man and spent his working life surrounded by young air hostesses who were hired based on their attractiveness. It wasn't hard to put two and two together and figure out that he was having an affair.

Sheila steeled herself.

'I don't doubt it,' she spat angrily.

There was a moment's pause as Sheila detected a change in the atmosphere, a tension.

'What do you mean?'

The voice, still deep and growling, was nonetheless robbed of some of its menace by the tiny undercurrent of surprise that rippled through it. Sheila managed to remember not to smile for although she could not see, she knew that she could be seen.

'The bastard's having an affair,' Sheila snapped. 'I don't doubt that he's gone to the police.'

Another long silence before the voice spoke again. *'How long have you known about this?'*

Sheila blinked in surprise. 'What the hell does that matter?'

There was a brief movement and then the voice roared in her ear with a volume and intensity that sent a lance of fear bolting up and down her body.

'Answer the fucking question!'

'I don't know,' Sheila cried out in response. 'Maybe a few months? I suspected something but there was never any real evidence.'

'Why have you not confronted him about the affair?'

Sheila's heart raced and her chest heaved as she sucked in air.

'I didn't want to rock the boat,' she replied, and realised instantly how pathetic the excuse sounded. How pathetic *she* sounded. 'We have a good life. I didn't want it to end.'

The voice returned to its original volume and position.

'You know the woman in question?'

Sheila shook her head. 'No.'

There was a long silence and then Sheila heard her abductor stand.

'Don't leave.' No reply came back to her. 'Don't leave me alone here again, I'll give you anything!'

The voice growled at her from directly in front of her face as her bonds were suddenly yanked tight again under her jaw.

'If he does not come up with the money, then you'll die here.'

Sheila choked on her fear as sobs burst from within her chest, but she snarled her response.

'He's not going to come up with any money, you asshole!' she shouted. 'He's gone to the police because he hopes that you'll kill me. He wants my money, nothing more! That's all he's ever wanted! It's all men ever want from…'

The gag was pulled tight again, cutting her words off into a stream of strangled cries that degenerated into sobs.

The voice spoke one last time into her ear, leaning close to her.

'Then you're better off dead, because your time is up.'

As her captor leaned over her, Sheila smelled a carnival of odours that flashed images through her mind. Long ago she had read an article about human pheromones, of how men and women could subliminally detect all manner of physiological and even psychological dispositions just from the natural body odour of other people.

Sheila McKenzie had a sudden, vivid flare of realisation as she smelled the scent of her captor on their shirt, and in an instant she realised not just their sex but recognised the unique scent of *them*.

Then the ear plugs were shoved back into place. Sheila heard the shutters doors open and close again and the silence of her world returned to consume her.

But this time, she feared it no longer. Sheila McKenzie knew exactly who her abductor was, and her only thought now was a burning desire for vengeance.

She relaxed her burning right wrist. She had clenched her fist tightly and angled it slightly upwards when the bonds were fastened in order to create a small gap between her wrist and the arm of the recliner. Now, although her bonds had been yanked supremely tight, she could just about move her right hand.

Slowly, carefully, she began trying to work it free.

***

28

Kathryn hurried into the precinct station, one eye always on her watch.

The detectives were consumed by a mad final rush to locate Sheila McKenzie, making calls, scouring data, scratching heads. The deadline was already a couple of hours gone and nobody was making any headway.

'You got anything on Griffin?' Olsen asked as she rushed by.

'He's not in today, right?'

'Called in sick. You been to his home?'

Kathryn nodded. 'He's not there, nor is his wife. I'd like to think that they've made up but…'

'Yeah,' Olsen replied. 'You got any idea where he's headed?'

Kathryn glanced at Maietta, who was sitting at her desk with a phone pressed to her ear, not looking at them but listening surreptitiously.

'I think so,' Kathryn replied. 'Captain, I need to borrow Detective Maietta.'

'For what?'

'Finding Griffin,' she replied, 'before, y'know.'

'It's too late?'

Kathryn did not reply, letting Olsen's words hang in the air between them.

'I've got a missed deadline and a missing woman who with every passing hour is more likely to turn up dead, and you want me to send one of my detectives to baby–sit Griffin?'

'The deadline has passed,' Kathryn said, 'and your detectives are up to their necks chasing their tails. Griffin is your best bet, and right now he's no good to anybody, much less himself. You want me to fix him, you're going to have to give me some help. If I can get Griffin on his feet, maybe he can solve this abduction for once and for all.'

Olsen stared at Kathryn for a long moment, and then at Maietta, who was off the phone and watching the captain expectantly.

'How long?' Olsen snapped.

'Couple of hours, no more,' Kathryn said.

Olsen considered the request for a moment longer, and then nodded.

It became a long morning, stretching through lunch and into the mid-afternoon before Kathryn had done what she needed to do. A long, straining, emotional conversation with two people whom she had never before met. Asking them to do something that she had no right to expect them to do, that few people would have the strength and the integrity to do in an age where vengeance and mistrust were the currency of mankind, the nobility of ages past now long lost to society.

The track, when Kathryn found it at the second attempt, turned off the main road and wound its way down toward a river. A handful of old farm buildings lay set back into the woods, Kathryn catching glimpses of rusting machinery entombed in coils of foliage and vines.

The sun was already sinking low behind distant hills, dark grey clouds scudding across a sky splattered with streamers and ribbons of molten metal.

Kathryn drove down to where the track opened out into what had once been a farmstead, maybe for cattle and other grazing animals as there were no crop fields anywhere nearby. It hadn't been used for decades but there was a car parked off to one side that Kathryn recognised instantly as she pulled in alongside it and killed the engine.

The air was cold as she got out of her car, the wind blustering over the nearby water, but it was otherwise silent this far out of town. The kind of place nobody ever visited unless they had bad business on their mind.

Kathryn walked down toward the farmstead, the wind rumbling through rotting timbers nearby and whispering through lonely trees as she walked up to the front door and peered into the gloomy darkness within.

She was reluctant to enter, as though this place was some kind of shrine to suffering, a place of sanctuary for the doomed where the living were not welcome. Kathryn took a breath and a pace into the interior, smelled the odours of dust and decay and saw the carcass of a dead rat lying on its back in a room to her left, teeth bared in rigor mortis.

She stepped carefully as she moved through the building, the floorboards groaning beneath her. Kathryn stopped, looking at the wall beside her where a handful of bullet holes peppered the cheap plasterboard, old scrawlings from police markers identifying rounds fired by police and by their quarry in that last, terrible shoot out.

She heard movement behind her and tensed, turned to see a strip of old police-scene tape twisting in the cold breeze from a doorway back up the hall.

'You shouldn't be here.'

The voice came from nowhere and she almost jumped out of her skin as she searched the gloomy shadows. Her heart leaped and then fluttered as her brain resolved the voice into that of Griffin's, coming from the darkness somewhere ahead.

Kathryn eased her way forward, through the rest of the hall and out into what must once have been a kitchen–diner that overlooked the lake and the brilliant sunset searing the horizon.

Griffin was sitting on a dilapidated old chair in the middle of the kitchen, staring out of the windows toward the west. The glow of the setting sun illuminated his face, scoured it of shadows as though he were laying his guilt out for all to see. In his hand, in a small plastic bag, he held a brass bullet casing that he gently rolled over and over in his fingers.

Kathryn stood silent and still as the cold winter breeze whispered through the lonely old house and spoke of how life had been ripped so cruelly from one little girl and one decent man in the time it had taken to blink.

'You followed me,' Griffin said, not looking at her.

'Jane told me.'

Griffin's head turned almost imperceptibly toward her. 'Jane?'

'She's worried about you,' Kathryn said. 'Everyone is. You keep disappearing and they thought that you might be…'

Griffin's eye met hers now. 'What, drinking?'

Kathryn swallowed. 'Maybe. She figured either you were drinking yourself to death or you were coming up here.' Kathryn smiled briefly. 'She tried here first.'

Griffin went back to staring through the gaping windows into the sunset. Kathryn edged her way toward him, folding her arms across her chest to keep warm as the cold air seeped beneath her clothes.

'What are you thinking?' she asked.

'You're the psychologist,' Griffin said.

Kathryn looked around at the farmstead and then at the bullet casing Griffin held in his hands. 'I think that you're trying to go back to that day, trying to figure out where it all went wrong. Not just the shooting. You're thinking about everything: your wife, your life, Maietta, the job, trying to understand when and why you stopped being you.'

Griffin looked down at the bullet casing. 'No,' he replied. 'I know when and why I stopped being me.' He held the casing up to her. 'This is the one,' he said. 'This is what they dug out of what was left of Amy Wheeler's skull.'

Kathryn tried not to look at the casing, instead keeping her gaze fixed on Griffin. 'You keep it. Why?'

Griffin shrugged. 'I don't know why. I just need it.'

'No, you don't,' Kathryn said. 'You need to let it go.'

'Just like that, huh?' Griffin said.

'Every journey begins with a single step,' Kathryn replied. 'We all have things that we wish we could change but no matter how bad those things are we can never, ever go back. We can only ever go forward, and if we don't the rest of the world leaves us behind.'

'Or we leave the world behind,' Griffin murmured.

Kathryn swallowed again, the primal fear of a nearness of death like something alive in the empty farmstead. She could not see a gun anywhere, but Griffin would likely have brought it with him, concealed in his shoulder holster perhaps.

'That doesn't achieve anything,' she said finally. 'All you'd leave behind is the same grief you carry now, for others to carry for you.'

'That's good,' Griffin admitted, pointing at her as his lips twisted in a tight smile. 'I kind of get why they hired you now. You've got a way with words, haven't you? All that quiet exterior, the soft voice and all, it's just a feint, right? Inside, you really are like stone.'

'I wish that were true,' Kathryn said. 'But it's not. It's all bluster to keep you from facing what you already know is true.'

'Yeah?' Griffin asked. 'And what's that?'

'That you can't leave this place because you feel responsible for that girl's death, and you can't resolve in your mind how to move on.'

Griffin stared at her, half of his face now cast into deep shadow wherein resided the unspeakable pain that must seethe through his soul. He watched her for a long moment.

'Maybe I'm tough enough to do that,' he snapped. 'I killed her, Kathryn. I *shot* her. I *pulled* the *trigger* of *my* gun, with *my* hand and fired *my* bullet that killed her! There are no words counsellor, not in this world or the next that will ever change that, because just like you said we can never ever go back.'

'I also said we can go forward,' Kathryn said.

'You can,' Griffin replied softly. 'I can't.'

'I know,' she replied. 'And I can't help you, Scott.'

Griffin frowned, confused. 'Then why the hell are you here?'

'It's not me that's come to see you,' she said.

Kathryn turned and stood aside. Behind her, holding hands, Henry Wheeler and his wife Mary walked into the house.

Griffin leaped out of the old chair and stumbled back and away from the door as though physically struck. He fumbled with the bag that contained the bullet casing, stuffed it hurriedly into his pocket as he shot Kathryn an angry glance.

'The hell's this?'

Henry Wheeler was in his late forties, Kathryn figured, but he was a former soldier and he carried himself with the pride of his service still running in his veins. He let go of his wife's hand as he approached Griffin.

'Get away from me,' Griffin said. 'I didn't mean to come here, I just...'

Kathryn saw the panic on Griffin's face spread like a disease, his movements uncoordinated as his entire psyche lost the ability to maintain the wall of silence that he had constructed around his soul. Henry Wheeler kept moving toward Griffin until the detective was backed into one of the dusty old counters. Griffin's face began to crease and crumble, folding in upon itself as his pain was likewise cornered and left with nowhere to go but out.

'Get away from me, man...,' was all that he could mumble.

He tried to look away from Henry but the old man stood resolute before him. One hand reached out and gently took the bag with the bullet casing from Griffin's jacket pocket. Griffin did not resist, unable to decide where to look.

Henry Wheeler looked down at the casing, and then slipped it into his own jacket pocket. He looked at Griffin, stared at him for countless long seconds until Griffin was forced to look into the eyes of the man whose daughter he had killed.

Kathryn flinched as Henry Wheeler's arm flicked up toward Griffin's face, and then wrapped around the back of his neck as he pulled the detective close to him, wrapped him up as though he were a kid. Kathryn felt tears prick the corners of her eyes as Griffin collapsed into Henry Wheeler's embrace as he cried great choking sobs. Griffin's legs gave way beneath him and he sank toward the kitchen floor, Henry Wheeler easing the detective down as Mary Wheeler dashed past Kathryn and dropped to her knees alongside Griffin, her arms wrapping around the detective as they folded themselves protectively around him.

Kathryn backed away from the kitchen and turned, walking quietly out of the farmstead until she could no longer hear the sobs that echoed through the lonely farmstead, dredged out in big, heaving chunks of grief and cast out onto the wind. She checked her watch as she walked. Stephen would be home soon and Kathryn knew somehow that she could not continue her charade any longer. Just like Griffin, she needed to confront her demons face to face.

Outside, Maietta stood beside her car, her arms folded against the growing chill as she watched Kathryn approach. She raised one perfectly arched eyebrow and Kathryn nodded.

'It's done,' she said.

'Just like that?'

Kathryn sighed, the wind blowing her hair across her face in ragged strands that for a brief moment she felt represented the tattered fragments of her life.

'It's what he needed,' she replied. 'What he wanted. He just couldn't see it.'

Kathryn walked past Maietta's car and headed for her own.

'You not going to hang around?' Maietta asked, watching her curiously. 'See how he makes out?'

Kathryn shook her head as she looked over her shoulder. 'I've seen enough grief for one lifetime, detective. I'll see him when he gets back to the office. Can you take him home for me?'

Kathryn got into her car and started the engine, then picked up her cell and dialled a number as she guided her car out of the track and onto the highway. The phone rang for only a second or two before Ally picked up.

'Hey honey.'

'Hi,' Kathryn replied. 'Listen, are you free to talk later tonight?'

'On a Friday night?' Ally asked. *'After work, now that the unbearable dragging lethargy of the working week is over? Does the proverbial bear shit in the proverbial woods?'*

'Can I stay at yours, tonight?'

There was a long pause on the line. *'Are you okay?'*

'Not really,' Kathryn said, and unexpectedly a seething ball of grief shook her and she fought back tears.

'What's happened? Has he hurt you?'

'No,' Kathryn said. 'But I need to end this. You were right, Ally. Stephen is not good for me.'

'*Good,*' Ally replied. '*Glad you're finally making some sense. Come straight from work, okay?*'

'I've got to get home and pack first.'

'*Don't,*' Ally said. '*Just leave, now, and don't go back there.*'

'I have to,' Kathryn insisted. 'I can't leave him piecemeal, I have to get out and never go back.'

'*Don't do it, Kathryn. You never really know people until they do something that you don't expect.*'

'I'll make it quick,' Kathryn said. 'I promise. Call me as soon as you get out of work.'

Kathryn tossed the cell phone to one side, only for it to trill once again. She picked it up, and was surprised to hear Maietta's voice on the line.

'Is he okay?' Kathryn asked.

'He's fine,' Maietta confirmed. 'He's coming back into work. I think you ought to be there.'

Kathryn bit her lip as she glanced at her watch. 'Okay, make it fast though.'

'You in a hurry now, counsellor?'

'Got another client booked in for this afternoon,' Kathryn replied. 'But I can make room for Scott. I'll wait at the station.'

***

Dean Crawford

29

Kathryn drove back to the precinct and sat in Olsen's office staring down at Griffin's file, trying to force Stephen's image from her mind. Calling Ally had in some way cemented in Kathryn's mind that it was time to finish everything.

Stephen is history, she told herself. Focus on the future.

Griffin's last proper appointment with her had ended with him storming from the office after making what amounted to a physical threat. For a moment, Kathryn had finally seen the detective for what he was: a man capable, indeed trained to kill who was living on the edge of an abyss of guilt, whose spouse had left him and who saw for himself no future other than one consumed by regrets. Then, she had seen his hardened exterior crumble and his innermost grief exposed for all to see before he had been shielded by the Wheelers' embrace.

What difference, he and I? What grief did she harbour, festering and poisonous inside her?

Kathryn shook off her maudlin thoughts. While she had been sitting and waiting for the detective to show, she had thought long and hard about her own life. Yes, she had made progress. But no, there was no future for her, not here, not any more. Stephen was lost to her, of that she was certain, and no longer just because he was seeing another woman. No. Stephen was lost to her because there was something inside of him that she had not seen before, something rotten and awful that she realised she feared.

In contrast to Griffin, Stephen was not a real person but a faÃ§ade and she knew it now.

There was nothing more that she could do for Griffin. His healing process would be his own now. He, like Kathryn, had been a slave to a past he could not change. Now was the time to sever her own ties with her past, and make a future of her own choosing.

It was time for her to leave. She had already packed everything that she could and jammed it into a suitcase, which she had then crammed into the trunk of her car, which was parked outside the precinct. There was very little left for her to do now that she had made up her mind. Sometimes, it was better to abandon something that was not quite right, than to labour it until it was sick and festering.

Time to go.

Kathryn got up from her desk and grabbed her handbag.

'Counsellor?'

Kathryn blinked and looked up. Griffin was standing in the doorway to the office, one fist knuckled at the door. He must have knocked and she had not heard him.

'Come in,' she said. 'Sorry, I was miles away.'

He looked different. He was wearing a fresh suit and had shaved in the time since she had left him with the Wheelers – probably Maietta had run him home on the way. There were still dark rings beneath his eyes but there was a glint of light and life in them that had been absent before.

Griffin shut the door and sat down. There was a long silence which Kathryn was happy to allow to draw out. Griffin, his hands in his laps, stared at them for a few moments before he spoke.

'That was some stunt you pulled there. Lawyers would be on your case if they ever found out.'

'Seemed like the right thing to do,' Kathryn replied.

'That how they train all you shrinks? Sink or swim? I thought that you were all for the softly–softly approach?'

'Tried that. It wasn't working.'

'I know.'

'I figured you just needed to hear what we were saying from Amy's parents instead. They...'

'Kathryn,' Griffin said. Somehow his use of her given name stopped her in her tracks. 'I know.'

Kathryn felt a little of the tension slip from her own shoulders. She nodded, a smile melting her features as Griffin went on.

'And I wanted to apologise, okay? I was out of order, blowing my top at you.'

'It's okay, detective.'

'No, it's not,' Griffin said. 'I could excuse myself for screaming at a perp' I've arrested, or at a judge for releasing a convict on nothing but technicalities, or even myself for being an asshole, but you didn't deserve that and I'm truly sorry.' Griffin sucked in a deep breath before he continued. 'I was trying to figure it all out up there, at the farm.'

'And did you?'

'Maybe,' Griffin said, and then shook his head. 'Not really.'

'I don't think that some things can ever be figured out,' Kathryn said. 'They happen, and we just have to pick up the pieces again and try to move on.'

Griffin nodded. 'I've been acting like a dick for the last few days.'

'That's true.'

Griffin looked at her, caught the smile, and shrugged. 'I've heard what you've had to say, and it's stayed with me. It kind of comes back when things are quiet, y'know? Especially when I sit out at the barn in the dark and replay in my mind all that happened up there.'

A brief smile flickered across Kathryn's features, gone as soon as it had arrived.

'Are you going to keep going up there?'

'No,' Griffin said.

'Why?'

Griffin's gaze was as piercing as ever but his features were calm, his shoulders relaxed, his hands clasped gently in his lap.

'Because there's nobody there,' he said.

Kathryn watched the detective carefully. 'What about Angela? Have you spoken to her yet?'

Griffin shook his head. 'I called her, asked if we could meet tonight. Just figuring out how best to go about talking to her.'

'There is no best way, just talk to her,' Kathryn said, 'make it your priority. No conditions, no surprises, no arguments. Let her hear what you have to say. Make sure you take the night off to do it. I've got the sense that everything else you both need to happen will follow all on its own.'

Griffin nodded. 'Seems simple if you say it quickly enough.'

'It *is* simple,' Kathryn said. 'You're good people, both of you.'

'You've never met Angela.'

'I don't need to,' Kathryn said. 'She would never have married you if you weren't the right guy, a decent guy, the kind of guy that all women wish they could have, because your problems are real and they make you all the more noble for it.'

Griffin watched her for a long moment. 'You've got a real way of putting things straight,' he said finally. 'I should have met you when I was younger.'

'So should I.'

A long silence filled the room and Kathryn felt herself blush as she spoke again quickly.

'You both want this to work,' she said. 'You'll both make it work, provided you talk rather than try to hurl each other out of a window.'

Griffin nodded. 'Yeah.'

Kathryn stood and put out her hand. Griffin, keeping his pride anchor firmly in place, stood up and shook it with his free hand.

'I gotta go,' Kathryn said. 'Just keep doing what you're doing now and everything will be okay.'

'You leaving already?'

'My work here is done, detective,' Kathryn replied, 'and there are other clients in need of my help. My case load is building up as we speak.'

Griffin nodded.

'Good knowing you, counsellor.'

Griffin strode out of the office and walked away.

Kathryn glanced at her watch as soon as he was gone, cursed silently, and then hurried out of the station.

***

30

Kathryn worked quickly.

To her relief, the apartment was still empty when she arrived. She felt exhausted, both mentally and physically, as she drove back to her apartment, but now she had to focus on herself. On her future. Kathryn showered, got dressed, stuffed some toast and coffee down her throat while simultaneously cramming her belongings into two suitcases that usually resided in the space beneath the bed.

Kathryn hauled her suitcases out of the apartment to her battered old Lincoln and jammed them into the trunk. She had to jump up and sit on it in order to force it closed. Satisfied, she then returned to the apartment and packed what else she could fit into a small holdall that she then stuffed under the bed, ready for a fast getaway.

Kathryn dashed back inside and grabbed Stephen's tablet computer, accessing it and logging in to his personal accounts. She worked feverishly, hurriedly accessing various accounts and doing what needed to be done. She would ensure that he was fully exposed, that he would lose not only Kathryn but also his wife and his life with her.

There was no more room for manoeuvre; things were black and white now. Stephen had a wonderful, luxurious life with his wife and a painful, struggling existence with Kathryn. There must be a reason why he remained with Kathryn, so what was that reason?

As she grabbed the last of her things, a long flowing dress fell out of her handbag where she had crammed it. Kathryn looked at it and recognised the sarong she had stolen from Stephen's other house, tucked in alongside the tickets that she had asked Ally to purchase for her.

Kathryn had to know.

The full length mirror in Kathryn's bedroom was hard to stand in front of because the bed almost filled the room, but now, she looked at herself and the flowing blue and green dress she wore.

It looked fabulous. No doubt about it. The fabric was as thin as mist, no doubt a factor in how much it had cost. Kathryn had Googled the dress and tracked it down to a designer named LeMarke, some French guy who ran a boutique in Singapore of all places. Painfully fashionable and hand crafted by local experts according to the website open on her laptop on the bed.

The one thing that Kathryn realised she probably had over Stephen's wife was her figure. With youth still somewhat on her side, and knowing what a gym was for and what food not to eat, Kathryn was still *slim and trim* as Ally referred to her. The dress hugged her waist and flowed over her hips as though it had been poured onto her.

Kathryn twisted and turned in front of the mirror, running her hands down the fabric as though she were caressing a wild animal, imagined what it would be like to walk down main street on a summer's day and see other men, and women, watching her. *She looks fabulous. I bet that cost a fortune. I wonder if she's single? I wonder if she's a movie star?*

The front door clicked loudly and Kathryn almost toppled backwards onto the bed in shock. She scrambled to one side and shut the lid on her laptop as the front door closed again and she heard Stephen make his way toward the bedroom.

Shit. She hadn't planned for him to see her wearing the dress and she realised that it was a fatal step too far. Kathryn yanked the dress over her head and hurled it across the bedroom to land out of sight on the far side of the room just as Stephen strode in.

He stopped and stared at her. Kathryn, wearing nothing but her underwear, sucked in a breath and put her hands on her hips as she smiled and peered at him with a gleam in her eye.

'That was good timing,' she said. 'Do you have a sixth sense for when I'm in a state of undress?'

Her voice tinkled innocently as Stephen stared at her. In a flash she noted his drawn looks, tired eyes and slumped shoulders. He looked as though he had not slept in days and his normally immaculate hair was ruffled and unkempt.

'I've got some bad news,' he said.

'What is it?'

'I might be laid off.'

'Oh,' Kathryn feigned surprise and cultivated an expression of concern. 'Oh no, that's terrible. When did you learn of this?'

Stephen sighed and sat on the edge of the bed. Kathryn mastered her fear and perched next to him, slipped one arm across his shoulders as he replied.

'Last night. They called us all in and told us that the company's profits were down by twelve per cent on last year. They can't afford all of us. I'll either get selected to continue or I'll be laid off.'

That he could lie, so smoothly, Kathryn presumed was because he was partly telling the truth. The phone call she had overheard the previous night certainly heralded bad news, but it wasn't a lay off. It had sounded more like Stephen had committed some kind of illegal act or perhaps been under–performing.

She glanced at the bedroom cupboard. The door was slightly open, but it was dark enough inside that he would not be able to tell that she had emptied it of her clothes.

'When will you know?' she asked him as she peered behind her at the crumpled dress on the floor.

'A few days, I guess,' Stephen said.

'Well, maybe I can cheer you up,' she said. 'Guess what I've got.'

'A winning lottery ticket?' he asked. 'The ability to foresee the future?'

Kathryn smiled as she slipped her arms over his shoulders and kissed him. 'Better than that.'

'Really?'

'No,' she shrugged, 'but I think that you'll like it. Your prize awaits.'

Stephen looked down and she saw him spot the small envelope tucked inside her bra. Stephen grinned faintly as he reached inside, brushing his hands across the soft skin of her breasts as he fumbled for the easily reachable envelope.

'There appear to be some obstructions,' he said.

'Later,' Kathryn replied. 'I want you to see this first.'

Stephen feigned disappointment as he retrieved the envelope and opened it. Two tickets fell out.

'What are these?'

Kathryn did not respond as Stephen held them up and read the labels on them. 'Hunter's Lake Lodge Vacation Station?'

'Tickets for two, this weekend,' Kathryn said. 'Out in the country, about twenty miles from here. Not too far to drive but far enough out of town to get some peace and quiet, time to ourselves, you know?'

Stephen managed to smile but he shook his head. 'Honey, I don't know if I'll be here. If I get a short–notice call I might have to fly half way across the country and with all that's happening I can't afford to turn down any work.'

'When did you last get to take some time off?' Kathryn asked, keeping her voice reasonable as she reached for his cell phone. 'Let me speak to them, I'm sure they won't mind me…'

'No, it's okay,' Stephen said. 'It's very kind of you and a lovely gesture, really. I'll call tomorrow and see if I can book the weekend off.'

'There,' Kathryn said smoothly as she fought for something, anything to distract Stephen, 'that wasn't so hard, was it? Although, correct me if I'm wrong, but I can feel something else that is very hard.'

Stephen's hands slipped around her waist and pulled her down onto him. 'Oh dear, what ever will we do about that then?'

Kathryn let him start loosening her bra as she gently kissed his neck and whispered into his ear as she now sought for something else to deter him.

'Something vigorous and worthwhile, so that I can use a pregnancy testing kit.' She felt Stephen stiffen beneath her in all the wrong ways. To his credit, or perhaps against it, he continued to loosen her dress.

'You've already bought one?' he asked as he fumbled. 'How long have you not been on the pill?'

'A while now,' she revealed. 'These things take time after all. And I bought a testing kit two weeks ago,' she added. 'Should get a result in soon.'

Stephen looked up at her, his hands suddenly no longer trying to release her bra. 'You're pregnant?'

Kathryn smiled down at him. 'I'm not sure, hence the tests. But *something's* going on.' Stephen almost blanched as he held her. She could see behind his expression the titanic will of effort it was requiring for him not to reveal any sign of panic.

'Something?' he echoed.

Kathryn, still smiling, tilted her head this way and that.

'Well, we did it last month, didn't we,' she said. 'Remember?'

Stephen's brow furrowed. 'Last month was a long time ago, and...'

'You were a bit drunk,' she said. 'You were watching that show, that one I don't bother with about the survival people. I asked you what we would do to survive if we were stranded on a desert island together.'

She saw the recollection appear on Stephen's face, although it was not joined by any signs of delight that she could see.

'I said that I could light a fire, and boil water to make it safe.'

'Yes,' Kathryn agreed. 'And I said we could have babies and create an army of little helpers to assist us. And then I...'

'Suggested we start right away,' Stephen completed her sentence as he leaned forward and nuzzled her breasts.

Kathryn felt her bra fall from her shoulders, and in silence she squeezed her eyes tight shut and hoped that it would be over soon.

The fact that she had actually never stopped taking the contraceptive pill was not one she would be sharing with him. Nor that his willingness to have sex with her, despite clearly being afraid of her becoming pregnant, said far more about his nature than anything she could write down in her day job. For the first time in their relationship, Kathryn realised that she was seeing exactly the kind of man he really was.

Maybe it was his exhaustion or perhaps stress, but their lovemaking was over within minutes. Kathryn positioned herself on her side of the bed and struggled to make sure than Stephen could not see the dress on the floor nearby.

'I don't like to sponge off of you all the time, it's not fair,' he said as he looked at the Hunter's Lodge tickets again.

Anger churned hot in Kathryn's belly and she fought to keep control of her features. 'That's okay,' she whispered. 'I'm sure we'll find the money to pay this month's rent from somewhere. I just wish we had some stashed away. You don't have any savings or anything, do you?'

Stephen sighed and shook his head. 'I'm sorry, no. I'm totally cleaned out.'

Kathryn, one hand resting on Stephen's shoulder with her long nails brushing gently against the skin of his neck, sought one last opportunity.

'Maybe I'd better cancel Hunter's Lodge then,' she said.

Stephen nodded. 'I'm sorry, honey.'

'Me too.'

Kathryn stood up. 'I need to get dressed,' she said softly.

Stephen got up off the bed, and then he turned to her wardrobe and before she could say anything he reached out for the door handle. 'Let me choose.'

Stephen opened the wardrobe to reveal the empty hangars and shelves. He stared at them for a moment and then looked at Kathryn. 'Where are all your clothes?'

Kathryn slapped an awkward smile onto her face. 'We were going away. I packed my clothes into my suitcase already.'

Stephen stared at her for a moment. He was smiling as though bemused, but a sinister little glow had appeared in his eyes. 'What, like *all* of them?'

Kathryn sucked in a deep breath. Now it was her turn to come clean, before things got out of hand.

'Stephen, I'm going away for a few days.'

Stephen gaped at her. 'Going away? Why?'

Kathryn stood up, took a deep breath and tried to maintain a sense of dignity as she stood in her knickers and bra before him.

'I know Stephen. I know about everything.'

'Know about *what*?'

'How long do you want this conversation to last?' she challenged. 'You want it to end here and now, or do you want to tell me what you've been up to?'

Stephen stared at her for what felt like hours before he replied. 'I'm not sure what you're referring to.'

Kathryn smiled tightly. Denial was a powerful weapon, in the right hands. It was likely, she realised, that Stephen actually believed in what he was saying, to the degree that he could fool a lie–detector, so entrenched was the fantasy he had constructed around their lives. In this moment in space and time Stephen's other life, even his *wife*, were probably to him figments of his imagination interchanged at will depending on who he was with at the time.

'Your wife,' Kathryn said finally. 'Your other home. Your other job. The money that you earn. I know everything.'

***

31

Time seemed to stand still.

Stephen and Kathryn stared at each other like gunslingers sizing each other up at dawn, fingers hovering over their mental triggers. Stephen appeared to be lost for words, and Kathryn guessed that he was struggling to concoct a suitable explanation for years' of lies and manipulation.

It didn't take him long to find his escape route.

'The restaurant,' he said. 'The big scene you created. The talk of babies and holidays and a house in the city. It was all bullshit, wasn't it?'

Kathryn, standing at the end of the bed barely six feet away from him, realised belatedly that Stephen was blocking her escape route from the room.

'It was to coax you out,' Kathryn said. 'I knew about your wife and I wanted you to admit to me that you were lying, to both of us. I wanted you to tell me who you wanted the most, to explain to me why you would do all of this.' Kathryn looked him up and down and decided to veil her fear with a facade of disgust. 'You didn't have the guts.'

Stephen glared at her in silence.

'What?' Kathryn asked. 'The great Stephen Hollister has no answer? The biggest liar in town, lost for words?'

Stephen took a pace forward. Kathryn couldn't help herself. She backed up, and in a flash her courageous front was shattered. Like a wild animal sensing fear, Stephen advanced toward her.

'You want to know why?' Stephen growled. 'I'll tell you why. Because I like to keep my feet on the ground, hold on to an anchor to remind of what my life used to be like when I lived in the gutter with white trash.'

Kathryn flinched as though physically struck. It wasn't just the words: it was the venom loaded inside them that shocked her, a cruelty and a fury that she had never seen before.

And then she remembered that she didn't really know Stephen at all.

Kathryn backed around the corner of the bed. 'You don't mean that,' she managed to say.

'You think you're important?' Stephen asked rhetorically. 'To me?' He shook his head. 'You're nothing to me. You're one of life's losers, Kathryn, struggling to make enough to eat and keep a roof over your head.'

Kathryn's rage reasserted itself. 'Then why the hell have you stayed with me for so long?!'

Stephen was about to answer when he turned his head as something caught his eye. Kathryn looked over her shoulder and realised that they could both now see the beautiful blue and green dress that lay crumpled on the floor.

Stephen stopped dead in his tracks and she saw his skin pale as he took in the blues and greens of the fabric.

'Where did you get that?' he asked.

Kathryn felt her heart skip a beat as her stomach plunged into freefall inside her. 'I got it in the market, in town.'

Stephen glared at her. 'Which part of the market?'

Kathryn, frozen to the spot, had to force her jaw to work as she replied. 'I don't remember. I..,'

She glanced at her cell phone where it lay on the bed, half concealed beneath the crumpled bed sheets. All she had to do was grab it and dial *911* and...

Stephen spotted the cell and grabbed it as he crossed the bedroom to her in a single stride. His advance was so utterly without compromise that Kathryn threw her arms up in front of her. Stephen grabbed her wrists and yanked them down as he shouted into her face.

'Where did you fucking get it?!'

He let go of her wrists and slammed one hand around her throat as he shoved her hard against the wall. Kathryn felt her throat crush as Stephen lifted her up onto her tip–toes, his face twisted with rage and his nose barely an inch from hers.

Kathryn struggled to reply, her eyes streaming and her breath choking in her throat.

'I... don't... remember.'

Stephen flashed her a shit–eating grin. 'You sure got lucky. It's from a Malaysian design house, very rare. They cost hundreds to buy, if you can find one. I'd be amazed if there's another like it in the entire country.'

Kathryn gagged as Stephen tightened his grip, and then suddenly he swung his other fist and thumped her deep in her belly. Kathryn's face felt as though it was going to explode as her legs tucked up around the throbbing pain that surged through her stomach.

Stephen released her and she slumped to the floor, coughing and wheezing and curling up into a foetal position on the carpet as Stephen stepped over her and reached down to pick up the dress. He lifted it to his face, inhaled deeply upon it as though savouring whatever odour it was he sought, and then his cold gaze flicked back up to meet Kathryn's.

Stephen looked Kathryn up and down again, and she realised something had changed in him. Now there was a hunger in its place, something primal that had burst into flame before she had had chance to realise it.

Stephen lunged toward her and one strong arm pinned her to him as the other reached down and gripped her behind like a vice and lifted her off the ground. Kathryn squealed as she felt herself toppled backward onto the bed and Stephen's forearm crushing against her throat.

'You look great like this,' he hissed at her.

Kathryn shuddered, Stephen's voice laden with hate.

Ally's words rang through her mind. *Don't push him too far.*

'Where are you going?' he demanded.

Kathryn saw him dangle the front door key in his hand as he pinned her to the bed.

'Let me go,' Kathryn gasped, he throat painfully constricted. 'It's over, Stephen.'

'Yes it is,' Stephen grinned back, a maniacal light twinkling in his eyes. 'It's over.'

Kathryn's hand found Stephen's tablet computer without even thinking about it. She swung the tablet with all of her might and the coalesced fury of months of being lied to. The tablet computer smacked across Stephen's nose with a dull crack and Stephen hurtled sideways off the bed and landed hard on his ass, blood spilling from his nose as he tumbled down.

Kathryn scrambled out of the bedroom and lunged for the front door, grabbed her key from the hall as she ran and shoved it into the door. She yanked it open and literally jumped down the three steps outside and into the parking lot. She dashed to her car on her bare feet, the asphalt cold and wet beneath her and the cold wind whipping up goose–bumps on her bare skin, and got in, locking all of the doors and praying that the tired old engine would start first time.

The battery whined and the engine coughed and spluttered as it tried to turn over.

'Get back here you bitch!'

Stephen's hand slammed into the window beside her head with a loud crack and she screamed as she tried the engine again. The Lincoln's tired engine coughed and then growled into life. Kathryn, still wearing only her underwear, threw the car into drive and pulled out of the lot for the last time.

***

32

Stephen staggered back into the apartment, wiping blood from his lips and nose with the back of his hand as his heart burned with vengeance. He strode into the bathroom and splashed warm water onto his face, cleaned off the blood. There was no bruising yet, but he knew that he could not stay in the apartment any longer.

Stephen needed to leave, fast.

Stephen rued the day he had first set eyes on Kathryn. Slim, elegant, a little anxious perhaps. She was waiting tables at a diner in town, scurrying about through the busy lunchtime crowds, eager to please, always smiling and clearly popular with the locals. It had made a change from the surly teenage girls who tossed meals in front of clients like they hadn't paid for them, or who idled by the kitchen doors texting their boyfriends as meals went cold on the serving hatch.

He had never been one for extravagant displays of affection, so he had simply quietly turned up at the same diner whenever he could until Kathryn got to know him a little. Stephen ensured that he was always polite, considerate, quick with a funny punch–line, everything that other male clients hurrying between meetings wouldn't think to be. As planned, Stephen started to stand out from the crowd. He got preferential service; the coffee was made more carefully, meals appeared more quickly. Kathryn was bumping him up the list ahead of the fly–by customers.

He had become the nice guy. The cool guy. The one who was easy to talk to, always friendly, never a threat.

They got to chatting from time to time. Stephen eventually worked his way into her confidence enough that when he suggested they seemed to get along really well and maybe it would be good to meet somewhere other than the diner for a drink or two, Kathryn had instantly accepted the invitation. Happily, excitedly, a little anxiously. Although Stephen had very carefully phrased the invite as just a friendly drink, not a date, he had also carefully avoided saying that it *wasn't* a date. Cool enough not to be a threat, interested enough to excite and intrigue.

First dates, in Stephen's experience, always went well. Most all men panicked over them, but then they didn't think about the fact that their date was also likely nervous. Everybody concerned wanted to be there, nobody wanted it to be a lousy night, but so many tripped themselves up by worrying too much and then acting like a first–grader.

Stephen made sure he presented a confident front, always something interesting to say, always perfect company. It put women at ease, he felt: if the man they were with was comfortable and not radiating panic, so they would begin to feel comfortable too. He didn't rush, didn't try to kiss her, didn't get her drunk, walked her to within a stone's throw of her home without ever asking to come in or force her to reveal her precise address. Asked her if he could see her again? Bingo.

Stephen had done it so many times now that it took a nearby death or an earthquake to throw him off balance. Good things come to those who wait, and Stephen was a very patient man who understood that it was not always a woman who held the reins of a relationship and that they could be mentally guided and controlled just as a man could be cajoled by a woman's physical charms.

By the time they decided to move in together a year had passed and Kathryn was without a doubt "his".

Now, two years later, he had realised belatedly that the happy, elegant, slightly anxious woman he had met in that diner all those years ago was not quite the person he had thought she was.

Stephen had been played.

Stephen moved into the bedroom and stood in the doorway. He scanned the room in silence, thinking about Kathryn and about where and how she would have gone about her despicable campaign against him.

Her laptop was on the bed near his tablet computer. Password protected, although he had seen her type it in enough times in the past. Stephen typed in her password, unable to keep the rueful smirk from his face.

KathrynandStephenforever

The computer hummed and Kathryn's desktop appeared. The background picture had for months been of them at a Christmas party, smiling for the camera. It had been one of the rare times when he had met her friends, including the excruciating Ally, a wobbling obese mess of self–denial who chortled and chuckled her way through life while transparently hating herself. Her rotund, pallid face was in the background of Ally's desktop image as it was in so many of her photographs, as though she were fucking haunting Kathryn.

Stephen scanned some of the desktop files for a moment, but he guessed that Kathryn would have hidden anything of interest deeper in her personal files. On an impulse, he typed his own name into the main search function. Moments later a series of folders appeared. One caught his attention.

Stephen: a meditation on life processes and motivational misconduct.

Stephen opened the file and found himself looking at a single document created within the last few weeks, which he opened and began to read with increasing fury.

Stephen Hollister is, it would appear, a classic example of sociopathic disorder. He is narcissistic, driven by a sense of his own importance over others, and compelled to deceive in order to maintain the illusion of superiority. Like many men, he has an inflated opinion of his own capabilities which are in truth woefully inadequate.

It has been, in some respects, extremely informative to watch Stephen squirm as I have applied pressure to his life, doing so in ways sufficiently subtle that he could not suspect my own true motivations. Stephen is used to orchestrating situations deliberately so that he has the upper hand, and I now believe he does so as a matter of daily routine. He has however proven himself unable to rise to the challenge of facing unexpected social situations, where he is deliberately caught off–balance. Whereas most decent men would laugh along, there is a glow of anger in his expression that I find most disturbing. Stephen hates being outwitted, outsmarted or in any way kept in the dark, especially by me. His reactions confirm my initial suspicions that he is, in some ways, a spoilt child who never grew up.

Stephen is, like me, an orphan. We should, all other factors being equal, possess a similar outlook on life. But we do not. Where I see friends and opportunities, Stephen sees threats and dangers. Whereas I am grateful for my life, Stephen is resentful. The bond we shared when we first met, in those first few wonderful months together that I have for so long cherished in my heart, I now believe to have been entirely fictional. An act. A charade. A deliberate, albeit long–term, version of the teenager's attempt to "get laid". Stephen was patient, kind, funny, gentlemanly and honest: yet it required him to be different in order to be so.

Now, I know his true colours. I know of his affair, of his lies and deceit, and I know that my life with him is over. The sooner I rid myself of his stain, the better my life will become.

P.S. Hi Stephen, I know that you frequently look at my laptop. My assessment above is confirmed by your presence reading this: you're not as clever as you think you are, and you never will be. We're done. Ciao.

Stephen slammed the laptop lid down, grinding his teeth as he stood up and looked around the bedroom. He stormed across to Kathryn's wardrobe and yanked it open again. Empty. He opened her bedside cabinet, her drawers and then hurried into the living room and opened the cupboards where she kept all of her books and DVDs.

Empty. She hadn't been packing for their weekend together. She had packed to leave entirely, before Stephen had returned to the apartment.

'You bitch,' he uttered to himself.

Stephen thought for a moment and as he did so his eyes settled on his own tablet computer, lying on the couch beside his briefcase. A sudden panic fluttered through his belly and he hurried over to it. He lifted the lid and to his dismay he saw that the screen was already alight and that the background image had been changed to a black screen with a single sentence written across it.

You see? You're not as clever as you think you are.

Stephen scrambled his fingers across the keys, bringing up his accounts and personal files. All had been opened the previous night, when he had been at home, after receiving the call from the flight director at... Stephen stared into space for a moment and then looked at the dress on the bedroom floor.

'Oh God, no,' he gasped. Kathryn had been there.

His bank account files. Stephen searched through them and his blood felt as though it were draining from his face as he accessed account after account and saw the same thing in each of them.

Empty.

'Bitch!'

Stephen hurled the tablet down, ran his hands through his hair as he screamed and kicked the walls and the furniture. He was halfway through what was becoming an epic rant when a phone trilled in the bedroom. Stephen stormed back into the room but then hesitated as he saw Kathryn's cell amid the crumpled bed sheets, the screen glowing with a name. *Ally.* The answerphone activated, and a voice tinkled down the line.

'Hi Kathryn it's Ally, I just got out of work. Where are you? Are you home yet? I can meet you at the usual place if you like?'

Stephen stood in silence as he listened.

'I'll wait for you in the town square and we can go from there. You know the place, opposite the diner where you met Mister Right, ha ha?! Don't be late honey, this will all be over soon.'

Stephen watched the phone until it fell silent and the screen went dark. Then he reached out and grabbed it, tucked it in his pocket and headed for the front door.

***

33

'Okay, have we got anything new on Sheila?'

Maietta glanced across at Griffin. He looked tired, but there was an air of calm about him that she had not seen for months. Despite the rings around his eyes his gaze seemed clearer, the tension and anger he had radiated for months absent now, a metamorphosis of grief into a cold determination.

She figured that he had changed all right, but then again she figured that he shouldn't be at work at all, especially not this late on a Friday afternoon. He had a wife to go to, to talk to. He should be at home. But then, of course, things had changed. The 48 hour deadline on Sheila McKenzie's life was well and truly over and there still had not been a single call.

Maietta had waited for him to emerge from the farmstead that morning. Griffin had not blown into a rage at the Wheeler's presence and somehow even Maietta had felt that witnessing Griffin's pain would be a step too far for her, that she would be intruding on a moment that only he and the parents of Amy Wheeler had any right to share.

She had then driven him home, and he had insisted on returning to work to see the shrink, Stone, and getting back onto the case somewhat more composed than he had been prior.

'Nothing,' a detective admitted from across the office. 'She's in the wind, no calls, no letters, nothing.'

'Where's the husband?' Griffin asked.

'Not at home, not answering his cell,' the detective replied. 'I'll keep trying him.'

'We've got this,' Maietta said to Griffin. 'Why don't you get your ass out of here?'

Griffin nodded. 'I will, just as soon as we figure out what the hell it is we've been missing. The deadline's gone and we've heard nothing.'

Maietta shrugged and gestured to the wipe board, where a picture of Sheila McKenzie and her husband were pinned. 'So far, nothing,' she said. 'No ransom demand, no calls, no nothing. It's like she's flown off the damned planet and nobody cares.'

Griffin nodded. 'Either her abductors have balls of steel…'

'Or they're not ever coming back for the money,' Maietta agreed.

'What about Dale McKenzie? You talk to him recently'

'He's sweating, but right now I just don't know why,' Maietta said. 'You know he got suspended from flying duties at Ventura? Nearly caused a mid–air collision. Is the pressure because he's abducted his own wife or is he worried about her?'

'Could be both?' Griffin hazarded. 'Maybe he is involved but somehow it's all gone wrong. We should have damned well put a watch on him when we had the chance, ruled him out or let him implicate himself. Now there's nothing to stop an accomplice from high–tailing it out of here with his wife and her fortune too.'

'Maybe it isn't just about the money.'

Griffin turned as Maietta handed him a sheet of paper. 'What's this?'

'You asked me to dig into Dale McKenzie's past a little, see what I could find out. I spent a while on it while you were…'

Maietta broke off. Griffin waved her embarrassment away. 'Don't sweat it.'

Griffin looked at the details on the paper. Dale McKenzie was thirty–eight years old. No Priors. An airline pilot for a decade.

'No parents or siblings,' Griffin said as he scanned the page. 'Worked for several different airlines over his career, mostly as a result of shutdowns?'

'Regional airlines,' Maietta explained. 'I made some calls. They tend to rise and fall with economic times, so I'm told, or are bought out by larger players. Pilots often move from one to another, sometimes losing their ranks as they do so.'

'First officers become captains,' Griffin agreed, 'then they move onto bigger, better paid jobs in larger aircraft and become first officers again on that type before becoming captains again. Learning on the job, so to speak.'

'McKenzie hasn't moved up in his career,' Maietta noted. 'He's just moved between regionals.'

'He's stayed with particular aircraft types,' Griffin said. 'Supposedly some guys don't want to do the trans–Atlantic stuff so they stick with regional and short–haul. It lets them go home at night.'

Griffin frowned as he pinned the page to the wipe board. 'So our guy Dale is a home–boy, likes to be with his wife. It doesn't jive with my instinct that he's the perp. I still like him for abducting his wife, or at least knowing about it.'

'That's what I meant when I said about this maybe not being just about the money,' Maietta said. 'The file we have on him says that he has no siblings, right? And you pulled those cold cases thinking there might be a connection? But I went a bit deeper and found out that Dale was not put up for fostering: he was abandoned as a child on the steps of an orphanage.'

'Ain't life cruel,' Griffin said. 'His folks not like him?'

'More likely,' Maietta said, 'that his folks could not afford them.'

'*Them*?' Griffin echoed.

'Dale McKenzie and his brother, Stephen McKenzie.'

Griffin almost laughed out loud. 'You're not telling me that there are two of them running about, surely? Like twins?'

'No,' Maietta said. 'Stephen McKenzie died of pneumonia when he was six years old. Dale was the oldest of the two by a few minutes.'

'Like attracts like,' Griffin said thoughtfully. 'His wife's an orphan too, right?'

'Yeah,' Maietta said. 'Maybe they thought they could be ruthless together. What if Sheila McKenzie really is in on this too? You remember what her assistant said, that the art gallery business was suffering because her competitors were acting against her. Maybe she was in deeper than we thought? Maybe she and Dale decided to play the system to their own ends a little, tease a ransom out of his airline or fake her death in return for the life insurances?'

'Or maybe we've been looking at Dale McKenzie the wrong way,' Griffin said as he apparently realised something important.

'You really think that he and Sheila orchestrated the whole thing?'

'No,' Griffin said as he looked down at the sheet of paper. 'But those four cold–case victims and Sheila McKenzie all have something real important in common.'

'Yeah, you said they're all orphans.'

'Not just that,' Griffin said. 'Come on.'

*

'I'm not saying it's a deal breaker, just hear me out.'

Griffin stood with Jane in front of Captain Olsen, who sat with his arms folded as he stared up at the detective.

'You shouldn't even be here,' Olsen snapped and looked at Maietta.

'We were just talking,' Maietta replied. 'He's got something.'

'Make it fast,' Olsen snapped at Griffin. 'It's Friday night and my wife's got a pie in the oven, a beer in the fridge and I'm on a promise. Unless you can beat that, I'm done here today.'

'We've got a lead on Dale McKenzie.'

'We've been here before, Scott,' the captain rumbled. 'Dale McKenzie's not on the cards for the abduction. He has a cast–iron alibi that he was airborne and hundreds of miles away when his wife disappeared.'

'I'm not talking about the abduction,' Griffin said. 'I'm talking about the suspicious deaths of four women over ten years ago, the cold–case you put me on after.., after I was pulled off active duty. They all shared the same characteristic death, cardiac arrest as a result of drowning, right? Two in the bathtub, two in the pool. Coroner's report in all cases cited a mixture of either drugs or alcohol with extreme exhaustion as the cause of death.'

'It happens,' Olsen said, losing interest already as he glanced at the dense stack of paperwork on his crowded desk. 'Sing me a new song or I'll get the next act up.'

Griffin tossed a wad of papers onto the captain's desk.

'What's this?' Olsen asked.

'Flight plans from the days of death of each of the victims. Two of the airlines are now defunct, but their flight plan records are maintained by the Federal Aviation Authority. Those plans state the captain and the first officers of each flight. Look at the names.'

Olsen scanned down the list of pilot's names. 'McKenzie's on all of them.'

'Now look at the destination cities for the flights,' Griffin added.

Olsen looked down, scanned the destinations, and then leaned back in his chair.

'McKenzie was in all of the cities on each murder date.'

'He had time to kill them,' Maietta said, speaking for Griffin. 'He was on overnight stops in all cases. We managed to figure out which hotels he was using, as they were booked by the airlines in advance of the flights. He's registered as staying there, but we could find no evidence that he actually *slept* in the hotels in question.'

Olsen scanned the papers for a moment longer before speaking. 'It's not enough to bring him in. There's no motive, no direct connection to the victims.'

'He was in the vicinity of *all* of the murders,' Griffin pushed. 'All of the victims were believed to have casual boyfriends, but nobody could identify who the boyfriends actually were. All of the victims had their bank accounts cleaned out either immediately before or immediately after they died, meaning that the person who did so had access not just to the victims' bank details but the passcode to their accounts. By the time the bodies were found, all of the cash had been withdrawn and the perpetrator had vanished into the wind.'

'Sure,' Olsen admitted, 'I'll buy that much, but it could be a coincidence. He's an airline pilot after all, they move around a lot.'

'Sure,' Maietta said, 'but I took a long hard look at McKenzie's career. Turns out that before he was an airline pilot he barely made it through high school let alone flight school, flunked college within a year and at the age of twenty he was flipping burgers and mopping floors at a small–town greaser. The guy was a total loser.'

Olsen shrugged. 'So? Maybe he got tired of life taking him up the ass and turned things around, got himself sorted out, made a future for himself?'

'He did,' Griffin said, and tapped the papers on Olsen's desk. 'He became an airline pilot. He had to train for eighteen months to do so, thousands of hours of study, hundreds of hours of flying. It costs tens of thousands of dollars to pay for that training, so how does a burger flipper pay for it all? He probably could barely make his rent and there's no evidence of loans from any banks.'

Olsen's moustache shifted position and settled down again. 'You want to sort through his financials?'

'It's worth a deeper look,' Maietta said. 'From what I can figure out from what local airlines have told me, they used to pay for their pilots' training but because they fronted the money they only took on stellar applicants like college graduates and the like, or former military pilots looking for civilian careers. Dale McKenzie would have been shown the door before he'd reached reception.'

'So how did he get into the cockpit?'

'Self–financing,' Griffin replied. 'If somebody puts up the money for their own training, either at a flight school or an airline, then all they have to do is pass the entrance exams showing that they have the intelligence and aptitude to become a pilot. McKenzie may have flunked college but he's clearly no idiot. If he showed up with the money and passed the exams, then he could have got in.'

Olsen frowned as he folded his arms again and leaned back in his seat.

'So he got himself some serious money from somewhere.'

'And all we need to do is track it down,' Maietta said. 'He must have had accounts that he would have used to pay the airline for his training. If he did kill those girls and take their money, then we could trace it all the way back to the accounts of origin. If McKenzie can't explain where he got it from…'

'… then it's enough to maybe charge him,' Olsen agreed. 'You think that he's pulling a similar stunt here with Sheila McKenzie?'

'She's worth a lot more than any of the other victims,' Griffin said, 'although he didn't previously marry and kept himself very much out of sight.'

'And Sheila McKenzie's an orphan,' Maietta pointed out. 'It fits the kind of target he'd go for, if he's our man.'

'Maybe he got what he wanted before, financially,' Griffin said, 'but this time he's got a new problem. We looked into Sheila McKenzie's financials at the gallery, and she's on the verge of bankruptcy. If her bubble bursts then Dale McKenzie loses everything too because he can't support their home on his captain's salary. What if he's decided to pull the plug on her before she loses everything and doesn't think we'll make the connection with the other homicides?'

'Suicides,' Olsen corrected, 'for now. Okay, I'll talk to the District Attorney's office and get the warrant. Where's McKenzie right now?'

'He's got himself grounded apparently,' Maietta said. 'We're looking for him.'

'We'll watch him,' Olsen said, 'but no arrests. Get some uniforms to locate him. If we've got the right man, let's make sure we can pin him for all the murders and not just his wife's abduction. And you, Griffin?'

'Captain?'

'I want your ass out of this office before mine, is that understood?'

'I can finish this,' Griffin replied, 'and we can…'

'Let the night shift handle the watch details and pick up the warrants,' Olsen interrupted him.' 'You have a wife waiting for you, or am I mistaken?'

Griffin's shoulders relaxed and he nodded.

'Good,' Olsen said as he slid his jacket on. 'Now fuck off home for a nice weekend or whatever it is you decide to do, and don't come back until your roster says you have to.'

STONE COLD

***

34

Ally stood in the rain beneath the shelter of an acacia and waited as the sky darkened and the streetlights began to glow against the onrushing gloom.

Her umbrella was useless in this sort of weather, and her raincoat did nothing to keep out the deepening chill that was sweeping in from the north. The clouds above tumbled and spat their freezing rain down on the town as though insulting it before leaving for more interesting climes.

She tried Kathryn's cell phone one more time, but once again caught the answerphone message. She grimaced and shook her head. Kathryn worked for the police and Ally knew that she was heavily invested in her first client, but it wasn't like her not to answer her phone or at least get back within a reasonable time.

A small, somewhat superstitious part of her wondered whether the storm clouds were some kind of cosmic warning, the universe's karma pulled out of synch by her decision to meet Stephen. Everything had gotten out of hand, everything had gone too far and she was the only one still thinking straight enough to put it right.

From out of the gloom a large, expensive–looking glossy black car pulled into the sidewalk. Ally did not recognise the car, but one of the windows wound down electrically and to her surprise Stephen leaned over so that she could see him.

'Get in, before you go and drown!'

Ally, already half drenched by the gusting squalls, hesitated. This was not something that Kathryn would want, but then if she refused would it alert Stephen to what was coming? Another sodden gust swept across Ally and she hurried over to Stephen's car and opened the door, which clunked heavily as though to demonstrate its expensiveness. She clambered in, slumping into the passenger seat alongside Stephen and slamming her door shut.

'Nice car,' she said as she looked around her. Leather seats, walnut veneer dashboard, sumptuous fittings, air con. 'What happened to that crappy old thing you and Kathryn were driving around in?'

'It's my company car, not our personal one,' Stephen replied. 'How's you?'

'Fine,' Ally said. 'You?'

Stephen sat back in his seat as though preparing himself. The wind and rain drummed on the windshield as he spoke. 'Ally, I think that I've made a terrible mistake and I need your help.'

Ally chose her words with care. 'Okay, what's happened?'

'I think that Kathryn is going to leave me,' Stephen said, 'and I wouldn't blame her if she did. Ally, I've been seeing somebody else.'

Ally's shoulders sank. 'For how long?'

'A while now. It's not serious, hell it wasn't even intentional. It just kind of happened, office stuff, you know?'

'Sure,' Ally said, wishing briefly that she had more amorous office encounters than she did. 'Happens to everyone.' Ally savoured the warm air billowing into the car's interior from the air–con. She took a deep breath, closed her eyes, let the breath out and started talking. 'Kathryn came to me a few days ago. She told me that you were having an affair.'

Stephen stared at Ally for a long time before he replied. 'It's been complicated.'

'But why cheat on Kathryn, Stephen? Why? She loves you, you know that don't you?'

Stephen grinned tightly. 'I don't think that there's been much love between us for a while now, Ally. Listen, I need to know: has Kathryn been trying to patch things up between us or something? I know that she's been trying very hard but it's been difficult for me. Work has been horrendous, I've not been there for her and I fear that if I don't do something soon I'll lose her forever.'

Ally sighed again.

'Kathryn told me that she'd decided to do something about your infidelity,' she said. 'I didn't know what she meant at the time, but then she started doing things.'

'Things?' Stephen echoed. 'What things?'

'She took you to a restaurant that she knew you loved going to with your other woman,' Ally said. 'Forced you into asking Kathryn to marry, knowing that you would be uncomfortable with everything. Then she decided to try to make you think that she was pregnant, and that you should buy a bigger house, anything she could think of to see if you would crack and explain to her what was really going on.'

Stephen was watching her with an intense expression on his features, as though studying a complex maths problem.

'Go on,' he said.

'She wanted to find out just how much she means to you,' Ally said finally. 'She wants you back, Stephen. She knows about the affair but she wants you in her life and I've been spending all this time worrying that she might go too far and drive you away.'

Stephen seemed so stunned that he could not speak. He glanced out of the windshield through the sheets of water blurring the streets outside. The sky was low and dark, the streetlights glowing. People running with their umbrellas held up against the torrent as rain started hammering the roof of the car.

'She wore a dress,' Stephen whispered.

'What?'

Stephen turned back to face Ally. 'She wore a dress that belonged to my wife. Does Kathryn know where we live?'

'Your *wife*? You mean that you're *married* to the other woman?'

Stephen glared at Ally. 'Like I said, it's complicated.'

Ally blinked in surprise and nodded. 'You see, this is what I was afraid of. She's gone too far. That's all I have for you, thanks for listening. I'm going to go now and…'

The door locks clicked as one, sealing her in. Ally knew what had happened but she still tried the door handle anyway. It was locked. She turned back to Stephen and saw him release the locking button on his key fob.

'Stephen, this isn't helping,' she said to him. 'Kathryn's who you need to be talking to. I just came here to let you know what was happening and…'

Ally was silenced as Stephen, smiling, reached out and pressed a finger to Ally's lips. She stared at him as his hand slid gently around to cup her jaw and he leaned across. Moments later, his lips were pressed against hers as he kissed her.

Ally tried to pull back, but her body would not respond as Stephen's arms slid around her shoulders and she melted into his embrace.

Then a sharp pain pierced the back of her neck and she squealed. Stephen's embrace became fierce as she felt something cold flood into her neck, some kind of fluid. She gasped, struggling against Stephen, trying to scream, but he held her firmly as he pulled away from the kiss and yanked her head deep into his chest.

Ally writhed and struggled, but then she felt her arms and legs weaken as though she were utterly exhausted. Her heart fluttered in her chest and her breath shuddered in her lungs as she felt her bladder suddenly empty onto the expensive seat beneath her. Her face slumped against Stephen's chest until he pushed her back into the seat and dragged the seatbelt across her, plugging it into place.

Ally's head sank back against the headrest and lolled uselessly to one side as her tongue drooped from between her lips.

'Don't worry,' Stephen said as he pulled out into the road again. 'We'll just go for a little drive and then you can tell me all about your adventures with Kathryn, and exactly what she's done.'

Ally managed to rotate her numb eyeballs up toward the top of her head, where she saw Stephen driving as he looked down at her and smiled.

'And if you don't tell me every single detail, I swear I shall carve that fat carcass of yours into a thousand tiny pieces and feed you to the fish.'

Moments later, Ally's consciousness slipped silently away from her.

***

35

Ally awoke to a throbbing sensation filling her face, as though it was swollen to twice its normal size. She blinked through tears that sprung unbidden from her eyes and looked around as she saw Stephen stand up from where he must have knelt and slapped her awake.

She was lying on her back on wet grass and her entire body was quivering in the cold. She felt the raindrops drumming on her naked skin and realised that her clothes had all been removed. Horror filled her with a dread chill and she tried to move, but her limbs did not respond. Even her head felt too heavy to move.

The night sky above was inky black, the falling rain illuminated by bright white beams from a vehicle's headlamps somewhere out of her sight.

'I'll make this as brief as possible.'

She tried to speak, but her lips seemed numb and her words sounded weak and distorted.

'Stephen… What the hell's going on?'

Stephen stood over her, and in one hand he held a small piece of paper that he had retrieved from her purse, which he now held in the other hand. He shielded the paper from the rain as he read from it.

'A ticket purchase,' he announced, 'from Ventura Air by credit card number…' Stephen read the number out and looked down at Ally. 'Does that number sound familiar to you, Ally?'

Ally felt her lips trembling along with the rest of her body as she fought over the cold to reply.

'Kathryn asked me to buy them,' she said. 'She wouldn't say what for, but I figured that she was taking you somewhere, that it was all part of her plan to punish you and then make it all up.'

Stephen chuckled heartily and slipped the paper back into his pocket. Abby realised with a lance of terror that he was wearing blue surgical gloves and in his right hand he held a knife.

'Oh, she was taking me somewhere all right,' Stephen chortled at her. 'For a fucking ride, and you had ringside seats, didn't you Ally?'

'It wasn't like that!' Ally snapped. 'She wanted revenge, but she didn't want to end things! Jesus, Stephen I'm just the messenger okay? I haven't done anything to harm you, let me go!'

Stephen stared down at her.

'Tell me, was there anything else that Kathryn asked you to buy for her? Anything else at all?'

Ally struggled to remember what had been on Kathryn's list.

'There was some food, cleaning materials, I don't know, just stuff. She didn't give me the details.'

'Tell me everything on that list!' Stephen bellowed down at her.

'I can't remember!' Ally wailed through her numb lips. 'The address of a lock–up storage company downtown, maybe some…'

'A lock–up?' Stephen echoed.

'Yeah. I figure that's where she would keep all her stuff when she moved out.'

'Where is the lock–up?'

'I don't know.'

Stephen knelt down alongside her shivering body, looking her up and down with interest.

'I can see why it might have been fun for you,' he said. 'I mean, since you let yourself go you haven't exactly had much in the way of excitement in your life, have you?'

Ally dredged up a feeble morsel of anger and spat it out at Stephen.

'Is that all you've got, Stephen? Childish insults?'

Stephen smiled at her. 'No.'

The blade in his hand flashed down and sliced through the flesh of her thigh as though it were not even there. Pain seared Ally's leg and she squealed in agony as Stephen watched her like an insect caught between finger and thumb.

Ally sobbed as what little courage she had left deserted her.

'Please, don't, why are you doing this?'

Stephen shrugged thoughtfully and looked at the blade in his hand. 'It's been long overdue, to be honest. Tell me, did you laugh and joke about me with Kathryn while she was running this charade with you?'

Ally squeezed her eyes tight shut and shook her head vigorously. 'No.'

'Are you sure, Ally?' Stephen quizzed her. 'You see, I know you well enough to know what a sharp little wit you are. I can just see it now,

Kathryn sitting down with you after what she pulled in the restaurant, or after she broke into my home, and having a good old chuckle together at my expense.'

Ally, her voice broken with sobs and shivers, tried to reply.

'You... started... it. You... were... already... married.. .to...'

'Sheila,' Stephen cut her off, bored already. 'Yes, my wife. Such a shame, don't you think, both of them having to be silenced? If only they'd remained good and quiet and faithful and not...'

Stephen sliced Ally's thigh again to a squeal of pain.

'...gotten..'

Another slice, deeper now, to more agonised cries.

'...involved...'

Stephen sliced her other thigh for good measure, and Ally felt warm blood spilling down her thighs in the rain as Stephen shifted position and held the knife vertically above her belly, the blade pointing down at her and dripping blood.

'Tell me, where is Kathryn's lock–up?'

Ally, paralysed with fear and pain, could barely speak.

'L..l...l...let.. me.. go...'

Stephen smiled down at her. 'You tell me where Kathryn is and I'll let you go.'

Ally gaped as words fluttered in broken pieces from her lips.

'I... don't... know...'

Stephen slammed the blade hilt–deep into Ally's belly. Ally's cries of pain descended into gagging noises, her eyes wide and her mouth agape as Stephen twisted the blade inside her and a deep rush of blood spilled from the wound and flooded down her quivering flanks.

'It's the Triple A, off 2nd Avenue!' Ally screamed in horror as her life blood poured from within her and she broke down into trembling sobs.

'A shame,' Stephen said, 'that you didn't see sense sooner.'

'Please..., help me,' Ally gasped.

Stephen stood up, turned and stalked away from her into the night.

Ally, pinned on her back and with blood pulsing around the edge of the blade buried in her stomach, heard the car drive away into the night as an intense, deep chill enveloped her shivering body.

***

36

Sheila McKenzie lay pinned to the recliner and shivered in the darkness.

Her right wrist was rubbed raw from where she had spent hours working it back and forth beneath the tight rope bonds, pain seething through her skin, but the pain merely drove her onward as she thought of her cheating, lying husband and his selfish plan to deprive her of both her fortune and her life.

She wondered how long he had planned all of this. Months. Years? Just waiting for the right time to orchestrate her downfall. She could picture him vividly in her mind's eye; his grief before television cameras at his beloved wife's disappearance; his devastation at the discovery by police of her dead body discarded in some obscure commercial storage unit somewhere or buried far out on some lonely plain; his long and difficult period of recovery and suffering while collecting on her life insurance and taking an extended leave of compassion from his airline. Selling her beloved art gallery for whatever additional profit he could make. Maybe taking a holiday using Sheila's money with that younger bitch of his and fucking her while laughing at his ex–wife's demise.

Sheila gritted her teeth and pulled harder against her bonds. Pain seared her wrist as it slipped further, tearing her skin another tiny fraction as though she were peeling it off by choice. She squealed through her gag as her hand slid a little further out, probably lubricated by the blood that must by now have drenched the cords.

A sudden ripple of vibrations trembled through the recliner and with a start of horror Sheila realised that her abductor had returned. There was no way that they would miss the damage to her skin or the blood on the bonds.

Sheila sucked in a deep lungful of air and then yanked her wrist as hard as she could.

She gagged and stars and whorls of light flashed before her as white pain burned her upper wrist and hand, but with a horrible sucking sound like water draining from a plug her hand wrenched free from the cords.

Sheila reached up to her hair and pulled a clip free, an inch–long pin that she immediately concealed in her palm as she dropped her hand back down. She slid her fingers and thumb back over the restraints and hoped that it would be enough to conceal, however briefly, what she had done.

The shutters rumbled up and then hit their stops as the smell of fresh air and rain filled Sheila's nostrils. She felt rather than heard hurried footsteps rush into the storage unit and this time the shutter doors did not close behind them.

For a moment Sheila thought that rescue might finally have arrived, that she was finally to be liberated from this living hell. She sensed the person move close to her and she tensed her body ready to drive the hairpin deep into their eyes.

Suddenly the ear plugs were yanked from her ears and a voice, a woman's voice, whispered in her ear.

'It's okay, don't move, I'm here to rescue you.'

Sheila closed her hand a little tighter around the pin in her hand as she felt the blindfold that had denied her vision for so long being loosened around her head. Suddenly it was pulled free and Sheila squinted against even the dull light that flooded into her world.

The recliner was in the centre of a storage unit, no more than twenty by eight by six feet, all cold metal walls and a thin rubber carpet that both helped to insulate the unit a little and deadened all footfalls. An old chair leaned near one wall to her right, and to her left was a pile of old paper bags from a supermarket or convenience store.

Outside the unit it was raining, the torrential downfall glowing in the brilliant headlamps of a vehicle parked nearby. The harsh white beams scythed through the rain and into the storage unit, illuminating the face of a woman in her thirties, long brown hair and business suit, a concerned expression etched into her features.

'We have to leave, right now.'

Sheila stared at the woman in disbelief. 'Who the hell are you?'

'It doesn't matter,' the woman replied. 'Your husband is going to kill you in return for your life insurance. We need to go, now.'

Sheila was about to scream and plunge the pin into the woman's eyes when she caught a waft of a scent that she had recognised and a shadow passed in front of the car's headlamps to fill the storage unit. Both Sheila and the woman looked up to see a man standing silhouetted in the entrance to the storage unit, rain dripping from his hair and gleaming on a pistol he held close to his thigh. Sheila blinked in surprise as she recognised the man watching them.

'Dale?'

**

37

Griffin sat in his car and waited.

It was an odd thing about police work that you got so used to sitting around waiting for something to happen. In many ways, it had been the same in the military. *Hurry up and wait.* Griffin was bored and a little anxious, but he shut his mind down and waited in stoic silence.

She appeared out of the drizzle, the streetlights reflecting off the damp pavements like glittering galaxies as she hurried across to the car and opened the door. Griffin watched as she climbed in and shook out her umbrella.

'Thanks for coming,' Griffin said.

Angela looked at him as though to snap a retort, but then her expression changed as she took him in. She started to say something, hesitated, then tried again.

'Something happened,' she said clairvoyantly.

'Yeah,' he replied, 'it did.'

Angela watched him for a moment. 'You look, better.'

'You look amazing.'

Griffin wasn't just saying it. Angela's strawberry blonde hair was hanging in curls to her shoulders, and he could see that she was wearing a jet–black dress cut just above the knee on one side and cut low to her ankle on the other. Black shoes to match. Earrings and a slim gold necklace that he'd bought her when he left the military sparkled in the light. She looked perfect.

'You look amazed,' she smiled back. 'When was the last time I dolled up for you?'

'It doesn't matter,' Griffin said as he started the car. 'You're here now.'

Angela yanked the mirror down to check her look.

'Damn it,' she muttered. 'I had my hair done.'

'What made you change your mind?' Griffin asked. 'I wasn't sure you'd come out.'

Angela fluffed her hair as she replied. 'I'm your wife. You asked nicely. What the hell else was I supposed to do?'

He drove her to the restaurant that Kathryn had recommended, which was only a few minutes away, and they walked in together. A wide reception area greeted them, all glossy black with electric blue lighting. A glass panel on one wall was filled with photographs taken inside the restaurant. The waitress took their jackets and guided them to their table, opposite a vast mirror down which flowed torrents of water through rainbow hues. Menus appeared, along with glasses of sparkling complimentary champagne.

Griffin, his collar feeling tight and his jacket scratchy, took a sip of the champagne as Angela arranged her handbag, checked her look in a little folding mirror, checked her cell phone and then her look one more time. Such things used to annoy the hell out of Griffin, but suddenly they had become endearing again, tiny little habits that he'd forgotten he liked so much.

'You're staring,' Angela said.

Griffin blinked. 'You blame me?' He looked around at the restaurant. 'Great place.'

'It was a good choice,' Angela agreed. 'Somewhere nice but neutral so we can talk.'

Griffin felt himself tense a little, but she raised a hand to forestall him.

'No arguments,' she said. 'No rows, no accusations, no blame. Just talking.'

Griffin relaxed a little and picked up his champagne again. 'Okay, I can deal with that.'

'Good,' Angela said. 'So, you've been a world class asshole lately.'

Griffin coughed on his champagne and shot Angela a look, only to see her grinning behind her glass. Griffin's face split into a smile that hurt.

'That your idea of no accusations?'

'I didn't say we couldn't state facts,' she replied. 'For the record I'm willing to state that, on occasion, I may also have acted without due consideration for your feelings.'

'Is that a confession?'

'It's another fact. I think that the problem here, and the one that's never come up between us, is that we're both suffering in our own ways but haven't been able to *share* that suffering.'

'You've lost me,' Griffin said. 'I don't mean that in a bad way, okay? I'm just not following.'

Angela set her glass down. 'You ever hear about that study, something to do with ordinary people in extraordinary situations, how they relate to others?'

'Yeah, there have been loads of them, we used to hear about them in the army,' Griffin replied. 'Everybody thinks that they're carrying the can while everybody else is doing less than them and... Ah, I'm with you.'

'We've been so wrapped up in ourselves that we haven't been able to share the load,' Angela said. 'We're always focusing internally on our own struggles and not talking about them like we should, not clearing the air enough.'

Griffin nodded, shrugged his shoulders. 'I guess I'm guilty of that.'

'Me too,' Angela admitted. 'Things get to the point where neither of us thinks the other is listening any more, or is even capable of listening or understanding any more, and before you know it, *zip – ping* and we're breaking up.'

'I don't want that,' Griffin said.

'Nor do I,' Angela agreed. 'I've never wanted that. I want my husband, I want our life together.'

'You want me to leave the force?' Griffin asked. 'I can do it, if you need me to.'

'Like hell,' Angela said. 'I want you out there catching bad–guys because that's what you do. It's what you've always done.'

Griffin looked at his champagne for what felt like a long time. 'I kept going back,' he said.

He sensed rather than saw his wife tense, as though she instinctively knew that something was coming that she had not heard before.

'Going back where?'

Griffin felt some of the tight knot in his chest tremble and loosen as he spoke through lips that seemed suddenly numb.

'Back to where I shot the kid,' he managed.

Angela waited a few moments before she replied. 'Why?'

'To try and figure out what went wrong. What I could have done differently. Why it was that the bullet just had to hit her instead of the asshole with the gun. Just two eighths of an inch to the right, Angie. Two eighths. I measured it myself. If that bullet had gone out of my gun a fraction of an inch to the right we'd have been celebrating the death of the abductor and the safety of that little girl.'

'But it didn't,' Angela said. 'There's nothing that you could have done about that.'

'I know.'

Angela chose her words with care. 'Is that what's really been bothering you?'

'I didn't know it until now,' Griffin said. 'I know I didn't kill her, and I know that the guilt over what happened is natural but misplaced. I know it wasn't my fault. But why, Angie? If there's any justice in the universe, why would an innocent little girl die and a drug–addled, murdering biker live?'

Angela sighed. 'Because the only justice we have is what we make for ourselves. This world can be both heaven and hell â€" it's how we make it that determines how it turns out. You're one of the people trying to make it closer to heaven than to hell and you're heavily outnumbered by the opposition.'

Griffin nodded but his expression was fixed into a grimace of disbelief.

'It makes me wonder if it's worthwhile, you know?'

Angela reached across to hold Griffin's hand.

'The reason you, and all people like you, do what you do is because if you didn't then we wouldn't be sitting here. This restaurant wouldn't exist. We'd be living in countries like Afghanistan or Sierra Leone, where you can die for just going to school or having money or believing in somebody else's wrong god. Without people like you, we'd all be unlucky.'

Griffin, his head bowed as he listened, looked up at his wife. 'This is why I love you.'

Angela smiled and squeezed back. 'And I you. I want this life, even with its tragedies, because it's so much better than the alternative. I want to be married to you, a cop, in a safe country where our child can grow up and have a future.'

Griffin nodded, squeezed Angela's hand back, and then his train of thought ground to a halt.

'Child?' Griffin echoed.

Angela said nothing as she smiled across the table at him. Griffin felt his heart skip a beat, felt a hot flush tingle across his face and down his spine.

'Oh, Angie,' was all he could say, his lips numb. 'Why didn't you…?'

'I've been too afraid to say anything,' she replied. 'I haven't known if we have a future together, Scott.'

Griffin closed his eyes and shook his head, cursed himself. He looked back up at Angela.

'We've always got a future together,' he said. 'I may be a world class asshole but I'm not going to run away from you. I just need some time, is all.'

'I know,' Angela said. 'That's why I went to my sister's, to give you some space. It was all I could think of to do.'

Griffin felt pain sting the corners of his eyes as he fought to keep his face from collapsing.

'How long?' he asked.

'Ten weeks,' Angela replied. 'I had to tell you because I'll be having a scan again in a few weeks. We can decide if we want to know whether it's a boy or a girl later.'

Griffin felt something escape from his lips that was somewhere between a cough and a cry. His eyes flooded and he felt like an asshole yet again but this time it was for all the right reasons as he covered his face with his hand.

Angela was beside him in an instant and he threw his arms around her and pulled her close to him.

'It's up to you,' he managed to mumble into her shoulder. 'You decide. You're carrying the load.'

Angela laughed as she held him. 'Always the poet, Scott.'

A waitress hurried up beside them. 'Are you guys okay?'

Griffin nodded, the smile still plastered over his face. 'Sorry, I get real emotional about champagne.'

Griffin took his seat opposite his wife as every muscle and fibre in his body seemed to unwind and the poison infecting him leaked away with his tears.

***

Dean Crawford

38

Kathryn froze as she saw Stephen standing behind her.

The rain tumbling from the darkening sky glistened in his hair. His shirt was drenched, raindrops falling from the tips of his fingers in one hand and from the barrel of a .38 pistol held tightly in the other.

Kathryn jumped behind Sheila's recliner and pointed at him. 'I knew it,' she snapped. 'I followed him here yesterday.'

'Dale!' Sheila yelped. 'What the hell is going on?!'

Kathryn felt a lump clench her throat. Her legs felt as though they had taken root in the concrete floor of the storage unit beneath her, her brain clouded in a dense fog of fear as she found herself transfixed by the pistol in Stephen's hand. Suddenly, and with a terrible clarity, she realised how Scott Griffin must have felt when facing down armed gunmen in the line of duty. She still had not moved. Neither had Stephen.

'Dale!' Sheila shrieked.

Stephen remained silent and still, but he blinked his gaze away from Kathryn and seemed to notice Sheila for the first time. A grim, almost rueful smile spread across the clean line of his jaw as though a dangerous thought had flickered through his mind and was trying to escape from his lips. He took a pace forward into the storage unit.

'Stephen,' Kathryn whispered.

The name had fallen from her lips as though of its own accord. She didn't even realise that she had spoken until she heard her own voice in her ears. Stephen looked at her, a fearsome gaze touched with a maniacal glint of humour, as though somehow he was both enraged and delighted at the same time. He shook his head.

'My name is Dale McKenzie.'

His voice was low, charged with a live current of menace. The index finger of his right hand stroked the cold, wet metal of the pistol as he loomed in the entrance.

Sheila glared at her husband. 'What are you doing?'

Kathryn swallowed, her throat dry and painful as she managed to force more words out past her lips.

'Who is Stephen?' she asked the man standing before them.

Dale stared at her for a moment longer, the smile still fixed to his face as rainwater streamed down his black hair.

'My brother,' he replied, sounding distant, suddenly hollow as words tumbled from his lips. 'He died when he was six. We were both orphans, Kathryn. They handed his papers to me after he died. I kept them to remember him by. They've come in most helpful for many, many years.'

Kathryn shivered. 'Why?'

Dale stared at her for several long seconds, and then Kathryn flinched as he suddenly burst out laughing. The confined storage unit amplified his deep laughs and made them shockingly loud, even above the drumming of the rain.

'Why?' Dale echoed, and then his voice turned cruel, and in a blink of an eye Kathryn realised that Stephen was gone forever. 'Why the *fuck* not?! Two lives, the chance to live any way I wish. To leave either of them at any time I please. To pick the best and make it my own. You really think I need a reason, or permission, to use my dead brother's identity to have a little fun of my own?'

Beside Kathryn, Sheila seemed to coil up like a cobra in her chair as she screeched at him. 'You adulterous bastard!'

Kathryn tried to keep calm as she spoke, but her eyes kept flicking down to the pistol Dale held close to his thigh.

'Your fun ruins people's lives,' she managed to utter.

'What *lives*?' Dale spat, and looked her up and down as though she had crawled from under a rock. 'You don't *have* a life Kathryn.'

It was as though he had shot her already. Kathryn felt a dense pall of shame and grief descend around her as she realised that everything she had done had been for nothing. All of the months of study, all of the money she had scrimped and saved, all of the times she had consoled "Stephen" on his misfortunes at work, all of the long nights and the long days and the charade and deceptions that she had planned and the misery of modern life, all of it and so much more, all for a lie, for a man who did not exist, for a liar, a cheat and a polygamous, murderous bastard.

The rage came all of its own accord.

Kathryn launched herself at Dale McKenzie with a shriek of hatred. She saw the briefest glimmer of surprise and panic flicker behind his eyes just as she plunged her hands into them and raked her nails with insane fury down his face.

Dale screamed and swung one hard forearm up and into her. Kathryn felt the world spin and the breath rush from her lungs as the blow connected with her belly. Dale swung her round as she clung to his face and she felt him hurl her backwards. The metal wall of the storage unit slammed into the back of her head and her vision starred as her legs crumpled beneath her.

Dale loomed up and something whipped past in front of Kathryn's face.

The hand smacked across her lips and Kathryn slumped sideways out of the storage unit into the rain as pain ripped across her lips and cheek and throbbed through her skull. She tried to haul herself further out of the storage unit, to make herself visible to anybody outside, but strong hands gripped her ankles and hauled her back inside.

Dale strode past her and pressed a button on the wall of the unit. Instantly, the electric shutter doors rattled down until they closed and Dale hit a switch on the wall, illuminating a small light bulb at the back of the unit. Kathryn struggled to pull herself up onto her knees and she heard Dale's voice frighteningly close behind her.

'You never did get it, did you Kathryn?' he growled. 'You couldn't quite understand it, despite everything you've done since. All those little games you've played, but not once did you stop to consider the fact that you were never *my* main play.'

Kathryn struggled to think straight, her voice strangled and poisoned with rage. 'What do you mean?'

'Poor little Kathryn Stone,' Dale snapped, 'all alone in the world, acting as though everybody in life owes you a favour. Just like all the rest, you figured that you were the most important one. Hell, you probably haven't even realised that you were not the *only* one.'

Kathryn was about to reply, but it was Sheila's voice that broke through.

'Dale, what the hell are you talking about?'

Dale was still towering over Kathryn, but now he seemed to remember that Sheila was there. He stepped back and turned to look at his wife, still strapped to the chair.

'Don't play dumb with me,' Dale snapped. 'You, you're the other way around. You had a chance in life. You earned a fortune. Yet you still spend it wallowing and bitching about how the world has dealt you a bad hand. Look at you. Even now you're wearing clothes that Kathryn here couldn't afford with an entire month's salary.'

'I don't understand,' Sheila complained.

'No, I know you don't Sheila,' Dale agreed, stalking toward her. 'That's because you've never understood. I can't stand you, Sheila. I can't stand either of you. You're both upstanding examples of how not to live a life: one crawling through the dirt just to make ends meet, the other drowning in money and doing nothing but complain about it.'

Dale stood back and looked at them both, as though satisfied with his assessment. Kathryn squinted at him.

'You've done this before,' she said finally.

'Many, many times,' Dale replied. There was pride in his voice, as though he were relating courageous military service or the glory days of his youth. 'You see, there's one thing that all three of us have in common, one thing that we share. We're all orphans. I know how it feels to face the world alone, and I know how to turn that to my advantage.'

Kathryn, her throat still dry, coughed bitterly. 'You target orphans.'

'No family to defend them,' Dale sneered, 'no other relations to inherit their money, a natural fear of the big bad world around them.' He chuckled. 'You should have found yourself a nice man to marry, Kathryn. You'd have been a lot safer.'

Kathryn stared at Dale for a long moment.

'I did find a nice man,' she snarled. 'But it turns out he died a long time ago and I ended up with his heartless bastard brother. Too bad it was Stephen who passed away and not you.'

Dale's face twisted upon itself as he stormed across to her.

'Dale!' The shout was loud enough to freeze Dale in his tracks. Sheila glowered at him from her seat. 'Stop this right now!' Dale peered over his shoulder at his wife as Kathryn watched. 'Untie me this instant!'

Dale backed away from Kathryn and straightened as he looked down at Sheila.

'Now, why would I do that?'

There was genuine hurt on Sheila's face. 'Why wouldn't you?'

Dale chuckled again as he looked at the pistol he held in his hand. 'Do you really think I'd bring this with me if I had any intention at all of letting either of you go?'

Sheila's face collapsed into panic. 'Dale, this is ridiculous! You haven't hurt anybody yet. There is still a way out of this for you, right? You can walk away, Dale. I won't press charges.'

Dale raised an eyebrow at her. 'Against whom?'

'Anybody!' Sheila yelped. 'I just want this to be over with!'

'So do I, Sheila,' Dale said calmly.

'I haven't done anything!' Sheila screamed. 'I've been abducted and now you're threatening to kill me!'

'I haven't abducted anybody,' Dale replied calmly. 'You have Kathryn here to thank for that.'

Sheila blustered a fearful laugh. 'You really think that I'm going to buy that, now?'

Dale shook his head as he strolled over to his trapped wife and replied.

'Oh Sheila, you're right. That's what makes this whole thing so tragic, but I can assure you that Kathryn here has not been in league with me at all.'

'Tragic how?' Sheila gasped in horror.

'I wasn't going to kill you,' Dale said. 'I would happily have just taken all of your money and disappeared. That was my plan, you see. That's what I do. It's only when somebody else interferes that things get messy. And now it's Kathryn here who will kill you.'

Sheila's panic mutated grotesquely into panic. 'What the hell are you talking about?!'

'I need Kathryn,' Dale went on calmly. 'You see, worthless piece of trash that she is, she is an essential part of my exit strategy.'

Sheila's arm whipped out from the restraints and Kathryn saw something thin and nasty in her hand flash in the light. Dale flinched away, caught off guard, but he was not quick enough. The needle–sharp pin, clasped in Sheila's enraged fist, punctured Dale's eyeball and he screamed in agony as he spun away, his hands flying to his face.

'Get me out of here!' Sheila screamed at Kathryn.

***

39

Kathryn lurched to her feet and dashed toward Sheila. Dale, still screaming, whirled and swung the pistol in his hand at Kathryn's face. The butt of the weapon hit her square across her temple and she reeled sideways into the metal wall of the unit and collapsed, her vision starring.

Kathryn turned, her face slumped against the cold metal wall as she tried to haul herself back up to her feet.

She looked over her shoulder in time to see a grimacing Dale, one hand covering his injured eye, lift his right boot and smash it down with all of his might onto the back of her left ankle.

White pain shrieked through her leg as she heard her ankle crunch as though she had stepped in deep gravel. Kathryn sucked in a lungful of air and screamed as agony pulsed through her and she slumped onto the cold, wet floor of the storage unit. Dale stood over her crumpled body. The rainwater on his face mixed with the bloody scratches she had gouged into his flesh and the blood spilling from his punctured eye, dripping from his chin in scarlet globules that stained her shirt as he aimed the pistol down at her.

Kathryn fought for something to say, anything to distract him further.

'How did you know I was here?' she asked.

'You keep the finest company,' Dale snarled with a cruel smile. 'Or used to.'

Kathryn's guts plunged inside her. 'Ally,' she gasped. 'Where is she?'

'She squealed like a pig,' Dale replied, 'sold you out in a matter of seconds. I don't suppose she'll survive long enough to learn about what's happened to you.'

'What are you going to do?' Kathryn gasped, one hand raised as though she could somehow stop the bullet.

'Me?' Dale asked rhetorically, his teeth gritted against his pain. 'I'm not going to do anything, Kathryn. You are.'

Dale knelt down on one knee alongside her. Kathryn recoiled from him and a fresh bolt of agony surged through her leg.

'Best you don't move,' Dale grinned coldly. 'In fact, let me help you with that.'

He moved far too quickly for Kathryn to stop him. She barely had time to register the syringe he pulled from his pocket before it plunged into her neck. She gasped and squirmed as a bitterly cold fluid was injected into her, and the words *Pancuronium bromide* flashed through her mind.

Dale yanked the syringe out and stood up, towering over her. His wounded eye was weeping tears of blood like some bizarre and hellish vision of evil.

'What have you done to her?' Sheila asked.

Kathryn felt a new fear flood cold and clammy through her as she felt her hands and feet tingling. Despite the pain soaring through her leg she realised that she could no longer move it. Within moments she realised that her arms had fallen limp by her sides where she lay.

'What have you done t....'

Kathryn's voice trailed off as her head slowly sank onto the cold floor. She was conscious and could feel everything, but was utterly unable to even blink her eyes.

'Pancuronium bromide,' Dale said, his hand back over his bloodied eye again. 'A sedative, strong enough to still every nerve and muscle in the body for an hour or two, not strong enough to stop the heart.'

Kathryn watched, trying to ignore her throbbing ankle as Dale squatted down alongside her once again. But this time, he cleaned the pistol on her blouse before turning it and placing in in her unresisting hand.

Sheila's face blanched and she shook her head. 'Please, no!'

Kathryn saw her yanking at her bonds, trying to escape the chair as Dale positioned himself behind Kathryn and lifted her hand in his, the gun clasped painfully within it.

'Dale, please don't!'

Kathryn saw Sheila's tears spill down her cheeks, saw more fluids spill down her legs as she thrashed and tore at her bonds with her free hand. Dale looked at her, and for a brief moment Kathryn heard something of the man she had once known in his voice.

'I'm sorry, Sheila,' he said. 'Really I am.'

Then Dale's fingers squeezed Kathryn's painfully hard.

The gunshot was deafening in the tiny storage unit. Kathryn smelled a whiff of smoke as her vision cleared and she saw Sheila slumped in the seat. Her long blonde hair was draped across her face, which hung sideways on her neck. In the centre of her chest was a dark red stain that spread slowly as it soaked into her blouse.

Kathryn, her body limp, felt tears trickle down her face as she lay on her side and stared at Sheila's corpse, still strapped to the seat.

Behind her, she heard Dale stand up. He carefully took the pistol from her limp hands and dropped it into a plastic bag that he sealed. Then he walked across to Sheila's side, and from his pocket he produced a small flick–knife. As Kathryn watched, Dale sliced a lock of Sheila's hair from her head and slipped it into his pocket. Then, he returned to Kathryn's side and squatted down before her.

The calm, quiet expression on his features did nothing to calm Kathryn's nerves. If anything, she felt even more afraid.

'Now, Kathryn,' Dale said. 'The police will be here soon. They will find Sheila's body and they will immediately assume that you have killed her. Of course, I could leave you here with Sheila. It would be the perfect crime scene, wouldn't it? I could use the same pistol to put a bullet in your head, stage your suicide. A woman on the edge, a cry for help, all that psychological crap that you enjoy so much.' He shook his head. 'But no. It would all be too perfect, too arranged, you know? Things need to look a little messier, a little more like you were totally deranged.'

Dale smiled. Kathryn felt her guts turn to slime within her.

Dale stood up and with a cloth carefully wiped the floor in front of her. It took her a few moments to realise that he was attempting to remove the gunpowder residue from the shot that had killed his wife. The low angle suggested by any residue might be considered suspect when firearms specialists examined the scene.

Dale then slid his arms beneath her body and lifted her off the floor. Agony surged through her ankle but she could not even scream, her breathing fearfully light and her vision fading in and out as she struggled to remain conscious.

Dale opened the shutter doors and carried her out into the rain. He shut the doors behind them and carried Kathryn across the parking lot toward her car. Kathryn saw from her awkward position in his arms that the CCTV cameras were still all twisted to one side, pointing in useless directions away from the lot.

Dale hefted her in his grasp and threw her over his shoulder in a fireman's lift, blocking her view of the parking lot. She heard him open the trunk of her car, and then he lowered her into the trunk. Dale then reached out and picked up a small, mahogany lock–box laying alongside Kathryn inside the trunk. He reverentially opened it with a key, and then with one hand he fished the flick–knife and the lock of Sheila's hair and placed them in the box before locking it once more.

'This won't take long, Kathryn. I promise it will all be over very soon.'

Kathryn, staring up at Dale, watched as he slammed the trunk of her car closed and she was plunged into absolute blackness.

***

40

Griffin walked out of the restaurant with Angela on his arm, feeling a little lighter on his feet than he probably should as they strolled into the lobby.

The waitress went to fetch their coats as they stood and held each other, surrounded by the blue lights and with the sound of whispering water from the restaurant display tinkling behind them.

'That,' Angela said, 'was the best night out I've had in a long time.'

'Me too,' Griffin said. 'That waterfall keeps making me want to pee though.'

'Ever the romantic.'

'Poet, romantic,' Griffin said. 'Where do my talents end?'

'We'll discuss that in the morning,' Angela said with a sideways glance and a playful smile.

The concierge returned with their coats, and as Griffin slipped Angela's coat over her shoulders and shrugged his own jacket on, his gaze alighted on the photographs filling the wall near the reception desk.

'Looks like they all had good nights too,' Angela said, catching his gaze.

'Yeah, looks like a lot of people enjoy coming here,' Griffin smiled. 'Maybe we should do the same and have our... photo... taken...'

Griffin's voice caught in his throat as his gaze settled on one of the images. A woman and a man, holding each other in a tight embrace, bright smiles painted onto their features as a slightly drunk cameraman or woman had taken the shot of them, the entire restaurant behind them smiling and clapping.

Griffin edged closer to the photograph.

'What is it?' Angela asked.

Griffin stared at the image for a moment longer and then his voice returned as the heady fusion of happiness surging through his veins was suddenly shut off.

'Oh shit.'

Griffin stared at the image of Kathryn Stone, held in the arms of Dale McKenzie.

'We've got to go,' he said as he yanked his cell phone from his pocket and dialled Maietta's number. 'Now!'

Griffin hit the street and the cold night air as Maietta answered the phone. He was talking even before she had the chance to ask what he wanted.

'It's McKenzie!' Griffin yelled. 'Call the DA and have them issue a subpoena for his financials, everything you can get! And then find out what life insurance company Kathryn Stone uses.'

'What?'

'Just do it!'

***

41

Maietta yanked the wheel of the pool car over as it pulled into the apartment block parking lot, the tyres screeching on the asphalt as two marked vehicles pursued her, their lights flashing like nightclub strobes in the darkness.

They leaped out into the rain, weapons already drawn as Maietta led four uniformed officers up to Kathryn Stone's apartment. Maietta rapped her knuckles on the front door hard.

'Police, open up!'

The rain splattered down in cold squalls from the black sky above, but she could hear nothing from inside. The uniformed officer beside her shook his head, and she turned to another of the uniforms who hefted an iron ram under his arm.

'Hit it!'

The officer hauled the ram up the steps and swung it twice before launching it at a spot alongside the door handle. The ram crashed into the wood and the door splintered around the handle, but it did not break. A second swing and the door burst open as the handle and locks scattered to the ground.

'Police, stay still!'

Maietta lurched into the apartment, her pistol cupped in her hands before her above a flashlight. The white beam swept the apartment, but nothing and nobody moved.

'Lights!'

The lights in the apartment blossomed into life, illuminating the living room as Maietta swept through the apartment and lowered her weapon.

'Clear!'

The officers joined her in the kitchen. 'Long gone, both of them,' one of them said.

'Shit,' Maietta growled. 'Search for evidence of a struggle or blood, then have forensics tear this place apart. We need to find them, both of them.'

The uniforms began hunting carefully through the various rooms, not moving anything as they searched. Maietta slipped on her gloves and walked into the bedroom. She saw the laptop on the bed and carefully opened it. A document awaited her.

Stephen: a meditation on…

A commotion at the front door alerted her in time to see Griffin burst in. Beneath his rain coat he wore a smart looking suit, his shoes were highly polished and his hair parted cleanly.

'Thanks for coming, Capone,' Maietta said.

The gag fell silent as Angela Griffin followed Griffin in, her coat huddled around her shoulders over her entirely too thin black dress as a uniformed officer accompanied her.

'You got her yet?' Griffin asked Maietta, his face pinched with concern.

'She's gone,' Maietta replied. 'So is McKenzie, hasn't been in contact with us for hours.'

'Looks like his concern for his wife's well–being has evaporated real fast,' Griffin said. 'How long since anybody heard from Kathryn?'

'We're trying to figure that out right now,' Maietta said. 'A couple of hours?'

'Shit.'

'I tried to call you when we realised that Dale McKenzie was missing,' Maietta insisted. 'We didn't know you were….'

Maietta glanced apologetically at Angela Griffin. Her husband nodded and waved Maietta down.

'Yeah, I know, doesn't happen much. My cell was in my pocket.'

Maietta watched as Griffin turned to his wife. 'Honey, I'm sorry, but if we don't find her she could be…'

Angela moved to Griffin's side and then up on tip–toe to kiss him. 'I know. Go do what you do, I'll wait. Call me, okay?'

Maietta saw Griffin nod and hug Angela tightly. 'I will,' he said, and then to the uniforms. 'Get her home safe, will you? We've got things here.'

As Angela was driven away in a patrol car, Maietta brought Griffin up to speed and she showed him the laptop, the tablet and the empty wardrobes.

'Check this out,' she said, and gestured to the laptop. 'I'll see your laptop and raise you a tablet registered to one Stephen Hollister.'

Griffin looked at the tablet screen as Maietta held it out to him.

'"You're not as smart as you think you are",' Griffin echoed the words written on the screen. 'Looks like our girl knew he was up to something,' he said. 'Makes me wonder just how much.'

'Either way, she was doing something about it,' Maietta said as she gestured to the empty wardrobes.

'Yeah, and probably getting herself into more trouble than she bargained for. And he either took her before she could leave or he's pursued her. We got her license plate out with traffic?'

'Everyone's watching,' Maietta said. 'But they could be a long way from here by now.'

Griffin looked up and down the bedroom, and then saw something half way down one wall. He moved closer, and squatted down by the wall.

'Blood,' he said. 'Not much.'

'Maybe a punch?' Maietta hazarded.

'They fight,' Griffin imagined out loud, 'she leaves. Is her car here?'

'No.'

'So either she fled or he caught her and took her with him.'

'Why do all of this though?' Maietta asked. 'Leaving him messages on his computer? She could have just left, gone to friends, whatever?'

'You ever hear that phrase?' Griffin asked her. 'Hell hath no fury?'

'Like a woman scorned,' Maietta nodded. 'All of Stephen Hollister's bank accounts were recently cleared out.'

'The modern day equivalent of cutting his ties in half and daubing his car with paint,' Griffin replied. 'She's getting revenge. She knew that he was involved with another woman.'

'Maybe she knew it was Sheila McKenzie,' Maietta hazarded. 'She could have maybe seen the incident board at the precinct, identified Stephen Hollister as Dale McKenzie.'

'Or maybe not,' Griffin countered. 'Either way, if McKenzie has a hold of her he'll have to finish the game now. He's already abducted his wife.'

'He had an alibi for that,' Maietta reminded Griffin.

'Yeah, so everybody keeps sayin',' Griffin shot back. 'That's something we'll have to look more closely at. Either way, we may as well presume that she's long dead. That means that Kathryn is a loose end he won't want to keep a hold of...'

Maietta did not say anything, both of them knowing that it could not end well. 'Did you get the insurance details for Stone?'

'Yeah,' Maietta said as she yanked a folded piece of paper from her pocket. 'Turns out she's on the same policy as Sheila McKenzie. It's handled by an agent, by the name of...'

'Stephen Hollister,' Griffin said as he looked down at the paper, 'of Hollister Insurance Incorporated. I'll be damned, that's how he moved money.'

'He's been using the Internet and acting as a sub-contracted legal agent for a non-existent claims company,' Maietta said. 'It's registered to a Postal Box in Sacramento. Zero physical presence, essentially a front company. He represents dead clients and organises their insurance pay-outs to Hollister Insurance, then launders the money out for his own use. A real neat little package, and by targeting orphans there's nobody to act in their defence. Everything's tied off via phone and e-mail.'

'Son of a bitch,' Griffin uttered.

'We got something!'

Griffin turned as a uniformed officer dashed up the steps outside to the apartment door and yelled inside.

'The hospital just called. Sheila McKenzie's been found after reports of shots fired out on the east side!'

Maietta dashed after Griffin as he ran from the apartment.

***

42

'She's right this way, detective.'

Griffin hurried along behind the nurse as she waved for him to follow her. As he walked he tried Kathryn on his cell phone again, but he couldn't get a signal inside the hospital. He cursed as he slipped the cell back into his pocket and followed the nurse through a door into a private room.

Sheila McKenzie was lying on a bed, her chest a mass of medical dressing. A ventilator sat near her bed, no longer active, and Griffin could see where they had intubated into her neck to keep her breathing and into her side to drain her ruined lung of blood. Her eyes were underscored with dark rings of bruised sclera as though she had been beaten half to death, but one of the eyes had opened wearily as Griffin entered the room.

'She's exhausted,' the nurse said, 'and has been prepared for surgery. Make it brief, detectives.'

Griffin nodded as he approached the side of Sheila's bed, Maietta beside him. Despite Sheila's injuries Griffin could tell that she was an attractive woman and he knew her to be both successful and determined in life. It made him wonder again what the hell she had seen in someone like Dale McKenzie, and why the hell she hadn't seen through his lies and deceptions. Then he remembered that Kathryn had likely been duped too.

'Been lookin' for you, Sheila,' he said softly with a smile that he hoped was sincere enough for her.

Sheila watched him through her bleary eye for a moment before replying in a voice that sounded rough as sandpaper.

'I think you missed the bus, detectives.'

Griffin's smile turned tight on his face and he nodded. 'By far too long,' he admitted. 'I'm so sorry.'

Sheila broke eye contact with Griffin and stared up at the ceiling. Griffin slipped his notebook from his pocket and pulled up a chair from nearby.

'Look, I know that this is a bad time, but we really need to ask you a few questions about what happened. Can you do that for me?'

Sheila swallowed thickly, winced at the pain, but Griffin saw her nod once.

'That's great Sheila, this won't take long I promise. Can you tell me what happened to you when you were first abducted?'

Sheila's voice croaked weakly as she replied.

'Somebody got into the house and hit me from behind. I didn't get a look at them.'

'No sounds at all, no hints as to who they might be?'

Sheila shook her head slowly. 'Too fast, covered up in black mask and a big coat. They put a sack over my head.'

'Was this at night or during the day?' Maietta asked.

'Night, after I got back from work.'

Griffin nodded. With the abduction occurring at night, and in a large house with its own garage and drive, it would have made it reasonably easy for Dale McKenzie to transfer Sheila from the house to a vehicle and away from the scene without being noticed. Even with their curtain-twitching neighbours, the foul weather of that night would likely have deterred most observers.

'Okay, and what happened next?'

'Car,' Sheila uttered. 'I was dragged into a car and driven someplace, it took a long time. I got dragged into a chair and that's where I stayed until you found me.'

'The storage units,' Griffin said, 'here in town. That's where we found you.'

Sheila nodded, coughed a little before speaking. 'I could tell there were people not far away during the day.'

'You could hear them?'

'Feel them,' Sheila said as she shook her head. 'Vibrations, through the recliner.'

'Did they move you at all from that place?'

'No. They kept me there the whole time.'

'Did they speak to you at all?'

'Yes.'

Griffin leaned forward in his seat. 'What did they sound like? Was it a man or a woman?'

'They spoke through a microphone of some kind,' Sheila replied, 'one of those stupid deep-throat things. I couldn't tell whether it was a man or a woman.'

'What did they speak to you about?'

Sheila swallowed, struggling to talk through her pain.

'They asked me about my life,' she said, 'about my husband, about our money and what we were doing with it. They asked a lot of questions about Dale in particular. They eventually told me he had contacted the police and that my life was in danger because of it.'

'Your husband did the right thing, Sheila,' Maietta said. 'Unfortunately, for all the wrong reasons.'

Sheila coughed again, louder this time. 'I don't doubt it,' she snapped with as much force as she could muster. 'He knew what would happen if I died. He'd get all of the money, every last penny. I bet he ran to the police the first chance he got.'

Griffin blinked in surprise. 'It didn't appear that way to us, ma'am. Your husband appears to have been extremely distressed by your disappearance.'

'Is that so, detective?' Sheila asked, and with a supreme effort she turned her head on her pillow to face him. 'Then where the hell is he now?'

Griffin frowned. 'We're not sure.'

'What a surprise,' came the bitterly whispered response.

'But you didn't see anybody, or hear anything at all that would help to tell us who your abductor was?' Griffin asked.

'No,' Sheila croaked. 'I was blindfolded, my ears were plugged and I was gagged.'

Griffin watched her for a moment, long enough for her to sigh and relax her head back into her pillows again.

'Did you smell anything?' Griffin asked.

To Griffin's surprise, Sheila McKenzie's dry, cracked lips widened into a faint smile as she stared up at the ceiling.

'Finally, detective, you're onto something.'

Griffin leaned forward on his seat. 'Tell me, quickly. Anything you could tell us might be of huge importance.'

Sheila turned her head and looked at him. 'What importance? My husband is a lowly airline pilot with an over–inflated opinion of himself. What could possibly be important about him?'

Griffin braced himself. 'Four women, who have died in suspicious circumstances in several states over the past fifteen years. All of them apparently drowned in the bath after random strokes and heart–attacks. It turns out that all of these women had one thing in common: they all are connected to the aviation career of Dale McKenzie.'

Sheila stared at Griffin for a long moment. 'Go on.'

'All of their bank accounts were emptied before they died,' Griffin said, 'and local police were never able to trace where their money went. The cases went cold despite hints at a boyfriend in all of the cases who was never identified. Every one of those women was an orphan with no family to support them. Are you seeing a pattern here, Sheila?'

Sheila gaped at Griffin. 'Are you saying my husband is a murderer?'

'Each of the victims died in cities where Dale McKenzie was known to have flown to during his career with various airlines at the time of their deaths,' Maietta explained. 'The connection was only made when we started digging into his past and working with other agencies and forces who had dealt with those murders.'

Sheila seemed to realise how close she had come to death, and some of the anger and determination returned to her eyes as she stared at Griffin.

'He was there, at the storage unit,' she said finally. 'Somebody came to rescue me, but Dale arrived before she could free me. I know it was Dale who abducted me, because the idiot still wore the same aftershave when he came to visit me. He figured he'd thought of everything,' Sheila smiled. 'I guess he's not as smart as he thought he was. I could even smell his scent, if you know what I mean, on his shirt?'

'You're sure it was him?' Maietta asked.

'I know my own husband,' Sheila hissed, but then her anger faded abruptly. 'At least, I thought that I did.'

'Somebody came to rescue you?' Griffin asked.

'Yes,' Sheila nodded. 'A woman, a pretty young thing. She said she had followed Dale and found the storage unit.'

'How did she know your husband?'

Sheila's anger broke through her pain again. 'Because the bastard was having an affair with her.'

'With the woman who came to free you?' Griffin asked, and was rewarded with a nod. 'Did the woman give you her name?'

'No, but Dale referred to her as Kathryn,' Sheila said, 'and the odd thing was that she didn't refer to Dale by his name. She called him Stephen.'

A uniformed officer poked his head around the corner of the door. 'Detectives? You're not going to believe this, but emergency services just pulled in with a woman who's mumbling about a Scott Griffin.'

Griffin leaped out of the chair and followed the uniform down the corridor outside, Maietta jogging to keep up as they rounded a corner into the emergency room as a gurney was being wheeled through, pushed by two nurses.

Griffin barged his way in alongside the gurney as it was wheeled along and looked down at the woman who lay beneath thermal blankets, her face flushed blue and her teeth clattering hard enough to send ripples through her jowls.

'What's your name?' Griffin asked.

'All.....yyyyy...'

The woman was in the throes of severe hypothermia and Griffin guessed she was naked beneath the blankets, her entire form trembling as though live currents were seething through her body.

'How did you know my name?' he asked.

'Kkkkaatthh....ryynn.'

'Kathryn?' Griffin asked as he jogged alongside the gurney. 'Where is she?'

Ally struggled to form words, her eyes quivering with the effort.

'Lllll...aaa....yyyy...'

'What?' Griffin urged. 'Come on Ally, say it!'

'Lllll..aaa....yyyyy...'

'She's out of it on some kind of drug!' a nurse yelled. 'We need to get her out of here!'

Griffin was pulled urgently aside by the nurses as they tried to get lines into the woman's flabby arms.

'Say it!' Griffin yelled as Ally was wheeled away.

'Lllll...aaaa... yyy... k.'

'Lake,' Maietta snapped. 'She's saying *lake*.'

'Hhunnnt..rrrrr,' Ally managed as she was wheeled away and her head slumped back onto her pillow.

'Hunter's Lodge,' Griffin snapped. 'There's a lake up that way, some sort of tourist resort.'

Griffin turned to Maietta and pointed at the gurney as it rattled down the corridor. 'Stay with her, find out more if you can and call me if you get anything useful!'

'Where the hell are you going?'

'To the lodge,' Griffin yelled as he turned and ran. 'Send back–up, then call in and set up roadblocks out of town to cut Dale McKenzie off!'

***

43

It was hard to keep track of time.

Kathryn's body was crammed into the trunk, enveloped by darkness. She could not move a single muscle. Pain throbbed in long, slow, agonising pulses through her ankle, and every now and again she felt a hole in the road shudder through the vehicle's suspension and jolt her painfully.

She had gone too far. She realised that now, could admit it to herself. In her fury she had blinded herself to what she was doing, had deliberately overridden her natural caution, her common sense, and become... what, exactly?

Occasionally in her life when she had faced crisis that had been of her own making, however indirectly, she had wondered: *how did it come to this? How did I go from living a happy life to having to deal with something like this?* Embarrassing moments from her history flickered through her mind like demons taunting her with past failures, all of which seemed so trivial now. Jilted lovers, offended friends, mistakes at work, schoolroom arguments – all overcome often with little more than an apology or a kind gesture.

Now, she was facing death. What *had* she been thinking? She suddenly felt more stupid and alone than she ever had, and a sudden realisation dawned upon her as she lay in the vibrating darkness: *nobody will miss me when I'm gone.* Her profound sadness deepened as she realised that even Scott Griffin would probably forget about her soon enough, his marriage likely saved along with his career. Kathryn's usefulness will have ended, along with her life.

The car suddenly bumped and rumbled as it left the road, and a fresh wave of panic flushed through her body. Kathryn tried desperately to move her fingers but they remained motionless, as though she were looking down upon someone else's body. Pain flared up and down her leg as she was rattled about in the trunk, and then finally the vehicle slowed and came to a stop. She heard the squeal of her car's brakes and the engine shutting off. A door opened.

Heavy footsteps walked to the rear of the vehicle.

The trunk clicked and then was thrown open.

The coal–black sky above Dale was spitting a hail of cold rain that gusted in sleety squalls faintly illuminated by the glow of nearby buildings. She could barely make out Dale's features as he stared down at her.

'Time for you to go for a drive,' he said.

Dale reached down and with a heave of effort he lifted her out of the trunk and carried her round to the driver's side of her car.

The vehicle was parked on a grassy bank, maybe a quarter of a mile from Hunter's Lodge, the yellow lighting around the resort glistening amid the blackness. Trees loomed dark and whispered as the wind hurried through their leaves. She smelled the scent of water and saw the lake, the even more distant lights from the city flickering on the dark water.

Kathryn gasped and tried to speak.

'Please… no…'

Her words were a ghostly whisper, as though her vocal chords had been whittled down to a hair's breadth.

Dale did not respond as he grunted with the effort of lowering her body into the driver's seat. He strapped her in, and then he reached across her to the passenger's seat. Kathryn swivelled her eyeballs enough to see Dale open the plastic bag with the pistol in it and let the weapon drop onto the seat beside her.

Dale produced the knife from his pocket once more. Kathryn's stomach turned over on itself as Dale lifted the blade to her ear, and then hacked off a chunk of her hair. He lifted the hair to his nose and closed his eyes as he smelled it, then he tucked it into his pocket along with the knife.

Dale carefully extricated himself from the vehicle and squatted down beside her. Quietly, he reached into his pocket and removed her cell phone. He tossed it onto the passenger seat beside her.

Then, he sat back on his haunches and admired his work.

'They'll find the car easily enough,' he said. 'Pull it out of the water. You'll be inside, somewhat more dead than you are now, with the evidence surrounding you. Your car. The pistol. Sheila's blood on you. The water will make it harder for them to find absolute forensic evidence, but I'm sure it will be enough to convict beyond reasonable doubt.'

Kathryn, her head lolling to one side and saliva drooling from her lips, struggled to speak.

'You…?'

Dale smiled again. 'Me? I'm the victim here, Kathryn. The poor grieving husband who lost his wife to the callous and mentally unstable hands of some loser by the name of Stone.' He held up two tickets for Hunter's Lodge. 'I've been up here all along of course. I'm surprised you left the apartment without taking these with you. I'll suffer of course, for a while, in the aftermath of so much death and tragedy. But I'm sure that Dale McKenzie will soldier bravely on, the life insurance policies from his poor deceased wife adding to the personal fortune he's been quietly amassing. Maybe I'll take some time off from flying, emigrate down to Mexico just in case any loose ends come back to haunt me, and try fucking eighteen year old virgins or something instead of middle–aged losers like you.'

Kathryn tried to respond, but her voice was not strong enough.

Dale smiled again and pressed one finger to her lips. A red line trickled from his eye like tears of blood where Sheila had stabbed him. 'Ssshh now,' he whispered. 'There's really nothing more to say, Kathryn. Your time has come.'

Dale reached across her and with one gloved hand he lifted hers and started the car engine. Kathryn squirmed desperately, felt her legs and arms jerk spasmodically.

'That's right,' Dale encouraged her. 'The drug is starting to wear off. Struggle if you like Kathryn, but it won't do you any good. It's far too late for that.'

He lifted her uninjured foot and placed it on the accelerator, then reached across her again and eased the handbrake off. Then, with one quick movement he flicked the car into drive and jerked back out.

The door slammed shut as the car rolled toward the lake. Kathryn strained and struggled to get her muscles to work again, tried to guide her hands down to the seatbelt release beside her as she felt the car move. The bank was steep and the tiny pressure of her foot resting on the accelerator was all it took.

Kathryn let out a strained cry of anguish as the vehicle rolled faster and faster, rumbling down the grassy hillside toward the bleak, black water ahead. Her hands twitched as her foot slipped off the accelerator, but the car was running under its own momentum now.

She tried to keep her lolling head up while guiding her hands toward the seatbelt release, but she could not take her eyes off her impending doom as with a rolling crash of water the car plunged into the lake. She saw a faint blue line of foam splash up across the hood and wash against the windscreen as the car rolled into the water.

The engine rattled as it was submerged, and she felt the wheels beneath the vehicle lose traction as the car began to float. Water rushed in through the door seals as the car drifted in blackness, icy cold against her throbbing ankle as it flooded the foot well. She saw the waterline creep up to the windshield, black and rippling. More water flooded into the rear of the car, and it sank lower in the water.

The engine coughed and spluttered and then fell silent, only the instruments before her glowing in the absolute blackness until they too flickered and blinked out.

The water rose up to her knees, sloshing bitterly cold and yet invisible in the darkness as though she were already dead and being swallowed by Hell itself. She cried out, fumbling beneath the fast–rising water for the seatbelt release. Her fingers fastened upon it, but they were not yet strong enough to depress the button and release her.

The water swelled in the vehicle and to her dismay she saw the lights of the distant city and their reflections on the water's surface vanish as the car became completely submerged beneath the blackness. The water pouring through the door seals became deafeningly loud, and she realised that what air was trapped within the car was vanishing in a cloud of bubbles through the tops of the doors and the sunroof.

The water flooded up to her neck as Kathryn strained to release the seatbelt. Her fingers were already becoming numb from the cold water and they slipped off the release button. She cried out, spitting water as she managed to crane her neck back for one last breath of precious air.

And then the water flooded over her.

***

44

Griffin let the car coast as he threw it into neutral, his eyes slowly adjusting to the darkness outside as he searched for some sign of Kathryn's car. He could see the lodge up ahead, a handful of bright lights glowing in the vast darkness of the plains, but the road was empty. He was about to give up entirely when from the gloomy night ahead a figure emerged from a bank onto the road.

A man. Tall. Walking.

Griffin waited until the last possible moment, the point when the man would hear the whisper of his car's tyres on the asphalt. Griffin saw the man's head shift position, turning toward the car.

Griffin squinted until his eyes were almost completely closed and then switched on the car's headlights, full–beam. Dale McKenzie's astounded face was briefly illuminated in a brilliant halo of white light as he threw his arms up to shield his face from the blazing headlamps.

Griffin swerved his car to one side. He yanked the handbrake on as he shoved his door open and leaped from the vehicle, rolling on the asphalt as he came up running.

Dale McKenzie staggered, briefly blinded by the bright flare of the headlights. Griffin ducked down as he ran and drove his shoulder deep into McKenzie's belly, just below his ribcage. He heard a rush of air blast from McKenzie's mouth as he was lifted clean off of his feet by Griffin's charge. McKenzie stumbled backwards off the road and onto the verge, tumbling onto his back as Griffin plunged down toward him.

Griffin saw the flicker of needle–thin light only at the last moment as he plummeted down to pin McKenzie on his back, a syringe in the pilot's hands.

Griffin landed hard on top of McKenzie and grabbed the wrist of the hand that held the syringe just before it sank into his chest. His weight as he fell drove the needle toward him and he was forced to roll aside to prevent it from penetrating his chest.

McKenzie let out a growl as he rolled with Griffin and scrambled to get on top.

'You're done McKenzie!' Griffin shouted through gritted teeth. 'We know everything!'

McKenzie did not reply as he kicked his legs and scrambled up on top. Griffin felt the pilot's weight pin him down onto the damp grass. McKenzie let out another strangled growl as he leaned all of his weight down upon Griffin. Griffin strained against the pilot's body weight, the syringe held barely two inches from his chest. Griffin had no idea what was in the damned thing but at a guess he figured some kind of powerful sedative or perhaps even a poison of some kind: whatever had allowed McKenzie to kill those other victims, their supposed suicides and accidental deaths neatly concealing his murderous tendencies.

McKenzie leaned further over Griffin, pushing his weight up over the syringe. Griffin's arms trembled and bolts of pain lanced through his wrists as they were bent backwards trying to hold the syringe away from his chest.

'Sweet dreams, detective,' McKenzie snarled.

The syringe eased its way toward Griffin's shirt. The detective let out a strangled groan as he felt the tip of the needle puncture his skin with an exquisite pain, and then he drove his knee with all of his might up into McKenzie's groin like a sledgehammer through a peach.

McKenzie screamed as his weight, precariously balanced over the syringe, was shoved upward and over Griffin's head. McKenzie writhed and then toppled sideways. Griffin jerked his head to one side as his arms gave way beneath McKenzie's weight and the syringe plunged down alongside the detective's neck, scraping the surface of his skin as it plunged down into the soft earth beside his ear.

Griffin released McKenzie's wrists as the pilot toppled onto his side on the grass and rolled away, scrambling to his feet as McKenzie struggled to regain his. The pilot was hunched over, tears streaming from his eyes and one hand clasping his genitalia as he tried to get up.

'Where is she?' Griffin yelled.

McKenzie glared up at him with defiance etched into every pore of his being. 'She's history.'

Griffin lunged at McKenzie again, saw the syringe flicker in the gloom as McKenzie tried once again to stab him with it, but this time Griffin saw it coming and he dodged to one side. The weapon flew past as Griffin lifted one boot and stamped it down hard on the outside of McKenzie's right knee.

The pilot gagged as his leg buckled and he sank down onto the damp grass. The syringe swung wildly back toward Griffin, who caught McKenzie's wrist and wrenched it to one side as he gripped the pilot's palm and twisted it savagely over. McKenzie cried out as the syringe span from his grasp.

Griffin picked the needle up with his free hand, flipped it over and slammed it up to the hilt into McKenzie's neck. The pilot cried out as Griffin yanked his head and snarled into his ear.

'You tell me where she is or I'll fill you full of this shit, you understand?'

McKenzie, his face twisted in pain, laughed out loud. Griffin yanked his head closer and stepped forward, keeping the syringe buried in McKenzie's neck as he head-butted the pilot hard across the nose. McKenzie howled as his nose collapsed with a crunch of crushed cartilage. Blood spilled from his ruined face, black in the harsh white light of the headlamp beams.

'Where is she?!'

McKenzie, crippled and still in pain, laughed again. 'It's just a sedative,' he spat. 'You'll get nothing from me.'

Griffin looked up at the bank and at the nearby lake, and in an instant he knew. He looked down at McKenzie and then squeezed the syringe. The remaining sedative drained into the pilot's neck, and with moments McKenzie slumped onto the wet grass in the darkness, his limbs loose and defenceless.

Griffin tossed the syringe aside, turned and sprinted up the bank.

His car's headlamps illuminated the edge of the lake in the faintest glow but he could see clearly enough the tyre marks in the grass, flattened stems leading down to the water's edge.

***

Dean Crawford

45

Kathryn felt her hair levitating in the freezing water, felt her heart pounding in her chest as she struggled to release her seatbelt. Her hands fumbled blindly in the pitch black and she realised that she could not even figure out where her door was, so completely disorientated was she.

She tried not to let the panic rise up and destroy her, but already she could see sparks and whorls of light spiralling in her vision. Her chest throbbed with each beat of her heart and her lungs felt as though they were swelling to twice their ordinary size in her chest as she fought for her life.

She released some of the air in her lungs, felt a dribble of bubbles leak past her lips, and some of the pressure eased.

Just one breath of air was all she needed. *Just one.*

The seatbelt release clicked, and in a frantic scramble Kathryn yanked the belt free and pulled it over her head. Her body floated free of the seat as her head hit the roof and her flailing hands smacked against the steering wheel.

She searched for the door handle but could not find it. Her limbs twitched erratically as she bumped against the car roof, more bubbles leaking from her lips, her hands flailing blindly for a release from her flooded prison. Panic flushed her as she realised that she had only seconds remaining, her lungs burning and her heartbeat squelching laboriously in her ears as it desperately sought oxygen in her weakening blood.

Kathryn banged the window of her door in a last desperate attempt to escape as sparkling galaxies of light flickered like phantasms in her field of vision and her senses contracted until she felt as though she were a tiny insect trapped in a vast black universe entirely deprived of air. The effort made her inhale a tiny amount of freezing water that scorched her nasal passages and leaked down her throat toward her lungs.

Her body convulsed as she tried not to cough and she doubled over, her hands falling away from the door handle as the last of the air from her lungs spilled from her lips in a feeble dribble.

In the freezing, flooded darkness and utterly alone, Kathryn's lungs convulsed inside her one last time and then she opened her mouth and sucked in a lungful of blessed air. Except there was no air. Her lungs filled with the freezing water, expanding once again as pain ripped across her chest and a final, bright white light filled her vision.

Bubbles streamed away from her as she saw the interior of the car illuminated as though by moonlight. As her consciousness slipped away she glimpsed the door being yanked open and a figure plunge into the vehicle, Griffin's face glowing in the light and pinched with a volatile mixture of determination and anxiety.

*

The pain returned, scraping at the insides of her chest as she gagged and coughed a splatter of cold water across her chest.

Strong hands grasped her body and rolled her over onto her side as she coughed and choked. She smelled the scent of grass, felt it touching her face. Felt the hands gripping her shoulders firmly but gently. She coughed a last mouthful of water out onto the grass as she felt her senses reconnecting themselves, as though she were awakening from a particularly unpleasant dream. Pain, from her ankle. Shivering, from the bitterly cold water. Fear, from reaching the verge of death and being yanked from it.

Kathryn slumped onto her back, her limbs still feeling as though they belonged to somebody else. Bright hazard lights flickered blue–white and red, headlamps cast beams of light through nearby trees and reflected off a sheet of thermal blankets onto which she was lifted by the paramedics swarming around her.

As she lay back on a gurney, she saw to her right the lake now illuminated by the headlamp beams of Scott Griffin's car, the driver's door wide open. In front of it, police were using a tow–truck to pull Kathryn's vehicle out of the lake.

Behind the paramedics treating her, watching silently, was Detective Scott Griffin. He observed her without expression as though she was somebody he had never met before. Somehow, through her weariness and pain, she managed to force one corner of her lips into a feeble smile as her eyes melted with a gratitude she was too tired to convey in any other way.

Griffin watched her for a few moments longer, made as though to say something, and then he offered her a curt nod in response before he turned and walked away.

***

46

Kathryn was hurried to hospital and fussed over by nurses for almost an hour before, finally, she was left in peace. She lay in a hospital bed in a private room and watched as nurses bustled past the door, which had been purposefully left open by an orderly who had recently visited her to check on her plaster cast.

Her ankle would take around four to six weeks to heal, she had been told. Fortunately, the X–Rays had revealed that Dale's brutally inflicted injury had not severed any tendons or broken any bones. The swelling would subside within a week or two.

Kathryn leaned back into her pillows, thoughts racing through her mind as she replayed the past few days of her life.

'Miss Stone?' Kathryn looked up to see Maietta walk into the room. 'How you holding up?'

Kathryn smiled. 'I've been worse.'

'Could've fooled me,' Maietta said as she pulled up a chair. 'You just got your ankle busted and nearly drowned.'

'It was a long day.'

'I'll say. Listen, I gotta ask you a few things, okay? Won't take long.'

'Shoot.'

'Did you have any idea that Stephen Hollister was living a double life?'

'No,' Kathryn whispered. 'I knew that he was cheating on me and that he had a woman in the city, but that was all. I didn't have any names or anything.'

'So you had no idea that the woman we were looking for, Sheila McKenzie, was married to the man you called Stephen?'

Kathryn chuckled bitterly. 'Hell, no. If I had, I could have helped you guys close the case far sooner. Is she okay, the wife?'

'She'll live,' Maietta said, 'just. Start at the beginning, Kathryn. How did this all come about?'

'When I learned that my fiancé was a lying, cheating bastard,' Kathryn smiled sweetly. 'I decided to check him out, see what he was really up to. I was hoping that I was mistaken, that he was secretly working two jobs to pay the bills or something.'

'But he wasn't,' Maietta said, as though possessed of clairvoyance.

'No. He was married to another woman. Not just seeing her – *married* to her. I followed them for a while at a distance, mainly because I guess I couldn't believe that it was happening.'

'And you never identified her?' Maietta asked. 'You didn't recognise her at all back at the precinct, in the photographs we had?'

'I never got that close enough to them to see her face clearly,' Kathryn said. 'I only saw her twice, from a distance. I knew that she was a blonde and maybe older than me, but that's about all.'

Maietta said nothing for a moment as she scribbled in her notebook. 'So, you decided to do something about the affair?'

'*I* was the affair,' Kathryn sighed.

'Okay, how did you end up in that storage–unit?'

'I followed Stephen,' Kathryn sighed. 'When I realised that he was cheating on me, I started looking into his life. I found things out. So I engineered this scheme to try to force him into a position where he would have to come clean and admit to the other relationship. I know it sounds stupid now but I wanted him back, really I did.'

Maietta looked at her notes. 'Okay, go on.'

'Anyway, I noticed purchases by him on his credit cards and did what I could to track them down, see what he was up to. One of them was for a Triple A storage unit in town near the airbase on the east side. I figured I could go take a look, see what else he was up to. I'd made copies of the bastard's keys, so it didn't take me long to figure out which one was needed. That's when I found her.'

'Sheila McKenzie.'

'Yeah, although I didn't know it at the time. I was trying to untie her from that chair when Stephen showed up. He had a gun. Then…'

'Then what?' Maietta asked.

'Then he attacked me, got me on the ground and stamped on my ankle so I couldn't run away. He injected me with something so I couldn't move. Then he put the gun in my hand, turned me around and shot the woman, Sheila.'

Maietta nodded. 'Then what?'

'He dragged me to my car, put me in the trunk and drove me out of the city. If Detective Griffin hadn't showed up when he did, I'd have drowned.' Kathryn looked at Maietta. 'How did he figure it out?'

Maietta leaned back in her chair. 'He was in a restaurant with his wife. Saw a picture of you with Stephen, or as we know him, Dale, on the wall. He figured you were about to become a victim and made his move.'

Kathryn sank back into her pillows. 'Jesus, too close.'

Maietta nodded. 'Just got a couple more questions for you. We've got traffic camera footage of your car in the vicinity of Sheila McKenzie's house in the city just a few days ago. You been there, Kathryn?'

Kathryn nodded. 'I drove past it more than once. Looks like a palace, doesn't it, compared to my little apartment? I had to go into the city because I wanted to find a restaurant to take Stephen to, a nice night out to help woo him back to me. I figure now that it was a lost cause, because he had far more to gain by staying with that other woman.' She shook her head. 'I should have just tossed the asshole out and found somebody else.'

'Serial killers and con men aren't known for their emotional attachments,' Maietta said.

'Thanks for the head's up.'

'And all this was before Sheila McKenzie was abducted?'

'I don't know,' Kathryn said. 'After I'd last followed them I never actually saw her again until I went to that lock–up.'

'Where Dale had been holding her,' Maietta said. 'She was alive?'

'Yes,' Kathryn said. 'She'd been cared for.'

Maietta nodded. 'Here's the problem I have. Dale McKenzie abducts his own wife in return for a ransom. He then makes no further ransom demands for delivery of the money. Then, he uses you to kill her. Why? Why did he not make a ransom demand?'

Kathryn stared up at the detective. 'You're asking me to explain the motives of a psychopath?'

'You're the psychologist, Miss Stone.'

Kathryn sighed and shook her head. 'I suspect that he had a plan, something more than just a ransom demand. I can't be sure but my putting him, or rather *Stephen*, under pressure might have upset whatever delicate little scheme he had in play.'

'So?' Maietta asked. 'Making a demand for the transfer of funds in return for Sheila's life was the next logical step but he never made it. If he wanted the life insurances, then he would just have killed her and avoided the whole hostage charade.'

'Like I said,' Kathryn repeated, 'I may have screwed up his itinerary. Maybe he figured he was better off just using me to kill her, framing my suicide and then sitting back and collecting the life insurances she had. He could go back to his airline job and his life with me would simply vanish into thin air.' Kathryn sank back into her pillows. 'I'm just glad you guys got involved when you did, or right now I'd still be ten feet underwater and that bastard would be sleeping it off back in his wife's bed.'

Maietta closed her notebook.

'You sure should be,' she said, 'because your ex is in fact a man wanted for four killings.'

Kathryn lay silent and still for a moment. She stared at the ceiling tiles. 'Say that again?'

'He's been linked to four murders committed a decade ago,' Maietta said. 'Dale McKenzie used the identity of his deceased younger brother, Stephen, to court young women before drugging them with a sedative called *Pancuronium bromide*, same thing he used on you, to fake suicide scenes and take off with their money.' Maietta gave Kathryn a serious look. 'He targeted orphans, Kathryn. You, and Sheila McKenzie, were both victims waiting in line. He carried a lock–box around with him, which we found at the scene of your attempted murder. It contained jewellery and a lock of hair from both a victim from several years ago and Sheila McKenzie, and connects Dale to the four unsolved murders. Your hair was in there too.'

Kathryn felt a shiver ripple down her spine like the cold touch of death. She lay back on her pillows as Maietta looked at her notes.

'So, how come you cleaned out Stephen's bank accounts?' she asked.

Kathryn smiled. 'Our accounts,' she replied. 'Stephen has been lying to me about his earnings for years, and I've had to pay our rent and food. That bastard was ripping me off from the moment we met. I just took back what he owed me.'

'You know that's theft, right?'

'It's justice,' Kathryn shot back. 'So arrest me. I'll fight for the right to the money in the courts.'

'Easy tiger,' Maietta said. 'I ain't sayin' I don't sympathise, but you can't be running off with his money if you want to see him go down for life.' Maietta scanned through her notes. 'Anybody else in on this with you, Kathryn?'

Kathryn was about to shake her head when she suddenly gasped in horror.

'Ally! Stephen might have…'

'She's fine,' Maietta said, 'a little shook up but she'll be okay. Right now all you've got to do is rest. Griffin's talking to Dale McKenzie right now. He's screaming to high heaven that he didn't abduct his wife and that he knows nothing about any murdered women, but I don't think anybody's going to buy it.'

Kathryn nodded.

'He's an expert liar, Jane,' she said. 'He had me fooled for years and his wife too. Don't let the bastard worm his way out of this one.'

'I wouldn't worry about that,' Maietta said as she got up from her seat. 'Time we're done he'll confess to starting World War Two.'

***

47

Griffin sat in silence as he stared across the table in the interview room.

Dale McKenzie sat opposite him, his wrists handcuffed to a steel restraint bolted to the table. His nose was bandaged with blood-stained medical dressing, as was his right eye which wept a thin trickle of blood down his cheek.

Griffin slowly placed a series of sealed, transparent evidence bags on the table between them. One contained the pistol used to shoot Sheila McKenzie; the next, a syringe; the next, a bottle of fluid labelled *Pancuronium bromide*.

McKenzie did not move, nor did his expression falter. He looked up expectantly at Griffin.

'Anything you want to say, Mr McKenzie?' Griffin asked.

'I want my lawyer.'

'Oh, you'll get your lawyer,' Griffin assured him. 'But not just yet. Reason is, we have so much evidence here that it's overwhelming.'

'What evidence?' McKenzie spat back at him. 'I've never seen any of those things in my life.'

Griffin raised an eyebrow. 'Is that so?'

'Go to hell,' McKenzie said. 'You've been after me for abducting my wife ever since I came to you. Since *I* came to *you*! Don't you find that a little odd, detective? That I would abduct my own wife and then come straight to the damned police?'

'If you were a very clever, scheming man, then no I would not,' Griffin replied. 'And being as you shot her, I'm guessing that you didn't care so much for her anyway.'

'Shot her?' McKenzie echoed. 'What do you mean? I haven't shot anybody!'

Griffin waved McKenzie down with lazy wafts of his hand. 'Yeah, yeah, we hear you. You didn't do any of it, right? It's all just a big set up and you're innocent of any crime.'

'I am innocent!'

'Yeah, that's not what your wife says.'

McKenzie frowned. 'She's dead.'

'Oh damn, didn't anybody tell you? She survived,' Griffin replied. 'She's fingered you for the shooter.'

McKenzie's face flushed with rage. 'I didn't abduct her!'

'Course you didn't,' Griffin agreed as he gestured to the bagged bottle, 'just like you didn't pump Kathryn Stone full of that shit and try to drown her in a faked suicide. Just like you didn't attack Ally Robinson.'

McKenzie strained against his cuffs.

'Kathryn was winding me up,' he snapped, 'and that Ally bitch was right behind her the whole way. They did it together, the two of them, set this whole thing up. I lost my temper, fair enough, but who wouldn't after what they put me through?'

'After what they put *you* through?' Griffin echoed again. 'Dale, all I want to know is the following; did you abduct Sheila, did she set the whole thing up, or were you in it together?'

McKenzie glared at Griffin.

'None of the above. I'm innocent.'

Griffin smiled and the reached down into his lap. He took out four photographs, each an image of a woman's face taken on a mortuary slab. He laid them down, slowly, one after the other in front of McKenzie, who looked down at them. Griffin saw the pilot's jaw tense, saw his gaze flick from one lifeless corpse's image to another.

'Recognise any of these?' Griffin asked.

McKenzie's mouth gaped as he tried to speak. 'I've never seen any of them in my life,' he muttered.

'Maybe not *your* life,' Griffin said, 'but how about in Stephen Hollister's life?'

Dale glared up at Griffin as though to retort, but the words were caught on his lips and Griffin smiled.

'Guess what, Dale? You're busted. As we speak these four victim's blood samples, saved in a cold–case chiller in a forensic laboratory, are being tested for Pancuronium bromide, the same stuff you used to incapacitate both Ally Robinson and Kathryn Stone. We also have here the flight plans from an airline you previously flew for, which places you in the same city, at the same time, as these women when they died. Moreover, Dale, how would you feel about letting us know how you came about the money that you used for your flight training?'

Dale's eyes flicked up to meet Griffin's, a flare of panic flickering in them as the detective went on.

'You see, we were able to trace it all back to an account that was set up when you first applied to become a pilot. That account was opened with cash, with more filtered in over time from other accounts belonging to you. Thing is, those accounts trace back to money stolen from the bank account of this victim, Meredith Turner.' Griffin tapped the photograph on the left. 'You were living within a quarter mile of her house at the time, Dale, flipping burgers in Las Vegas.'

'This is entrapment,' McKenzie growled.

'No,' Griffin said, 'it's called beyond reasonable doubt, and it's enough for a charge sheet and happy faces at the GFPD cold–case unit. You know it Dale, so forget the theatricals okay? You're under arrest for the murder of four women, the attempted murder of three more, extortion, kidnapping with intent, assaulting a police officer, misdirecting officers of the law during an investigation.... You want me to go on?'

'It's all circumstantial,' McKenzie hissed.

'Is it?' Griffin challenged. 'Then maybe you could explain how it is that your alter–ego, "Stephen", purchased a month–long lease on a storage unit downtown, the same one we found your wife shot half–to–death in?'

McKenzie's jaw gaped open as he stared at Griffin. 'I didn't buy any such thing and...' McKenzie's eyes flared with alarm as a realisation flashed across them. Griffin thought he saw a glimmer of horror there. 'Oh no.'

'Not so much the innocent man now, are we?' Griffin growled, and shoved another plastic–sealed item across the table in front of the pilot. 'Strange, how this tablet computer was used to access the same website as that which *Stephen* used to buy the storage lease. This is *your* tablet, correct?'

Dale McKenzie seemed to shrivel as he stared at the tablet computer. Griffin reached down to the floor beneath the table and produced a small mahogany lock–box sealed in a plastic bag that he placed in front of Dale. The pilot looked at the box, his eyes drawn to it as though by some unseen force and his lips parted as he drew an intake of breath.

'That's right, Dale,' Griffin said. 'This one little box ties you to everything, doesn't it? Four murders. You think a judge is going to have any problem with your conviction, based on the evidence we can put in front of them? Based on your little box of mementos here? You think a jury is going to shrug and say that we got it all wrong?'

'I didn't abduct my wife,' McKenzie whispered, his eyes still fixated upon the box.

Griffin leaned forward and tapped the photographs.

'I don't give a damn about the abduction, McKenzie. Your wife will survive, Kathryn Stone is safe and Ally Robinson will also recover from what you did to her. The four women in these photographs will not and you're in the frame for murdering all of them. What's the chances Pancuronium bromide will be in their blood–work, Dale? And we've got sufficient motive for the abduction: that your wife was on the verge of bankruptcy and poor little Dale McKenzie didn't fancy taking on the mortgage she had lumbered you both with in better days. Hell of a life insurance program you guys bought into. If Sheila was to die, all of those debts would just flutter away… Make this easy on yourself, Dale. Now's the time to decide whether you want to spend the rest of your days in a cell or fry in a chair.'

McKenzie's shoulders seemed to sag as he stared vacantly at the images of the four dead women on the table before him. Griffin leaned forward and tapped the images one by one.

'They may not have had families but they all had lives, Dale,' he said. 'Friends, people who cared about them and have spent the last decade suffering, wondering what on earth happened to them. They had lives that you took. Why? You lost your twin brother, Stephen. You *know* what it's like to lose somebody close. Why the hell would you put these people through that same pain?'

McKenzie did not look up as he replied, his gaze affixed to the photographs.

'Stephen never died,' he whispered. 'I gave him life again. Haven't you ever wondered detective, what it would be like to live a life without rules, without laws, without restraint? A life that you can just walk away from at any point, when you're bored of it or when it just gets too difficult?' McKenzie looked up at Griffin finally. 'A life where you don't have to care?'

Griffin shook his head. 'You could have lived that life without wrecking half a dozen others.'

McKenzie shook his head.

'No, detective, I couldn't. Tell me that you wouldn't kill if you could do so without fear of the law, or rape or steal or plunder. Tell me you wouldn't invade lives just for the thrill of it, control and dominate and then cast aside the old life for a new one.'

Griffin stared at McKenzie for a long moment before he replied.

'The only mind that would really think like that is the kind that isn't strong enough to face real life. You're a coward, McKenzie, nothing more and nothing less, and what's left of your life will be spent behind bars because even if the prosecution hire a fucking chimpanzee to handle this case the jury will still send you down.' Griffin looked up at the sergeant standing by the door. 'Get this asshole back to holding.'

***

Dean Crawford

48

Griffin walked through the hospital ward just as the morning nurses were starting their shifts, brilliant sunshine beaming in golden shafts between the rows of beds as he searched for Ally Robinson. Maietta walked alongside him, having met him at the hospital entrance, and he could tell that she was watching him with interest.

'You've got a bounce in your step all of a sudden,' she observed. 'Got lucky in the end last night, did we?'

'None of your business,' Griffin replied, but he couldn't help the smile twisting the corners of his lips. He felt like a clown.

Maietta made a soft whistling sound and nudged him with her elbow as they walked. 'Load off your mind?'

'Cut it out.'

'Seriously.'

Griffin glanced at Maietta, saw the genuine smile on her face. 'Sure, things are looking up.'

They walked into the ward and saw Robinson laying on a bed, propped up on pillows and staring out at the sunshine. The surgeon who had operated on her the previous night had informed them that the only thing that had saved Robinson from bleeding out was her obesity: the knife had not penetrated her deeply enough in any of the wounds to cause a fatal bleed.

Ally Robinson had dragged herself almost a quarter of a mile once the drugs had worn off, along the side of the road on which she had been abandoned, before a passing motorist had spotted her and called 911.

'Miss Robinson?'

Griffin introduced himself and Maietta. 'We'd like to ask you a few questions.'

Ally nodded. Her eyes were tired and her body was bandaged where she had been struck repeatedly by Dale McKenzie.

'Can you tell us what happened?' Maietta asked, all of the hard-edged street–kid attitude stripped from her voice and making her sound surprisingly gentle.

'I got a call from a friend of mine,' Ally said, 'last night. She's been having a hard time lately. I wanted to meet with her after work, to help her sort things out. Anyway, she didn't pick up, but her boyfriend did.'

'Kathryn Stone,' Griffin said, identifying the friend. 'How did you know my name, when you arrived at the hospital?'

'Kathryn mentioned you once,' Ally said. 'She was helping you.'

'And Kathryn's boyfriend did this to you?' Griffin asked, gesturing to Robinson's wounds.

She nodded, closing her eyes and looking away from them for a moment. 'Yes.'

Griffin looked at his notes for a while.

'Do you recognise this woman?' Maietta asked, holding out a picture of Sheila McKenzie to Robinson.

Robinson squinted at the image and then shook her head. 'No, I don't think so. Why?'

'You're sure?' Griffin pressed. 'You don't know who she is?'

'No, I don't know her.'

'So, why would Kathryn's boyfriend do this to you?' Griffin asked.

'Revenge,' Ally whispered. 'Kathryn was kind of abusing him after she found out that he was seeing another woman behind his back.'

'And you were involved,' Maietta said.

'Yes,' Robinson replied. 'Not directly, but I kind of helped a little. Kathryn was about to leave her boyfriend, Stephen. She'd been able to access his laptop after he started lying to her, and she figured he was having an affair. She looked at his financials, and was able to figure out where this other woman lived.'

'And you were helping her with all of this?' Maietta asked.

'I was her confidant,' Robinson replied. 'She told me all about the affair her boyfriend was having, and about how she was kind of playing tricks on him using her knowledge of his lies.'

'Okay,' Griffin said. 'Here's where I've got a problem. You see, last night we found the woman in the photograph lying in a pool of blood in a storage unit. She'd been shot.'

Robinson stared at Griffin as her lips parted in horror. 'What?'

'She nearly died,' Maietta added. 'Attempted homicide, twenty to life.'

'I didn't shoot her!' Robinson almost yelled. 'And Kathryn hates guns!'

'Then you'd better tell us everything,' Griffin said. 'Because somebody here is lying to us, and we need to find out whom.'

Robinson sank back into her pillow. Her reply, when it came, was barely a whisper. 'I don't know anything, only that Kathryn was taunting Stephen.'

'How did you get involved with her, with all of this?' Griffin asked.

'She asked me to buy some stuff,' Robinson replied. 'Said that she couldn't get it herself without her boyfriend getting all suspicious of what she was up to.'

'What kind of stuff?' Griffin demanded.

'Tickets to a holiday resort,' Robinson replied, 'uh, some particular kind of aftershave and an engagement ring, of all things. She got him to propose to her in front of about a hundred people.'

'Aftershave?' Maietta asked. 'What would she want with that?'

'A gift I suppose, I didn't ask too many questions.'

'Anything else?' Griffin asked.

'I don't remember. Tickets to a vacation spot.'

Griffin stared at Robinson. 'Hunter's Lodge?'

'Yeah, that was it. She was planning a weekend away.'

'And you paid cash for all of this?' Robinson nodded. 'And she told you what she was doing?'

Robinson stared up at the ceiling as she replied. 'Not all of it. I suspected she was up to something and that things might turn nasty if she continued. I kept telling her just to leave, to not get involved.'

'And you didn't find that odd at all?' Griffin asked Robinson. 'That she stayed put?'

'Sure,' Robinson replied. 'But Kathryn's been acting all kinds of strange lately. Like I said, she's been under a lot of pressure with work and her relationship, or what was left of it.'

'Yeah, her boyfriend,' Griffin said, and pulled out a photograph of his own. 'You recognise this man?'

Robinson took one look at the photograph and then shuddered. 'Yes, that's Stephen.'

'Stephen,' Maietta echoed.

'Stephen Hollister,' Robinson said. 'They've been together about three years.'

'Dale McKenzie,' Griffin corrected her.

'Who?'

Griffin slipped the photograph back into his pocket.

'Stephen Hollister does not exist,' he replied. 'His real name is Dale McKenzie, and he's currently in custody for the murders of four women.'

'Oh God,' Robinson gasped. 'Is Kathryn okay?'

Griffin smiled. 'She's safe. Is there anything else that you can tell us, anything at all?'

Ally Robinson sighed and pinched her eyes with one hand. 'I'm sorry, I just can't think straight right now. Kathryn was up to something, definitely, but I'm pretty sure she only told me what she needed to.'

'Okay,' Griffin said as he stood to follow Maietta from the room. 'Take it easy, okay? We'll need a statement from you at the precinct when you're discharged.'

'Sure,' she replied.

Griffin walked out of the room. Maietta shut the door behind them and looked up at him. 'Well, what do you think?'

'She's got no reason to lie,' Griffin shrugged, 'and if I'd just been stabbed half a dozen times I'd be screaming for justice. McKenzie did it.'

'Fine,' Maietta agreed. 'That's it, enough for one weekend. Get your ass home to Angela, I'll see you Monday morning, 'kay?'

'You got it,' Griffin nodded. 'I'm just going to swing by Kathryn, see how she's holding up.'

Maietta didn't reply other than to wave over her shoulder as she headed for the hospital exit.

***

49

It was going to take time to get used to limping about using a walking stick.

Kathryn struggled around her bed as she packed her things back into her suitcase, which had been retrieved by the police from the back of her car when it had been pulled from the river. Her plight had reached the ears of the nurses tending to her, and to her amazement they had done their best to dry her clothes out on radiators all around the ward.

A small act of kindness in a world that so often didn't seem to care.

She could not stay in the apartment any longer, that much she knew, even though Stephen was gone now. Too many bad memories. The place would always haunt her. At least she had somewhere else to go now. The thought of that warmed her soul a little as she worked. She was almost finished when she heard a knock at the door. She limped across and opened the door. Detective Griffin stood outside waiting for her.

His stood with one hand in his pocket, and for the first time since she'd met him he was wearing casual clothes, jeans and T–shirt and a dark leather jacket. She waved him in and he closed the door behind him. He kept the one hand in his pocket, trying to be casual. Pride anchor.

'You look different,' she said as he followed her into the room.

Griffin shrugged. 'New day, new dawn and all that.'

Kathryn smiled. 'Angela.'

A tiny smile curled from one corner of Griffin's lips. 'She's come round to my way of thinking.'

'You mean you grovelled and apologised until you were blue in the face.'

'Yeah, pretty much.'

'And she was happy about that?'

'Several times.'

Kathryn blushed and stuffed the rest of her things into her handbag. 'That was more than I needed to know.'

'You been discharged?'

Kathryn closed her handbag and lifted it onto her shoulder. 'An hour ago, doctor says I'll be fine. I heard you got your man?'

'Well, we know it was Dale McKenzie who abducted his wife if that's what you mean,' Griffin said.

'Make you feel better, to have closed another case?'

'Sure it does,' Griffin chuckled over his shoulder as he grabbed Kathryn's bulging bag off the mattress and carried it to the door for her. 'But it makes me feel on top of the world to know I've closed four.'

'Four?' Kathryn asked as she passed through the doorway. 'The earlier victims?'

'Yeah,' Griffin followed her out to a corridor, nurses bustling to and fro as they walked. 'Turns out he was some kind of serial killer with four unsolved murders to his name. Maietta fill you in on all of that?'

'Yeah,' Kathryn said as she limped down the steps outside the hospital and walked toward the taxi ranks. 'I had no idea.'

'He did it before his career took off,' Griffin quipped. 'The money he took them for paid for his flight training.'

Kathryn reached the taxi rank, a driver spotting her walking stick and climbing out to help her. Griffin opened the taxi's trunk and carefully lowered her suitcase into it.

'You think you'll be okay now, detective?' she asked him.

Griffin shrugged. 'Maybe. It's you I'm worried about.'

'Me?'

'Yeah, you,' Griffin said as he slammed the trunk shut. 'You were recently abducted, witnessed an attempted homicide, beaten and nearly drowned. That's gotta take some kind of toll, right?'

Kathryn sighed and jangled her keys thoughtfully in one hand. 'A lot has taken its toll recently, detective. Right now I'm just glad to be moving on with my life and not stuck in that apartment, rotting with Stephen.'

'Dale.'

'Whatever his name is,' Kathryn replied. 'He won't get off, will he?'

'Of this?!' Griffin laughed out loud. 'Mankind will be living on the moon by the time Dale McKenzie gets out. There's no way the finest prosecution team in all the land could unhook him. Best chance he's got is avoiding the electric chair, and that'll be an achievement.'

Kathryn nodded. 'So I can sleep with the light off?'

'Yeah,' Griffin smiled. 'You'll be fine. I owe you one, though.'

Kathryn smiled. 'You don't owe me anything, detective, it's my job.'

'I wanted to thank you for putting me onto McKenzie's tail,' Griffin said. 'All your talk about how important family was, it kind of got me thinking about the creep, you know? Where was his family? Where was his history? He targeted orphans, you know?'

'I didn't know that,' Kathryn said. 'All I know for sure is that's he's a world–class bastard.'

'Yeah, he is,' Griffin said. 'There ain't nothing people like him won't do because they don't have any family. They don't have anybody to embarrass, nobody to keep them on the straight and narrow, nobody to betray or apologise to. The McKenzie's of this world owe nobody anything but themselves.'

Kathryn looked at Griffin for a long moment.

'I've e–mailed Captain Olsen that, provided he agrees, you should be returned to full duties and your firearm returned to you,' she said finally.

'I appreciate that.'

'That doesn't mean you're fully recovered yet,' she cautioned him. 'But it does mean that you're on the mend and you're thinking straight. The rest will be up to you and your wife.'

'I think we've got it covered,' Griffin said. 'What about you? Where will you stay?'

'I've already arranged something,' Kathryn replied. 'I'll tell Olsen on Monday that your case is officially closed, detective.'

Kathryn offered Griffin her hand. The detective shook it firmly, and then to Kathryn's surprise he threw his other arm about her shoulders and pulled her close to him, the soft scent of her perfume wafting across his face.

'Take it easy,' he said.

Griffin noticed that the skin at the nape of her neck was flushed red, and her green eyes had lost a little of their hard edge.

***

Dean Crawford

50

'Well aren't you the damned hero?'

Olsen leaned back in his chair as he looked at Griffin, who was standing resolutely to attention before the captain.

'Nothing more than my job, captain,' Griffin replied.

'For Christ's sake, relax will you? Take the stick out of your ass and sit down.'

Griffin sighed. He pulled a chair out from beneath the captain's desk and slid into it, the morning sunlight streaming through the blinds across the office window and painting the room in alternating shades of gold and black.

The events of Friday night were still fresh in Griffin's mind, but after a weekend spent entirely at home they seemed to have occurred a decade ago.

'You heard from the hospital yet?' he asked.

'Sheila McKenzie's fine,' Olsen replied. 'She's already confirmed that she'll testify against her husband. How about you?'

'I'm fine,' Griffin replied. 'Just glad I got to her in time is all.'

Olsen let out a blast of air from beneath his moustache. 'Yeah, well, you've made me look a damned idiot in public. The media, not to mention the commissioner's office, will have a field day dragging my name through the mud once this all gets out.'

'You did what you had to do.'

'So did you. The difference is, you were right and I was wrong.'

'There is no right or wrong: my hunch just turned out better than yours.'

'Mighty noble of you to say so,' Olsen replied without humour, 'though I doubt the mayor will share your sentiments. A state–wide, decade long search for a serial killer is nearly derailed by a small town captain who is then put right by a rookie detective who saves the day in a dramatic rescue, right after said captain has suspended him. My career is over, thanks to you.'

Olsen opened a draw and hefted something out of it.

Griffin stared at Olsen for a long beat. 'Is that a gun in your hand?'

'If I were going to kill you Griffin, believe me I'd be using my bare hands, not this gun.' Olsen stood up from his desk. 'The simple fact is that heads will have to roll and as I'm on the verge of retirement, I'll get to bow out in disgrace after a blemish–free thirty five years on the force. You, detective, will be riding high after just five years. There is no fucking justice, as they say.'

'I won't let you be hung out to dry, captain,' Griffin promised, feeling suddenly guilty. 'I'll tell the mayor that you were…'

Olsen raised a hand to silence Griffin and shook his great craggy head. 'Save the sunshine Griffin, ready for when *you'll* need to blow it up the mayor's ass. Truth be told I can't stand the self–serving son of a bitch so I don't give much of a damn. Marjorie wants to move anyway, somewhere new. Sick of the winters so she says: too damned cold. I could do with a change of scenery and being retired from the force isn't going to affect my pension any. So, frankly, detective, I'd like to shake your hand.'

Griffin blinked as he stood. 'That so?'

'That's so,' Olsen agreed as he shook Griffin's hand. 'You did a damned fine job son, no two ways about it.'

In his other hand, Olsen held Griffin's service pistol. He held the weapon out to Griffin, who looked down at it for a long moment before he reached out and took it.

'Good,' Olsen said. 'If you'd refused to take it back I would have turned you round and shoved it up your ass.'

Griffin hefted the weapon thoughtfully in his hand. 'McKenzie?'

'In custody,' Olsen said. 'He's been charged and the District Attorney is handling the case personally, probably to advance her own damned career. I think it's safe to say McKenzie won't feel the soft caress of sunshine on his face for many a decade.'

'Why did he marry Sheila McKenzie? Why change his MO?'

'It looks like his marriage to Sheila McKenzie was a keeper and that he'd settled down. It's only when the money looked like it was going to run out that he decided to make some changes. Fucking tragic, eh? If he'd just stayed low we'd probably never have caught him.'

'Where did Kathryn fit in to all of that?'

'A get out of jail free card,' Olsen replied. 'An entire life, far removed from that of his career as a pilot and professional lunatic. If things got too dicey he could just vanish into his other life and start over, or alternatively kill Kathryn and launder her life insurance policy. We haven't even begun to dig out just how many lives that guy might have forged over the past decade or so using his dead twin's name, but most of what we do have is all down to Kathryn Stone requesting her assignment to you.'

Griffin glanced up at the captain. 'She requested me as an assignment?'

'Sure she did,' Olsen replied. 'Picked you out of a line–up of potential new cases over at the clinic she works for. I figured she must have a thing for ex–soldiers in need or something. Lots of women get wet over uniforms and shit like that.'

Griffin gazed out of the windows into the bright strips of sunlight. 'McKenzie swore that he didn't abduct his wife.'

'He's as guilty as they come,' Olsen said with a shrug of his shoulders. 'Forensics already found gunpowder residue on his clothes, and Kathryn's testimony to where they would find it and what he did in that lock–up fits perfectly with what they're uncovering at the scene. Blood screen on Kathryn has revealed traces of Pancuronium bromide, just as she claimed, proving that he drugged her and then forced her to hold the pistol that shot Sheila McKenzie.'

'I know all of that,' Griffin said. 'But why would he keep denying involvement in the abduction of his wife?'

'Who cares? He's come up with some bullshit story and says that he found Sheila at the same time as Kathryn, having followed her.'

Griffin stared into the middle distance for a long beat.

'You checked traffic camera footage of the area around the lock–ups, see who turned up first?'

'We didn't need to,' Olsen said. 'But as it happens the cameras were all down. Kathryn's story adds up, it's all sealed and delivered.'

Griffin's mind raced with words, scenes, pieces of evidence and fleeting hunches that competed for his attention in a flurry of dawning realisations.

'Yeah,' he agreed, 'all except one.'

'What?'

'Kathryn was working here at the station when we were e–mailed the picture of Sheila McKenzie with the abduction note.'

Olsen stared at Griffin for a long moment. 'Okay, I get what you're hinting at but she said she didn't see her close up …'

'She admitted to Maietta she knew where they lived,' Griffin said. 'Did Dale McKenzie's computer have the house alarm code on it anywhere?'

Olsen's jaw hung open. 'Yeah, saved in a file, but how would she have accessed it?'

Griffin didn't reply. He heard Maietta's words drifting through his mind from days before: *It's the dip of their eyes, to the right and down, that betrays the liars. They have to think about what they're saying. It's like a poker player's tell.* And then Kathryn's words, later just before he had blown up in her face. *You know how to spot a liar detective, and so do I.* And then the words written on Dale's lap–top.

"You're not as clever as you think you are."

Like an old movie playing on a flickering black and white screen in his mind Griffin saw a succession of images flash through the field of his awareness. Revelations hit him like mental body blows as he saw Kathryn in his mind's eye, back on the first day she arrived in the station.

Requested assignment to Griffin personally.

Her unhappiness. The removed ring on her finger.

The ransom note. The photograph, taken on a street.

Kathryn followed Dale and Sheila, knew where they lived.

I made copies of all of his keys.

Dale McKenzie's access to Sheila's personal wealth.

Sheila McKenzie smelling her husband's scent while a captive.

Ally Robinson buying aftershave on Kathryn's behalf.

The lock–up, paid for with Stephen Hollister's credit card, which Kathryn had access to.

I was raised in Nevada.

The realisation hit Griffin like a sledgehammer. 'Where is Kathryn right now?'

'She's probably on another case by now.'

'Did she and Stephen share a bank account?'

'Yeah, she cleaned it out, why?'

'Call her cell,' Griffin said as he whirled from the office. 'Send officers to wherever she is as fast as you can! And freeze Dale McKenzie's accounts and cards!'

'What the hell for? What's going on?'

'Do it!'

***

51

Griffin drove hard toward Kathryn's apartment, the hazard lights on his car blazing as his siren was joined by two more patrol cars that swerved into line behind him.

'Jesus Griffin, ease up!' Olsen shouted. 'She's not the anti–Christ!'

The three vehicles streamed into the apartment complex, and Griffin saw a further two cars already there. He pulled into the lot to the sound of screeching rubber and leaped out of his vehicle as Maietta appeared and waved him down.

'We've already gained access to the apartment,' she said. 'She's gone.'

Griffin ran up the steps to the apartment door, a uniformed officer standing back against the wall as Griffin rushed past.

The living room of the apartment appeared unremarkable to Griffin, the home of a couple who did not have much money. Pictures of Stephen and Kathryn adorned the walls, taken at bars or social gatherings, the couple smiling for the camera. Griffin felt rage surge through him, knowing how false those smiles were.

'You got anything from in here?' he yelled back down the hall at Maietta.

'Nothing out of the ordinary,' came the reply. 'The bed's not been slept in though.'

Griffin did a brief calculation. Kathryn was questioned by Maietta at the hospital while Griffin took the Friday night off on Olsen's orders. He had visited her on the Saturday morning.

I've already arranged something.

Griffin closed his eyes and cursed. She could have been on a plane within a couple of hours.

'You find any ticket stubs? Flight or holiday brochures, stuff like that?'

'Yeah,' Maietta said. 'Holiday brochures, two or three of them, all resorts in Mexico.'

Griffin looked around at the apartment, seeking some clue. Captain Olsen strode inside.

'You may want to cancel your retirement,' Griffin said. 'You weren't quite as far off the mark as you thought.'

Olsen's moustache twitched.

'Both Dale and Stephen McKenzie's bank accounts are empty, cleared right out,' the captain replied. 'We're tracing the money right now but I don't hold out much hope that we'll find it.'

'How much?' Griffin asked.

'Stephen Hollister's accounts, not much,' Olsen replied. 'Dale McKenzie's accounts, significant sums, six figures at least, all tucked away over the years.'

Griffin gritted his teeth and thumped one fist on the back of an aged sofa. 'Damn it, what the hell did we miss?'

'Nothing,' Olsen said. 'We weren't looking in the right places, and had no reason to do so. We just did a check of flights out of the regional airport and found a connecting flight to an international hub booked under the name Kathryn Stone. It departed Saturday afternoon. Neither Kathryn nor Dale McKenzie purchased any airline tickets that we were aware of, so they must have been bought with cash well in advance.'

Griffin chuckled bitterly. 'Robinson, her friend must have picked up the tickets for her.'

'Kathryn took off?' Maietta asked. 'She won't make her testimony against McKenzie. It doesn't make any sense. She wanted to nail that bastard.'

'She will,' Griffin replied. 'She already has. Sheila McKenzie's testimony and the forensic evidence is more than enough to sink Dale. Kathryn doesn't need to help them.'

Maietta glanced at Olsen. 'She did it?'

Griffin let out a long, weary breath of air as he hung his head for a moment. 'She set the whole damned thing up.' Griffin straightened, looked around at the apartment for a moment. 'She finds out that Stephen is already married to another woman,' he said out loud. 'She follows him, checks him out, sees them together. She gets upset about it, decides she's going to do something to make him regret going behind her back.'

'Worse than that,' Olsen said. 'She was the spare part in the *triage*, the cheap girlfriend. She'd have likely been enraged, desperate for revenge.'

Maietta nodded slowly.

'So she plots a series of encounters, chance events, things that threaten to expose Stephen's affair.'

'So,' Griffin said, pacing up and down, 'she puts Dale under pressure, tests him, keeps pushing him. But it still doesn't explain why Dale abducted Sheila unless...' Griffin looked at Olsen, and the captain's expression said it all.

'You're shitting me?'

Olsen emptied the envelope and held out a handful of grainy CCTV images, of Dale McKenzie's car at his wife's house, and those of a second car in the long–term lot at the airport.

'Kathryn knew how he was moving about and both of his identities, while we only knew about Dale McKenzie.'

Griffin clasped one hand to his head. 'She used Dale's double–life against him.'

'Which means that she must have learned about his history,' Olsen said, 'which means that she may have abducted Sheila McKenzie...'

'... to protect her,' Maietta finished the sentence. 'Holy crap, this whole thing was about pure revenge? I didn't know the shrink had it in her.'

'Kathryn lays in wait,' Griffin said, 'gets inside, clouts Sheila McKenzie and gets her out of the house, then sets us all in pursuit of Dale.'

An officer hurried into the apartment and whispered to Captain Olsen, who closed his eyes as though the worst day of his life had just begun.

'There's one more thing,' Olsen said. 'Sheila kept a diary. Had it locked away in a little tin box.'

'How much did it say?'

'Enough. Sheila knew about her husband's second life and had done for months.'

'She *knew*? And she didn't do anything about it?'

'She was worried about the social consequences, if you can believe that. She preferred to keep quiet about it all. Cursed Dale to an early death in the diary, but said nothing about it to any of her friends.' Olsen shrugged. 'I guess it happens all the time, women putting up with their husband's infidelity, suffering in silence and all that. But what's really interesting is that Kathryn slipped up, just once.'

'How?'

'She must have got really fascinated reading the diary, because her prints are all over it.'

Griffin sighed. 'That's not enough to push for a warrant.'

'No,' Olsen admitted. 'But at least we know now that she was in the home.'

Griffin nodded.

'She abducts Sheila, sets up the ransom letter and leaves a trail of evidence leading to Dale.'

'Who realises what she's doing and moves in, probably follows her to the lock–up, and then figures out a way to turn it all against Kathryn,' Maietta said.

'Damn it,' Griffin cursed. 'It would have worked, if I hadn't burst in there and stopped him...'

'Stopped him from murdering Kathryn as well as Sheila,' Maietta cut across. 'Think about it. Kathryn never set out to murder anybody: it's Dale who's the killer, and he's now sitting in jail awaiting a trial that will probably see him serving life with no parole.'

'Yeah,' Griffin nodded, 'it's perfect isn't it? She played us, every last one of us.'

'Yeah,' Olsen replied. 'She did. We could probably chase the money, track her down over time. Question is, are you going to expose what she's done and try to get her back here for trial on conspiracy charges, and maybe undermine the trial of Dale McKenzie for the multiple slaying of women across the country? Dale McKenzie's defence team would love any possible evidence of unstable testimony. Or are you going to ask yourself whether maybe this result is the better end of a lousy deal? We caught a killer, Scott, and we lost a fraudster who'd been wronged herself by that same killer.'

'It could have been a lot worse,' Griffin shot back. 'Who knows what could have happened, who might have died if her insane little plan had gone awry?'

'It did go awry,' Olsen said. 'But you saved her life, remember? Maybe that was why she picked you. Two birds, one stone, if you'll forgive the pun.'

'Fleeing in itself is enough to raise questions over McKenzie's trial,' Maietta pointed out.

'We won't need her,' Olsen insisted. 'McKenzie's previous murders will be more than enough to convict him, you know that. Personally, I think that you just want her back here for yourself, detective.' Olsen gave the apartment one last glance. 'You write your report, but you make damned sure you don't hand it in until I've left the force, you understand? It's your call but don't make it mine too, not now.'

Griffin nodded wearily and waved the captain away. 'Thanks for the support.'

Olsen left the apartment. Griffin remained for a few minutes, looking around at the apartment that for so long had held a woman captive by her own will, imprisoned by the world that she had tried to create for herself and seen so utterly destroyed by one man.

He knew that she would not be coming back.

Griffin took one last look at a photograph of Kathryn Stone on the wall of the living room and then turned and walked from the apartment.

*

Ally Robinson eased herself out of her hospital bed and reached for a glass of water on her bedside table. She was drinking from the glass when a nurse entered the room and handed her a brown envelope.

'Delivered here by a courier,' the nurse explained.

The envelope was addressed to her in big, round letters that she recognised immediately. Ally hesitated, unsure if she really wanted to open anything that had come from Kathryn, but her curiosity quickly got the better of her.

Ally waited until the nurse had left before she opened it.

That Kathryn had gotten her into this mess could not be denied, but then Ally too had gone against her own better judgement, as well as ignored Kathryn's wishes, when she had agreed to get into Stephen's car. That Kathryn had lived with the insane bastard for so long amazed Ally.

Inside was a carefully folded note. Within the folds, as she opened it, was a rectangle of stiff paper. Ally caught it and turned it over. A cheque, she realised, written to her, for eight thousand dollars.

Ally's breath had caught in her throat, and she looked at the note.

Sorry to get you involved.

Hope this helps and makes up for what happened.

Yours,

KS

P.S. You never really know people until they do something that you don't expect.

Ally smiled, and slid the envelope into her handbag.

***

Dean Crawford

52

The world drifted by as Kathryn watched through the window, a flare of sunlight in the hard blue above that was too bright to look at directly. She leaned back in her seat and shifted her leg slightly, giving her ankle more room.

There was only a little pain now, and what little there was had been suffused not just by the painkillers she had taken but by the sense of calm permeating her soul in a warm embrace. Sometimes, all it took was the realisation that one had to change in order to find happiness: that it wasn't the rest of the world that was at fault, but one's self.

She had tried so hard to conform, to be a part of a society that expected of her the things that it demanded of others. A loving husband, a good job, a nice house, new car, two point four children. Pets. Holidays twice a year. Team Family.

But some people just were not meant to be that way. Kathryn had realised, belatedly perhaps, that she was not one of those people. There would never be children, or pets, or a white wedding. Such things had passed her by. Even a good job was almost out of reach at her age. Too long on the bench, too long waiting for her chance to shine, and the last opportunity stolen from her by a murderous asshole.

Kathryn had finally realised that it was not her job to conform, not her responsibility to fit in with other people. Her only responsibility was to herself, and the sooner she started thinking that way, the better her life would be.

The tickets she had bought for Mexico were not for a getaway with Stephen, mainly because she had only bought the one. There had been no sense in showing it to him too clearly when she had revealed the purchase over breakfast, so she had waved the ticket airily, making sure that he *assumed* there were two. No reason for him not to, really. The fact that they were *Air Ventura* tickets was enough to preoccupy his mind anyway. As she had learned, sometimes Stephen's self-obsession could be an asset.

Picking up Sheila's credit cards when she had visited her home had been another decision made on an impulse, along with a handful of bank statements and access codes to Sheila's on-line banking. Katheryn had moved the money into Dale's accounts long before he had realised his wife was missing, enough to place suspicion on him right from the outset.

She was hardly a master criminal, but she knew enough to be sure that Stephen would have access to accounts both in his own name and Dale's. It took her little time to find them in Sheila's house.

Kathryn had never intended that her escape from the drudgery of her life had become so complex. Stripping Dale of his money and fleeing had been her main aim. Equally, she had never intended her abduction of Sheila to end with her being shot, yet it remained that Sheila had known about her husband's duplicitous life and had been quite happy to let it continue. They had both willingly and knowingly danced with the devil, the consequences of doing so to be born on their own shoulders. For Sheila, that had meant the end of her life as she had known it.

For Kathryn, it had meant the beginning.

Katheryn looked down at the letter she was writing, saw it quiver as a thump reverberated through the bus as it rumbled along the asphalt road. She glanced out of the window at the brilliant sunrise, the perfect blue sky, the palm trees and the airport terminal emblazoned with *Aeropuerto Internacional de la Ciudad de Mexico* as the bus pulled away. She smiled to herself, and then looked down again at the letter and read it one last time.

I'm like you. And you're like me. Like you, I've made mistakes.

Like you, I just wanted to escape them.

We were both enslaved to our pasts, to the tragedies and histories of other people, not by our own choosing but by events neither of us could do anything about.

I suppose that's what all of us want to do, in our own way, shake off our histories and start afresh. Sometimes it seems to me that people are not really meant to spend their lives together, that enduring life's rigours is easier when there's only yourself to worry about. I didn't always think this way. Maybe it's because I'm an orphan, but I used to dream of the perfect life. Team Family, I used to call it, the perfect little bubble that a fortunate few find themselves cossetted inside, like those charming old couples who have been together since the Dawn of Time and seem effortlessly to sail life's turbulent seas before cruising on into an afterlife of eternal peace. That was all I really wanted.

But in reality it's all a damned sight harder. We all want that perfect life, but none of us really know what a perfect life should look like. We all want do the right thing, and yet we all want to be free. And what is the "right thing" to do anyway? We struggle to adapt to each other, and when a thousand tiny irritations finally blossom into enraged conflict, where no compromise can quench the anger that courses like acid through our veins, so begins what so many of us call "the rest of our lives".

I made a stand. I decided that "good enough" wasn't good enough, that I had one life and I would damned well make sure it became the best I could ever live because life isn't a rehearsal and I'll never get another shot at it. If I failed, I failed.

Don't tell me you've never dreamed of doing it too.

Kathryn slipped the letter into an envelope and addressed it to Scott Griffin. She hoped that one day he would understand.

***

Also by Dean Crawford:

The Atlantia Series
Survivor, Retaliator
Aggressor, Endeavour
Defiance

The Warner & Lopez Series
The Nemesis Origin

The Ethan Warner Series
Covenant, Immortal, Apocalypse
The Chimera Secret, The Eternity Project

Independent novels
Eden, Holo Sapiens, Stone Cold,
Revolution, Soul Seekers

ABOUT THE AUTHOR

Dean Crawford is the author of the internationally published series of thrillers featuring *Ethan Warner*, a former United States Marine now employed by a government agency tasked with investigating unusual scientific phenomena. The novels have been *Sunday Times* paperback bestsellers and have gained the interest of major Hollywood production studios. He is also the enthusiastic author of many independently published Science Fiction novels.

www.deancrawfordbooks.com

Printed in Great Britain
by Amazon